W9-ANN-259

Live
and
Let Grind

Also available by Tara Lush

Coffee Lover's Mysteries
Cold Brew Corpse
Grounds for Murder

Live
and
Let Grind

A COFFEE LOVER'S MYSTERY

Tara Lush

CROOKED
LANE

NEW YORK

Published in the United States by Crooked Lane Books, an imprint of The Quick Brown Fox & Company LLC.

Crooked Lane Books and its logo are trademarks of The Quick Brown Fox & Company LLC.

Library of Congress Catalog-in-Publication data available upon request.

ISBN (hardcover): 978-1-63910-112-2
ISBN (ebook): 978-1-63910-113-9

Cover design by Brandon Dorman

Printed in the United States.

www.crookedlanebooks.com

Crooked Lane Books
34 West 27th St., 10th Floor
New York, NY 10001

First Edition: October 2022

10 9 8 7 6 5 4 3 2 1

For Dino, my heart dog

Chapter One

My Shih Tzu had murder written all over his furry little face. "Geez, he's serious about ripping that toy bunny apart, isn't he? That's the second one this week." My best friend, Erica, took a sip from her coffee mug as she eyed the dog. A lock of her chin-length hair flopped over her face, and she pushed it back with her hand.

The pupper was between us on the large sofa, shaking his head furiously while clamping his jaws around the neck of the bright blue, plush toy. The stuffed bunny was nearly as big as he was, but that didn't matter because he was on a mission of destruction.

"Stanley, come on, dude." I leaned over and tried to grab it from him, but my fluffy dog jumped down with a growl and ran out of the room, his apricot-colored tail wagging in excitement. My dad was in the kitchen, making some delicious-smelling muffins. Stanley probably wanted to enlist Dad in a game of tug-of-war. Or beg for treats. Dad was an easy mark for my dog's machinations.

I sank back into the overstuffed cushion. The sofa had been a sweet, recent find at a secondhand store, with buttery-soft, stainproof microfiber fabric. Combined with the botanical palm tree wall prints and mid-century modern accent pieces, it really tied the room together.

"Oh well. What's another toy bunny? Listen, Erica, what are we going to do for the drink of the month? It's the end of January, and we need to change the menus and chalkboard signs this week."

My friend stretched her legs on the lounge part of the sofa sectional. She was the best barista at Perkatory, my family's coffee shop on the island of Devil's Beach, Florida.

Well, my coffee shop. Technically I was only the manager, but Dad, who was the owner on paper, insisted the business was mine. After being a journalist for almost a decade—then laid off from my dream job at a paper in Miami last year—I was still getting used to the fact that I had a different career than I'd planned, one that brought me back to the charming, weird island where I was born and raised.

One that involved my favorite thing in the world, aside from Stanley: coffee.

This morning Erica was wearing what I called her tropical goth loungewear: black tank top, black sweatpants, hot pink fuzzy socks. She reached for her phone. "Hang on. It's a text from the boat mechanic."

"Really? On a Sunday?" Erica normally lived on a sailboat at the Devil's Beach marina, but the vessel had been in dry dock for the past two weeks. It made sense that she'd stay with me. We were practically inseparable as friends, we worked together, and my house was only a few blocks from Perkatory.

"Lana, check this out. He says he has to order a new part for the generator, and it still might take a couple of weeks. Is that okay?" Her voice rose slightly as she tucked the phone next to her hip.

"Of course, it's fine." I lifted my legs onto the sofa and gently pushed her knee with my bare foot. I was in gray sweatpants and a long-sleeved blue T-shirt that said "Welcome to Florida" next to a cartoon alligator. "It's been great having you here. We've had a blast. Movie nights, Cards Against Humanity, our failed attempt to make limoncello." The latter had ended in a large jar of foul, astringent, macerated lemons.

As much as I loved living alone, life had been more exciting with Erica around. I was a natural introvert, and she coaxed me out of my shell. Plus, on my day off, she happily took Stanley for walks at five thirty in the morning, an hour when I preferred to sleep.

"You're sure I'm not cramping your style with your man?"

I shook my head. I'd been dating Noah Garcia for almost five months now, and it was going better than I ever dreamed. Okay, he was up there as one of my favorite things, along with Stanley and coffee.

But between my managing the café and his duties as the police chief of Devil's Beach, we only had quality alone time a couple of nights a week. Usually we hung out at his beachfront condo, but he did spend the occasional evening here.

He also visited his mom in Tampa, frequently, for a family issue that he hadn't yet fully explained. The rest of the time, we'd grab coffee at Perkatory or eat a sandwich together on a bench at the beach.

We were taking things slow, and that was fine with me. I'd only been divorced for two years and didn't want to rush into anything serious. Noah and I had the perfect relationship, as far as I was concerned. Respectful, hot, and fun—and monogamous. Fidelity was a big issue for me, since my ex had cheated during our marriage.

"Not at all. Noah's been so busy with the department accreditation." And the family issue. Admittedly I was a little salty he hadn't told me more about why he needed to go to Tampa so often on his days off. Surely he'd reveal the details soon, I figured.

Erica looked at me over the top of her earthenware mug. "And that monkey situation. Dunno how he's going to resolve that. He's in quite a pickle with that one."

"Yeah, they've really been a pain in his butt. It's a total public relations nightmare for the police department and the entire town." A colony of wild monkeys lived on the island's nature preserve. Lately they'd been aggressive with tourists, who clamored to take selfies with the primates. So far no one had been bitten, but there had been multiple close calls, including one incident that resulted in a viral video that the island's Chamber of Commerce had quickly tried to distance itself from.

Neither man nor beast was fully innocent, in my book.

State wildlife officials wanted to capture a few of the more hostile monkeys and relocate them to a sanctuary on the mainland in the eastern part of the county, and Noah agreed with the plan. But that led to a protest from local animal rights folks, who wanted them to stay put.

I saw both sides of the issue. But as an up-and-coming business owner in town, I'd tried to stay out of the fray, which had recently escalated to people dressing in monkey costumes and parading down Main Street in a silent protest every week. While holding bananas.

"The monkeys should stay here, but not if they're going to bite people," Erica said, shrugging. "Let them live their best monkey lives at a preserve or primate colony or something."

My dad walked in, followed by Stanley toting the de-stuffed bunny in his mouth. Dad carried a plate of muffins and set it on the coffee table, and the scent of vanilla filled the living room. My father had his own house on the beach, but lately on weekends he'd taken to coming to my place—which used to be his, back when Mom was alive—and making brunch. He said he liked my gas stove better, but I suspect he probably missed Mom, whose cozy touches were everywhere in the farmhouse-style kitchen.

"Stanley massacred that toy. I had to throw away all the cotton innards. Are you two talking about the monkeys?" he asked.

I winced. Dad was one of the leaders of the pro-monkey faction on the island, and he'd lobbied hard for Noah and state officials to allow the animals to remain in their habitat. It had made for some tense meals recently. Come to think of it, this was probably why Noah had stopped coming over for Sunday brunch, choosing to head to the mainland to catch up on county gossip with his friend Vern, the medical examiner.

Duh. I should've put two and two together quicker. I made a mental note to ask Noah if this was truly why he was avoiding my house on Sundays.

"Nope, we were talking about Erica and her boyfriend," I lied. I didn't feel like getting into another conversation about primate social structure. Dad had become something of an expert on monkeys in recent weeks, spending hours watching NatGeo documentaries and scouring Jane Goodall's website.

"Yeah, I have to get a move on. I wanted to start on my cushion upholstery project, and Joey and I are driving to Orlando later today." Erica stretched. She was fixing some of the cushions on her boat in my garage.

"Oh, right, it's your big water park trip," I said. Erica had the day off tomorrow, and she and Joey planned to visit a new, volcano-themed water park that was holding an after-dark rave-type party.

"Yeah, can't wait. Not sure if Joey's on board with those big slides, but we'll find out."

"About those monkeys—" Dad started, but I interrupted.

I had to divert his attention, so I pointed at the muffins. "Whoa! Those look delicious. Nice job, Dad. You really do bake better with my oven. Must be the gas."

"Heck yes, I can smell them from here. They definitely look better than the ones you made at your house, Peter. Gimme," Erica exclaimed, knowing I didn't want to get Dad going. She reached for one, and I followed.

"I put my special sauce in." Dad grinned.

"Wait. Do these have weed in them?" I paused. Dad had a medical marijuana license for his "eye pressures," claiming he had pre-glaucoma, whatever that was. In reality, he was an old hippie who liked to get high from time to time.

"Oh my, no. I wouldn't waste the good stuff on you two." His voice was stern.

I exhaled. "So what's the special sauce?" I raised one to my nose. "Smells citrusy."

"Exactly. Orange juice. Fresh squeezed. From a friend who has an organic grove on the mainland."

Erica took a bite and chewed. "Oh my god, these are amazing."

They really were delicious. Fluffy and cake-like, just sweet enough, with a fragrant tang that was made even better with the addition of crunchy poppy seeds and a hint of vanilla.

Erica and I each grabbed a second muffin and munched in silence as we watched Dad sit on the floor and play tug-of-war with Stanley and the deflated bunny. After a couple of minutes, Dad rolled onto his back. Stanley dropped the toy and climbed atop Dad's chest, letting out a short, sharp bark.

"This is it," I said to Erica between the final bites of the muffin. "I've got it. This is our new drink at Perkatory."

"What? A muffin?" Dad asked, sitting up. Stanley stopped his wuffing and sprinted out of the room.

"No. Citrus. We can do an orange-flavored coffee drink."

"Hmm?" Erica took a third muffin. She was a coffee purist. I was as well, but in my brief time as manager of Perkatory, I'd come to realize we needed to offer customers a rotating selection of sweet, novel concoctions. They kept people coming back for more, and folks were starting to anticipate the drink of the month.

Erica usually came up with the monthly recipe; she'd done lavender, rosemary, and blueberry. The latter she'd dubbed "brew-berry," and it was a hit all throughout the month of January. It had been so popular that I was considering extending it into February, which was only two days away. But that seemed like cheating somehow.

Erica swallowed and held her hand up. "I was actually thinking of . . ." she swept her fingers in the air, "chaga."

My brows twitched toward each other. "Cha-*what*?"

"Chaga. It's a mushroom. It's all the rage in Seattle now—I was reading about it online. Basically you delicately grind mushrooms along with beans. Or we could use reishi, lion's mane, or turkey tail. There are a bunch that go well with coffee."

Dad perked up. "Like magic mushrooms? I once tried some of those before Lana was born, at a Dead show. Trippy."

"No, not those kinds of mushrooms."

Dad began to hum the song "Sugar Magnolia," which made Erica dissolve into giggles.

Ignoring him, I tried to imagine the earthy, full-bodied taste of mushrooms along with coffee, but couldn't. "What's the point, though?"

"Antioxidants. Mental clarity and focus. Also it's an interesting new flavor, and probably no one in Florida's serving it."

I finished my muffin while pondering this. "We could try it, but also consider the flavors of chocolate and orange. They're complementary. But not common, at least with coffee. We could use the Perkatory house blend. It already has notes of chocolate and spice, with a hint of citrus aftertaste. Adding orange to that will only enhance the drink." I lifted my mug for emphasis.

"It's quite a European flavor profile," Dad chimed in.

"Exactly." I pointed at him.

"So what would we use? Orange extract? Juice? Hot or iced, or both?" Erica asked. I loved how we debated and decided on new drinks for Perkatory as a team.

"Hmm." I tapped my fingernails against the mug. "It's been pretty warm this winter. I'd say iced. We need something light, something that makes tourists think of the beach and Florida. The iced coffee and the cold brew are still strong sellers, especially with the snowbirds from the north."

"Let's see. I don't think juice would work. Too overpowering and acidic." Erica began swiping on her phone screen, her pale face pinched in concentration. "What about seltzer?"

I tilted my head. "Like a nonalcoholic coffee spritzer? Is that weird and gross, or innovative and awesome?"

Erica ran her tongue over her teeth. "I think it's—"

Her answer was drowned out by a high-pitched mechanical roar, and she groaned. "I can't believe Gus is leaf blowing again. He used that stupid thing two hours ago. And last night at eight PM."

"He started leaf blowing at seven thirty in the morning on a Sunday?" Dad asked.

I rolled my eyes. "That he did. You're sure it's not Jeri?"

Jeri was the silver-haired retiree across the street, the only other neighbor on the block who used a blower. She'd never used hers much until Gus moved in next door to me several months ago, and she fired up her machine out of spite. Now it was like the Indy 500 on the weekends, and sometimes I couldn't hear myself think over the roar of engines.

Erica twisted her body so she could look out the window, which was directly behind the sofa. She parted the white, wooden blind with one finger. "Nope. It's Gus. He got a new blower. It's more powerful than the last one. Loud as heck. The kind that straps to his back, like a professional landscaper's. Jerkface."

Dad rose and mimicked Erica while sitting in the middle of the sofa. He, too, raised one of the blind slats. "You know what I heard about Gus?"

"What? That he has to remove every piece of organic material from his driveway three times a day because he wants to drive everyone on the street out of their minds?" Erica snorted.

I, too, flipped in my seat and shifted a slat an inch and peered out. There was my neighbor and his industrial blower. With a slow movement of his hand, he ran the blower nozzle in a methodical pattern over his cement driveway.

"I don't see anything he can even blow," I said, scanning his vibrant green lawn and lone palm tree for any evidence of leaves, dirt, or grass clippings, and finding none. "He has a lawn service come once a week. They use lots of chemicals."

"Don't let Stanley pee on a lawn that's been chemically treated, it's bad for him," Dad cautioned.

"Don't worry—I won't. Gus already told me to keep the dog off his property." That had been my first encounter with my new neighbor, and it hadn't been a particularly friendly one.

Gus was of average height and wore the unofficial male uniform of Devil's Beach: sandals, cargo shorts, and a T-shirt. He acted curmudgeonly, like he was in his seventies, but had a muscular build and the face of someone much younger. I'd once overheard him talking on the phone about CrossFit on his way to his Corvette convertible.

I hadn't had much contact with him, mostly because of his curt command to keep Stanley off his lawn.

Still, I'd tried to be friendly and, even after that rough beginning, brought over a tray of Nutella brownies to welcome him to the block. He'd grunted a thanks, then slammed the door. A woman, whom I assumed was a wife or girlfriend, had waved at me once, and I'd barely seen her since. I pegged her as a nurse or someone who had an overnight job. Or perhaps since I'd stopped being a journalist, I wasn't that observant anymore.

Dad parted the blinds even wider.

"We might as well open the blinds and stare at him," I deadpanned.

Dad reached for the string to lift the blinds but I grabbed his wrist. "I wasn't serious."

He chuckled. "Oh. Anyway, his wife is a hot roller."

"Dad"—I thwacked him on the arm—"don't be a pig."

"No," he scoffed. "I'm not saying that in a pervy way. She's quite talented."

"At what? I've only seen a woman over there a couple of times. Long blonde hair, much younger."

"That's her," Dad said. "She roller-skates."

I turned to grimace at him. What was he talking about? *Did he just say that she roller-skates?*

"How long have they been married?" Erica chimed in before I could ask my question.

"Can't be that long, since she's about twenty years younger than him and would've probably been in high school a few years ago," I snarked. "Now that you bring her up, I haven't seen her in a while."

"She's around your age, so pushing thirty. Not that young," Dad replied.

"Thanks, dude," I muttered.

Dad ignored me. "They've been married for three years. Met online while he was still in Fort Lauderdale. They've only been here about six or seven months. But she travels a lot for work."

"It's been six months? That long?" Jeez. I was losing track of time. Come to think of it, his leaf-blowing habits had increased in the last month or so.

I shot Dad a side-eye. "How do you know all this about her?"

"My crystal bowl meditation group."

I let this sink in while watching Gus pay meticulous attention to the area around his mailbox with the blower. Unlike others on the block, his mailbox was a plain black container on a white post.

Dad was into all kinds of new age woo. Reiki, yoga, chakras. It didn't surprise me that he'd attend something called a crystal bowl meditation group.

"Shouldn't you be meditating and listening to the healing sounds of the bowls instead of—I dunno—gossiping about Gus and his foxy young wife?" I asked.

"Well, she was a member of the group for a while, then she stopped coming. She said she was traveling a lot, so we didn't think much of it."

"I wonder if it was clarity from the meditation or Gus's leaf blowing that finally pushed her over the edge," Erica said in a dark tone, and I laughed.

"Her name's Honey. Have you seen her Instagram channel? I follow her. Her posts are wild," Dad offered.

I let the blind slat drop and turned to face him. "Are you on Insta?"

"Yeah, I am. I didn't tell you? I've posted some photos of Stanley. A company even wants to send me some dog clothes for him. Anyway, Honey roller-skates. She does videos of skating on the sidewalk by the beach to seventies tunes. She's really good. I'm surprised you haven't seen her. She's got millions of followers and sponsorships. It's her full-time job, and she goes all over the place to roller-skate. But she said in our group that she loves Devil's Beach the most because of that long sidewalk by the beach."

I climbed off the sofa and picked up my now empty coffee mug and other dirty dishes. It was hard to tell what was more unbelievable: that my tech-inept father was on Instagram, that he was posting photos of my dog without telling me, or that someone my age was making a living from roller skating to vintage disco beats. "I'm getting another cup. Anyone want anything?"

Neither Dad nor Erica answered because they were too busy talking about Gus.

"And I tried to make nice with him about a week ago when I asked him politely not to use the blower before eight in the morning," Erica said.

Dad pulled the cord and lifted the blind all the way. Their noses were now practically pressed against the glass. "What did he say?"

"'Tough luck.' That's what he said, in a real nasty tone. Tough luck. Can you believe it? Total loser. And did you hear what he did to the mailbox?"

"No," Dad said.

"Apparently the previous owner had a manatee-shaped mailbox. Like everyone else on the block. He removed it and put up that plain mailbox. Then he stuffed the manatee into his trash can on garbage day—that's what Jeri across the street said. Who would do that to a manatee statue?" This fact seemed to be a great injustice to Erica.

"That's terrible. Lana didn't tell me about that, and I guess I've been too ditzy to notice it myself."

"I didn't notice," I called out.

Dad launched into a detailed explanation of how a group of neighbors one year thought it would be hilarious if everyone on the street bought five-feet-tall, fiberglass manatee-shaped mail containers. "Our block was even on the network news one year for our manatee mailboxes."

I shook my head and wandered into the kitchen. Erica had asked me last week if it was okay that she approach Gus; I'd had no issue with it. Truth be told, I disliked the sound of the blower as much as she did, but I hated confrontation with neighbors even more. Mostly, I wanted my peaceful street back.

I poured myself another mug of coffee and watched Stanley wolf down his bowl of kibble. My phone was on the kitchen island, and I grabbed it, wondering if Noah had texted. A little zing went through my body when I saw that he had.

Happy Sunday, cupcake. Vern says hello.

Vern was the county's medical examiner, someone I'd met when I'd written a freelance article for the local paper about a murdered yoga teacher here on the island several months back. That was around the time Gus moved in, I recalled. Perhaps that's why I hadn't paid much attention to him and his manatee mailbox disposal, because I was so caught up with that homicide.

Say hi to Vern for me. What's on the agenda for the rest of your day? I texted back.

I just got back to the island. At the station, doing some dreaded paperwork, he replied.

You want to come over for coffee? Dad made some delicious muffins.

There was a pause and three flashing dots on the screen for several seconds. *I'll take a raincheck. I've got a ton of work. See you later? My house, sunset? I'll make dinner.*

Absolutely! Unless you want to come here. Erica's going away for the night with Joey, I responded. We would be alone, and it would be the perfect time to ask him if he had a problem with Dad. And about his trips to Tampa. Perhaps I'd propose a dinner with our families, since I hadn't met his yet.

Let's do my place. I already bought those shrimp kebabs you like from the Whole Foods on the mainland.

I beamed at the phone. Noah normally disliked Whole Foods, so it meant a lot for him to stop on his way back to the island.

I cannot resist shrimp kebabs or you, so I'll be there at five thirty. Because it was late January, the sunset—and our dinners—had shifted to earlier hours.

Noah immediately texted back, asking what I was doing, and I gave him the rundown of the Gus drama. Noah responded by sending a laugh emoji.

Let me know what you want me to bring to your house tonight, I typed.

Just your beautiful self. I'll take care of the rest.

A little, swoony sigh escaped my lips. Noah really was the best. I couldn't be annoyed about his weekends in Tampa or how he might be avoiding my dad. As I was giving myself a pep talk about not prying too hard into Noah's life during our date, I heard Erica shriek.

"That's it! I'm giving that guy a piece of my mind."

Stanley and I rushed out of the kitchen in time to see Erica stripping off her hot pink socks and shoving her feet into a pair of my flip-flops near the front door. "I'll be right back," she spat as she flounced out the door, slamming it behind her.

She moved so fast that Stanley didn't even try to dart outside. He and I froze, wide-eyed. I knew Erica had a temper but had never seen her like this.

Chapter Two

The door slammed shut, and Dad joined me in the hall.

"What happened?" I asked.

"Gus saw us looking at him—"

"Which is why I suggested you not open the blinds."

"And he gave us the finger."

"Great. Now we've started a full-blown feud with the next-door neighbor. Exactly what I need."

"After he flipped us off, Erica made her own gesture, and then Gus pointed at her. He did this." Dad raked his index finger across his throat.

I pressed my hand to my chest. "Good lord. That's rather extreme." I'd only talked with Gus a few times, and sure, he was a tad surly on a good day, but I didn't think he was capable of threatening a stranger with bodily harm.

"Erica wasn't going to put up with that, and nor should she. We should probably go back her up." Worry lines sprouted between Dad's brows.

I rubbed my forehead. It was nine thirty in the morning, and I still hadn't read the Sunday paper. My fault for sleeping in on one of my two days off this week. "Yeah, I guess we should. Let me secure Stanley first."

I barricaded him in the kitchen, and by the time Dad and I walked outside and rounded the front of the house, Erica and Gus were engaged in a full-blown spat. They stood in his driveway, and Gus gestured forcefully with the nozzle of the leaf blower.

Dad and I skidded to a halt and watched in horror from a few feet away, standing on our side of the lawn. The argument marred what was otherwise a perfect winter morning in Florida: bright sunshine, a clear, vibrant blue sky, and dry air were rare and fleeting in these parts, and should be cherished. Instead, we were mired in a neighborhood feud.

So much for this year's block party. When was that, anyway? I turned to ask Dad, but the situation in front of us escalated.

"Don't you aim that stupid thing at me," Erica yelled.

Gus pointed the nozzle of the blower in her direction. "Stay away from me, you crazy witch. I'm trying to clear my driveway of debris. I can't help it if your friend Ms. Lewis doesn't care about her yard."

I frowned. "I hired a landscaper," I muttered to Dad.

"I know you did, munchkin. The property looks beautiful."

Erica pointed at Gus. "You're the crazy one, blowing leaves at all hours of the day and night. All we hear is that stupid engine. Give it a rest!"

"Yeah, she's right," cried a voice. Everyone looked across the street. It was Jeri, standing next to her manatee mailbox. Funny, I'd never noticed that she was about the same height as the mailbox. Next to the potato-shaped gray manatee, though, she was quite trim and rosy cheeked.

Clad in a lime green polo shirt and a matching golf skirt, Jeri clutched a rake. To say she looked agitated would be like saying Kim Kardashian looked sultry.

"Stay out of this, woman," growled Gus.

Jeri responded by brandishing the rake in the air. Thankfully she stayed on her side of the street, but for good measure I suggested Dad try to calm her down. Instead, he was glued to my side, mesmerized by the drama unfolding before us.

For a solid minute, Gus and Erica bickered, calling each other names. The sixty-something Jeri watched, waving the rake in support of Erica's sharp words.

"We need to stop this," I whispered to Dad.

"They'll work it out between themselves. I have faith in Erica."

"I'm going to file a complaint with city hall against you," Erica threatened.

"If you do, I swear I'll—"

"If you all don't pipe down, I'm calling the cops! It's Sunday, for Pete's sake. Don't you people have better things to do?" The faint, disembodied female voice bounced off the palm trees lining the street.

"No, we don't," hollered Erica.

"Shut up, lady," yelled Gus.

"Who was that?" Dad asked.

I lifted my hands into a shrug. "Not sure. Might be Mrs. Williams, the person who lives next to Jeri."

Gus, whose angular face was now red, told everyone to shut up again. He gripped the blower handle so hard his knuckles were white, and the veins popped in his muscly forearms.

Jeri walked across the street, wielding the rake like a weapon.

"You!" Gus pointed with the blower at Erica. "Get off my property or I'm going to invoke the Stand Your Ground law. And Jeri, don't take another step toward me, or you'll regret it. I've already threatened to get a restraining order against you and your wife."

"Don't you touch her," Jeri said, taking a wide-legged, martial-arts stance.

"Holy cannoli," I whispered.

Erica grabbed the blower nozzle and shook, similar to what Stanley had done with his toy. I let out a little gasp. This needed to end before it turned into an all-out neighborhood brawl.

"Stop it, all of you, now!" I ran toward them as the blower roared to life.

As Gus blasted air in our direction, I pulled Erica away. Well, dragged her, with the help of Dad, who spoke in soothing tones about "calming her chi."

We'd managed to reach the sidewalk when two police cars roared up—with lights and sirens—and parked at the curb.

We were safely on our patch of the sidewalk. Out of the corner of my eye, I spotted Jeri scurrying back into her house.

"I guess Mrs. Williams, or someone, called the fuzz," Dad declared. "Erica, don't talk to them. We'll get you a lawyer. You have constitutional rights."

"I've got nothing to hide. Anyway, he threatened me first." Erica shook Dad and me off while shooting bullets at Gus with her eyes.

"Remember, in the spirit of temporary victories, violence never brings permanent peace. We can fight this with the right vibe."

"Dad, stop quoting Martin Luther King. Erica, hush for now." I watched as my boyfriend, Noah, climbed out of one of the cruisers. Holy fluff. This was embarrassing. "Please let me handle this, okay? I don't want to have to bail either of you out of jail."

I started to head toward Noah, then stopped when I realized Dad and Erica were following me. I pointed at the ground and spoke in a tone I occasionally used with Stanley when he jumped on people with muddy paws. "Both of you. Stay here. On our property. Neither one of you move."

"But—" Dad and Erica said simultaneously.

"No," I said sharply.

I marched over to Noah, who by now was standing in Gus's driveway, with his hands on his hips. He turned in my direction with a stern face. "Lana, what the heck's going on here? We got a call from the neighbor about—and I quote—'a ruckus.'"

The word *ruckus* almost made me chortle because it was such an old-fashioned thing to say. What was next? *Malarkey?* But I refrained from laughing because of Noah's displeased expression. I opened my mouth to speak, but he continued while squinting at me, "And what happened to your hair?"

My hands went to my head. During the melee, Gus's leaf blower had blasted my hair with hurricane-strength wind. My normally curly locks were poufy and matted. At best I looked like a member of an eighties hard rock band. At worst, like Edward Scissorhands.

"There was a little communication breakdown between Gus and Erica. She—well, the entire block—is upset at how much he uses his leaf blower. Then Gus turned his blower on us. That pretty much explains everything, including my hair."

He let out a long, exasperated sigh. The other officer, one I vaguely recognized because he came into Perkatory from time to time, walked up. "Chief, do you want me to take the main perps into custody?" He gestured to Gus, then Erica and Dad.

"No!" I yelped.

Noah shook his head and briefly closed his eyes, as if he were exhausted. "No need. You can head back to the station. I've got this under control. This is a minor dispute between neighbors."

He was silent while the officer walked to his car, got in, and drove away. His lack of words made me a bit nervous, because usually Noah was warm and chatty.

"All right, gather round, folks. Erica, Peter, Lana, and you." He pointed at Gus. "Take the leaf blower off and come here."

I'd seen Noah in a variety of situations, but never when he was taking charge like this. He was simultaneously respectful, stern, and commanding of this tense situation. It was both reassuring and attractive, and yet part of me knew I should feel at least a little guilty for being involved in a near-brawl.

But Noah's dark hair, flashing eyes, and sharp jaw made me feel things. Womanly things. I cleared my throat and studied a mini mound of dirt, an indication that that fire ants had invaded this part of the lawn. I shuffled closer to Noah.

Erica and Dad inched toward us with sheepish looks. We all stared as Gus wrangled the leaf blower off his muscular body. He walked over.

"And your name is?" Noah asked.

"Gus Bailey, sir." They shook hands.

"Okay. Here's the good news. I'm not taking any of you to the county jail today. I'm not writing you a citation. But I am giving you a warning. If I, or any of my officers, have to return here, we're not going to be as kind. I will not tolerate a feud between neighbors. Am I clear?"

I nodded enthusiastically. Erica said *yes* in a clear voice. Gus took a deep breath and grunted a word that sounded like *okay*.

Dad raised his hand like a schoolboy.

Noah pointed. "Yes, Peter?"

"Chief, my daughter and her friend are disturbed by the incessant leaf blowing."

Noah pinched the bridge of his nose. He, of all people, had heard Gus's blower and had expressed his annoyance more than once. Still, I could tell this entire situation was vexing him.

"Gus, I'm going to ask you to keep your leaf-blowing activities between the hours of nine AM and five PM on weekdays."

"Sir, I can't do that, because I work. I need to be able to blow on weekends. And it helps calm me down."

A long sigh escaped Noah's lips. "Fine. Let's say Mondays, Wednesdays, Fridays, and Saturdays. Nine to five on weekdays, and nine to noon on Saturdays."

Gus's nostrils flared, and I expected him to protest. To my surprise, he nodded. "Fine."

"See?" Noah smiled, and it was like the sun was shining through clouds. He had such a gorgeous smile, something out of a toothpaste commercial. Everyone visibly relaxed and basked in his beauty. Or at least I did.

"How difficult was that?" he asked.

Gus strode off, picking up his blower along the way. He went into his garage and slammed the door.

Noah looked at Dad and Erica. "Would you mind if I chatted with Lana alone?"

The two of them shook their heads and scampered back inside.

"Let Stanley out of the kitchen. But no more kibble," I called after them.

Noah turned to me. "Lana, I didn't take you for someone who would be involved in a melee."

I belly-laughed. "Melee. Ruckus. I've never heard anyone use those words out loud before. Other than journalists and cops. Do you know it was my goal when I was at the paper to use those words at least once a week in a story?"

"Lana, I'm serious. I don't want you going around picking fights."

I rolled my eyes. "I wasn't picking a fight. I was trying to calm Erica down. And attempting to keep Dad from getting involved."

"Erica is . . ." he sighed and looked in the direction of Main Street, which was only two blocks away. "Your father is . . ."

"What? A bad influence?" I crossed my arms over my chest.

"No—well, yes. No. Listen. I love both of them. But together, they can be"—he paused to lick his lips—"a lot to handle."

"Erica wasn't wrong. All she did was ask Gus not to blow early on a Sunday." I wasn't entirely sure of what she'd said, of course, but the way Noah was acting, I felt as though I should defend my best friend.

"I know. But here's the thing: I don't want you, or Erica, confronting Gus. Or even talking to him, really. I'm not as worried about your dad because he's a big, old peace-loving hippie, but—"

I cut him off. "Wait. Are you telling me not to talk to my own next-door neighbor? Why? Is there something I should know? Or is this some latent sexist trait that I'm just discovering about you?"

He gnawed on his bottom lip. "Lana, I'm not being sexist. Sometimes I can't tell you everything. You know that. Stay away from him."

I stepped closer to him. "So you know some interesting details about Gus?"

He nodded once. I placed my palm flat on the muscular plane of his chest. Today he wore a sapphire-colored T-shirt, orange board shorts, and Tevas. Not exactly the best color combo, but it was Sunday in Florida, and he was technically off duty. Plus, he looked adorable in anything.

"Can you give me a hint?" I purred. As a former reporter, it physically pained me when I knew people had information that I didn't. Especially if it had to do with something illegal; I'd been a crime reporter for years, and pumping cops for clues and color while on stories was second nature. Even if that cop was my boyfriend.

He kissed my forehead and wrapped his big hand around mine. "Nope. I have to get back to the station. See you tonight at my place."

With a squeeze of his hand, he walked away and climbed into his cruiser. I waved as he drove off, but my mind was now on the mysterious man next door. I hadn't gotten to know him since he'd moved in, mostly because I'd been busy running Perkatory, training my puppy, and navigating a new romance.

But who was Gus Bailey, and why had Noah so sternly warned me away from him?

Chapter Three

The winter sun dipped below the horizon of the sparkling blue Gulf of Mexico, and I settled into Noah's sofa, my stomach full from his expertly grilled shrimp. We'd laughed so much over dinner, with him telling a story about how, as a patrol officer, he'd responded to a report of a baby in a trash can—and it had turned out to be a burrito.

I described Erica's latest project in my house. She was working in my garage to reupholster some of her boat cushions. She made a mess with swaths of cloth, a sewing machine that had been my mom's, and dozens of pieces of cutout pattern paper, but I didn't care.

A busy Erica was a happy Erica, and she was deep into her project when I'd left this afternoon.

I'd spent several hours at Dad's house, helping him prepare for a small dinner party he was hosting. He'd also agreed to take Stanley for the night, since my furry friend was a social dog and loved gatherings. In fact, since Dad and Noah lived close to each other on the island's North Beach, I hadn't been home since noon.

Which was probably why I had that beachy, lazy, vacation feeling. Being near the water always did that to me; it was as if I was a tourist in my own hometown, without a care or a responsibility in the world.

In my hand was my first glass of crisp, apple and-cedarwood-tinged, pinot noir. I liked to drink a dry glass of wine after a meal, not with it. Sweet wines gave me a headache.

Noah knew this and had bought an expensive vintage from my favorite winery in California. We'd actually visited there together for a long weekend two months ago, and it had been the most romantic trip of my life.

I held up my glass, smiling at the memory of how we'd walked through the rows of grape vines, holding hands. "You remembered."

"How could I forget?" He sat next to me, his own drink in hand. It was his first drink too. "Are you ready for the dessert cheese? I bought several kinds today."

We'd also started indulging in dessert cheese. Could we be any cuter? Plus, cheese was my weakness. "Maybe in a few minutes," I said.

We sipped in companionable silence.

"That sunset is something else tonight," he murmured, leaning in to kiss my cheek.

I glanced out the sliding glass doors, to the orange-sherbet sky, and hummed pleasurably. "So was dinner." I paused and took a second sip. "You know, I wanted to ask you something."

"I'm not telling you about Gus."

I laughed. In the hours after the melee at my house, I'd set aside what Noah had said about my next-door neighbor. Now, like Stanley with a toy, I was latched on to a couple of other mysteries, ones that were awkward and possibly uncomfortable for both of us.

"No, I wasn't going to ask about that."

"Okay, good."

"Are you avoiding my dad?" I blurted. "Because of the monkey situation?"

He half smiled, half grimaced. "Maybe a little. You know I adore Peter. But he's getting to be a little much with the Jane Goodall activism. There are a couple of monkeys who could really hurt people if they got too close. And you know they have that strain of primate herpes. Not exactly what the town's Chamber of Commerce wants in the news, a tourist getting infected from a wild animal."

"I know. And I agree with you, I think they should be safely relocated. But I really want you to get along with my dad."

Noah drew me close. "I know you do. It's not your fault. I don't like confrontation. Well, personal drama-slash-confrontation. And your father has a way of hammering on a topic in a very gentle way."

"You're not kidding."

"I don't want to get in a position where I might say something that offends him, and inadvertently upset you. You're my top priority."

"Aww." I snuggled into his side, reveling in the warmth. It was January in Florida, which meant it was warm as summer for the Canadian tourists, who were probably still swimming in Speedos and bikinis at this very moment. But us Floridians thought of this as cozy season. If Noah had a fireplace, I'd have insisted we light it, even though the temperature was all of sixty-five degrees outside.

"I'll have a serious talk with Dad and ask him to simmer down. I think if I explain it to him in basic terms, he'll see the logic in not harassing you about the monkeys. At least when you're off duty."

"I hope. Because I do miss Sunday brunch at your house. And he does make excellent muffins."

I'd brought a few of the citrus-flavored baked goods over to Noah's house, and he'd wolfed one down while cooking the shrimp. I swear, that man had a bottomless pit for a stomach.

I trailed my free hand over his knee. "There's another reason I wanted to make sure you were on good terms with Dad."

"Oh yeah? Why?" Noah tilted his head and studied me.

"I was hoping Dad and I, and you and your mom, could all get together for dinner sometime. Maybe for . . ." My voice trailed off for a second. "Easter?" I finished.

He let out a swoosh of air. "Easter's a pretty big deal in my family, being Catholic and Cuban and all."

"Oh, right. Well, . . . um . . . Valentine's Day?"

He frowned. "I kind of had secret plans for you on that night. Something involving a weekend away and the Bahamas."

Eeep. Exciting! "Okay, well, that's out. How about a nice, Saturday evening dinner at my place? Don't you think it's time I meet your mom? I'd really like to get to know her. She seems so interesting and fun, from everything you've said. I'll cook a couple of lemon chickens—the ones you love—and you can make the side dish of arroz . . . arroz . . ." While I couldn't think of the Spanish word for the dish, I was impressed at how I'd sandwiched into the conversation my desire to meet his mom.

"Congri?"

"Yes, that's it." Noah made the most flavorful black beans and rice, probably because he added a hunk of salt pork while cooking. "You could make that, and your flan, and I could make my Nutella brownies. Plus a salad, so we get some vegetables. It would be a huge feast. Wouldn't that be awesome?"

His jaw moved from side to side. My heart plummeted.

"You don't want me to meet your mom? We've been dating five months, and you still haven't introduced us. How come?"

His fingers went into my hair and stroked gently. "Lana, cupcake, it's not that. It's—"

Right at that crucial moment, his cell phone rang. It was a shrill, old-school ring, and it shattered the tense mood that hung in the air. My breath rushed out in a groan.

He let out a soft, gentle swear and hoisted himself off the sofa. "That's the station. I need to grab that."

Blergh. What timing. Cool air replaced the warmth on my left side, where I'd been happily pressed against him. I clenched my back teeth, chiding myself not to say something sarcastic like *Saved by the bell* or *Isn't that convenient.*

"Garcia," he barked into the phone, sounding as annoyed as I felt. His back was to me. Then he practically yelled in an incredulous tone: "*What?* You're kidding!"

My ears perked up, and I shifted into a rigid, upright position.

"You're sure? The same location I responded to this morning?"

I held my breath. How many places had Noah gone this morning—other than my own block? He hadn't mentioned he'd had any other calls today.

"I'll be right there. Make sure the scene is secured, and don't let anyone near the area." He turned to fix his black eyes on me. "Especially the neighbors."

I pressed my hand to my chest and played with the charms of my sea glass and dolphin necklace that Barbara, one of my baristas, had made for me.

Noah tapped the screen of his phone with his finger and licked his lips. "I need to go. You stay here."

I held up my hand. "Hold on. What's happening?"

"There's been a report of a body."

I narrowed my eyes. Noah using passive police lingo—a report of a body—was unusual during regular conversation. He reserved that for official business. "Okay. So why would I stay here? You'll be gone for hours. I can head over to Dad's or go home."

His expression mirrored the stern look I'd seen earlier in the day. "Your neighbor, Gus Bailey, was found dead."

"What? Oh my goodness." My mind raced at the news. "So why do I need to stay here?"

"Because I don't want you interfering with the investigation."

I jumped up, my insides feeling spiked with adrenaline. "No. That's my home, and I'm free to go to my own house. Or are you telling me that my place is a crime scene?"

"No. Your home isn't a crime scene." By the way he paused I half expected him to follow up with the word *yet*.

"Good." I strode across the room, my A-line pink dress swishing around my knees. For some reason, his bossiness, combined with the fact that he'd been evasive about his parents, irked me. "Then I'm going back to my house. You're not the boss of me, and you can't keep me here against my will. I'll make coffee for you and your officers. And at some point, we're going to have to talk about us. Our relationship."

Noah sighed and hung his head.

Feeling wounded, I flounced out of his condo.

* * *

As expected, my neighborhood was a hotbed of law enforcement activity. Officers were stationed at each end of the block, and I came to a stop next to an orange traffic cone, then rolled down my window.

"Ma'am, we're only letting local traffic onto the block."

I smiled patiently. The officer was a guy I'd gone to high school with, and was new on the force. "Jorge, don't pretend like you don't know me. I live here. You know that. And I'm dating the Chief."

Jorge Aguilar, who was three years younger and had been a band geek, like me, in high school, sighed. "Oh, jeez, Lana. I didn't recognize you at first. You're all dressed up with makeup and stuff. You don't look like that at the coffee shop. I'm a little nervous because this is my first suspicious death."

"It's a homicide?" I yelped, jumping to conclusions.

He grunted. "No. Yes. I don't know yet. It's really suspicious, and the crime scene guys are crawling around. There's talk of the sheriff's department coming over from the mainland to help. The Chief was on the radio a couple of minutes ago and sounded super on edge. Listen, please don't put that in the newspaper, okay?"

Jorge knew I occasionally did freelance articles for the *Devil's Beach Beacon*. And I figured Noah sounded anxious because of our fight, but I certainly wasn't going to share that with Jorge.

"Don't sweat it. I won't. This is between us. I haven't been asked to write an article or anything."

He smiled gratefully. "Thanks."

"But listen." My voice dropped an octave. "If you find out anything interesting and want to share the deets, come on by Perkatory tomorrow. I'll be working the early shift. And you know I'll give you a free latte anytime, regardless."

After thanking me, he nodded and moved the traffic cone aside so I could drive down the street. Why had I said all that to him? I wasn't writing an article. It apparently was instinct after years of being a crime reporter in Miami. Whenever I saw a cop on duty, I felt compelled to pump them for information.

Still, it was strange. I hadn't felt the need to report or investigate in months, and now my curiosity was churning the wheels inside my brain.

As I pulled into my driveway and saw all the police cars, crime scene vans, and the medical examiner's SUV, an idea blossomed. I hustled inside and went to the sofa, where I could spy on the goings-on from the comfort of my living room.

I grabbed my phone and dialed Mike Heller, the editor of the *Beacon*.

He answered on the first ring. The background sounded as if he was in a club with thumping electronic music. "Lana, good to hear from you. You'll never guess where I am," he yelled in his deep baritone.

"Uh, are you in Miami at a club or something? It sure sounds like it. Can you hear me?" I hollered back.

He chuckled. "I can hear you fine. I'm at your father's house, enjoying some delicious veggie burgers. Hey, Peter," he called out, "I'm on the phone with your daughter."

I scratched my head. Dad, who had taken Stanley for the night, had told me he was having an "intimate dinner party." He'd called it a "full moon gathering," but this sounded more like a rave.

"Uh, Mike, I wanted to tell you that something's happening here. On my block. My next-door neighbor's dead. And it's suspicious."

The sound of the music grew louder.

"Your next-door neighbor's a Peeping Tom?" he yelled.

"No," I screamed. "He's *dead*. And it looks suspicious."

"Oh! Well golly. Keep me posted. Let me know what you find out, and I might be able to—" He was interrupted by a series of muffled noises. "Sorry, Lana, your dad and Barbara are trying to get me to do shots. Someone brought over a bottle of mezcal from Mexico."

"What?" I snorted. I knew the over-sixty set in Devil's Beach was a bit wild, but to have my dad's house be the party epicenter of the island was a bit much to bear, especially considering I was almost thirty-one and had barely drunk two sips of wine all night. "Is Stanley okay?"

There were more clicks, then footsteps. "Munchkin?" Dad's rumbly voice came over the line.

"Dad?" I shut my eyes, exasperated. "Is Stanley okay?"

"Yeah, he's snoozing in my room. We tired him out with a game of fetch. What's going on?"

"Gus Bailey's dead," I cried, opening my eyes and flipping the blinds open so I could watch the action next door. "My cop sources tell me it might be suspicious."

"Whoa, whoa, whoa. I'll ask around to find out some intel. But I'm in no shape to drive over now. I'm sorry, Lana. I could take one of those Ubers, if I figure out how to use the app."

"No. Do not drive over. Do not get in an Uber. Stay where you are. Let's not complicate matters. I only called to tell Mike in case he wants a story for the paper."

"I'll ask him about that. In the meantime, gather what you can."

"Ten-four. Oh, and Dad?"

"Yeah?"

"What music are you listening to? You're usually a Grateful Dead kind of guy."

"Oh, someone put this satellite radio on. It's called BPM. Or EDM. Or BFD. It's dance music. Pretty groovy. I think the DJ is named . . ." His voice crackled, and I didn't get the name.

We hung up. In his late sixties, my widowed dad never ceased to amaze me. First the new age stuff, the yoga and crystals and full moon bathing. Now he was into club music?

I'd covered dance music festivals back in Miami (well, the arrests), but I didn't know Tiesto from Trick Daddy. My taste in music was squarely in the yacht rock category, with a strong undercurrent of eighties hits and retro-sounding new bands like The Weeknd. I was a Gen Xer trapped in a millennial's body.

For a few minutes, I watched as more police cars and officers filled the block. Noah drove up, and I studied his handsome profile against the flashing blue and red lights. He was only about thirty feet from my window, standing in Gus's driveway. Did he know I was watching? Probably.

But I wasn't going to glean any information staring out my living room window. It was time to get to work. In my kitchen, I brought out my industrial-sized drip coffee maker and five pounds of Perkatory House Blend, which was my preferred grind to drink at home.

I also had a few portable, disposable cardboard carafes, the kind with a plastic spout. It was best to keep these around for impromptu parties, my mother had always told me.

When the coffee was finished brewing, I filled a carafe. Feeling purposeful, I toted it outside along with a sleeve of disposable cups and a plastic bag with little tubs of creamer and packets of sugar. Although I missed Stanley's presence at home, I was kind of glad he was with Dad tonight because I sensed I'd be going in and out a lot, and wouldn't want him underfoot.

I rounded the corner of my house and approached a group of officers who were all guys. Jorge was among them.

"Gentlemen, hey," I said warmly. "I've got some coffee for you. I live next door, in case you didn't know."

Of course they not only knew where I lived but also that I was dating their boss. Our relationship was well known all over town. Everyone thought it was adorable that the town's (relatively) new police chief was with the owner of the most popular coffee shop. We were invited to parties, fundraisers, and political events— although we always politely declined the latter.

"Wow, Lana," one of the officers said, "you didn't have to bring us this. But dang, it smells delicious."

"Aw, I wanted to. All y'all work so hard. Plus it's colder than a gravedigger's heart out here. Officers need coffee because it's going to be a long night, right?"

Jorge scurried over and took the carafe out of my hands, and I gave the stack of cups and condiments to another officer.

"It probably *is* going to be a long night." The tone was stern, and I whirled around.

"Chief, why hello," I exclaimed innocently, as if I hadn't huffed out of his condo a half an hour ago.

"Lana, what did we discuss?" He walked over and gently took my elbow, steering me back toward my house.

"I figured your officers deserve some good coffee."

"It's much appreciated. But stay inside, please."

"C'mon. Tell me what's going on. How did he die?" I batted my eyelashes.

Noah sighed.

"I'm going to find out one way or the other. You'll have to put out a press release."

"Are you writing a story?" He squinted at me in disbelief.

"Well. No, not exactly . . ." I bit my lip.

"But you called Mike Heller already."

"I mean, yeah. How could I not? Mike's actually at my dad's. They're having some sort of full moon party."

"You didn't answer my question. Are you writing a story? Did Mike hire you to freelance an article for the *Beacon*?"

I tilted my head back and forth. "He didn't explicitly instruct me to write a story. He merely asked me to fact-find."

"Fine. Here's what I can tell you officially, on the record. I'm working on a news release anyway, and I'll be sending that to the media soon. So I might as well tell you."

"Should I run inside and get my notebook?" I asked, excited.

"No. it's quite short. "Gus Bailey, a fifty-two-year-old white male, was found deceased at his home, near downtown, in the Beach Oaks neighborhood at approximately eight thirty PM."

About two hours ago, right as Noah and I had been enjoying our shrimp kebabs. "Who found him?"

"Neighbors."

I looked around. There were a group of people standing across the street, gawking at Gus's house. I spotted Jeri and her wife, Perry. "Really? Who?"

"I can't tell you that right now. They heard something, noticed the unusual, and called nine-one-one."

"How did Gus die? Natural causes?"

Noah shook his head. "No. Definitely not natural causes."

"Yikes. Someone killed him?"

"Perhaps. Perhaps not. That's what we're investigating."

"Come on, give me more than that. What did the neighbors hear?"

"An explosion."

Chapter Four

I reared back, anxiety surging through me. "What? Huh? His house and car are still here. What exploded? Are we at risk here? Should you evacuate the area? Is it a gas leak? Those can be quite dangerous. Did you call the utility company?"

"Hold on a minute, Lana. Calm down. There's no threat to the area. A single device exploded and killed him."

"A device? A bomb? Or like a firework?" I wrinkled my nose. None of this was making sense. "How did it kill him?"

"It appears that pieces of metal from the device pierced his back at the right angle, striking his heart and lungs."

"What device?"

Noah ran his hand through his dark hair. "The device he was using earlier today."

I opened my mouth in a silent gasp. "Gus was killed by his own leaf blower?"

"From the looks of the body, and the angle of the shrapnel, that's what we've determined."

"I've never heard of such a thing. How awful." Although I hadn't known Gus well—really, I'd only had those handful of brief, curt exchanges with him since he moved in—I felt terrible. No one deserved to die in such a violent, weird way.

"Me neither." Noah looked toward Gus's house. "Now we have to figure out if it was a faulty engine that accidentally killed him, or . . ."

"Or if someone tampered with it?"

He nodded, his mouth in a grim line.

"Who would want him dead?"

Noah raised his eyebrows and took a deep breath. "I need to make some calls. I want you to go back inside and stay there. Please."

He walked off. I stood and blinked. What a bizarre day. "Wait, I have more coffee—should I bring it out?" I called out to Noah.

He turned. "When we're ready, I'll come get it."

From his commanding tone, I knew he wasn't playing around. Probably I should've taken that as my cue to go back into the house immediately, but I've never been great with following orders. I sprinted across the street, to where my neighbors were clustered together.

They immediately surrounded me and lobbed question after question.

"What did the chief say?" Jeri asked.

"Did he tell you that Gus died when his leaf blower blew up?" Perry asked.

"Did he tell you that we found him?" Jeri added.

"You know how he died? You were there?" I asked, a bit incredulous. The way Noah had explained the cause of death, it had seemed like he was revealing the information for the first time.

"Oh, sure. Gus started up his leaf blower at about seven PM. We were about to go over and give him a piece of our mind when we heard the explosion. It was loud. Rattled the windows, like a thermonuclear explosion," Jeri said in a high-pitched, excited tone.

I frowned. "A thermonuclear explosion?"

"She's being dramatic. You know that she's writing crime fiction these days," Perry added, and the rest of the neighbors nodded.

"Oh, right, I forgot about that." Jeri had recently retired from the Devil's Beach Public Works Department and had been taking a class on writing novels. Perry was a retired sports radio announcer. "Anyway. What happened after you heard the explosion?"

"We ran over there." Perry screwed her face into a grimace and gestured to the side of Gus's house that was only feet from my own home. "And it was pretty bad. He was dead when we arrived."

Jeri shook her head. "Gruesome. That's when we called the cops. He looked like—"

"You don't need to go into details," another neighbor chimed in.

"Definitely not," I said. "Goodness. That's terrible. Do you think we're in any danger?"

A few neighbors shrugged. We all stared at each other with a mix of wariness and confusion.

"No," Jeri said quickly. "It was probably a faulty machine. Or he put too much gas in it, or something happened with the engine. He used the darned thing so much that it probably overheated."

The other neighbors nodded. "Yeah, that sounds most plausible. I mean, who would tamper with a leaf blower to kill someone?"

I glanced across the street, and locked eyes with Noah, who was standing next to a fireplug-shaped man several inches shorter than Noah. It was Vern, the medical examiner. He waved. I smiled and waved back.

"How are you, Lana," Vern called out in a friendly voice.

"Not bad. Nice to see you, Vern," I said.

"Lana," Noah called out, then pointed at my house.

"Ooh, he's got you on a short leash, girl," Perry said.

"He does not," I said, a touch defensive. "He's worried that I'm going to poke around and write a newspaper article and blow this story wide open."

"Well, are you going to?" Jeri asked, putting her hands on her hips. They both knew about my former career as a journalist and that I'd freelanced a bit for the *Beacon*.

"Perhaps. Listen, I've got to call my dad and tell him all about this."

The group chimed in and agreed that my father would probably be able to find out more than any of us here could. One person suggested I get Dad over here, and I demurred, not wanting to say that my father was likely in no shape to show up at a crime scene.

"See all y'all later." I walked across the street to my house, feeling Noah's eyes on me the entire time.

"I'm going inside now," I called to him. "Making more coffee for my favorite officers."

I hustled back indoors, eager to call both Dad and Mike to tell them the news. There was something more to Gus's death. I could feel it, and it further awakened the old reporter instinct in me—so much that I was almost out of breath by the time I dialed Dad.

"Munchkin!" he cried when he picked up. The music was even louder and pulsing with a disco-like beat. "What's the scoop?"

"Get Mike and go on speakerphone in a quiet room. I can't hear you with all that noise. I've got a lot to tell you."

"What you hear is Avicii," Dad said, spelling the name. "Hang on."

Who was Avicii? Some new friend? A DJ? I rubbed my forehead and waited, while I heard Dad and Mike yelling for each other over the sound of the thumping bass.

"Okay, we're outside. Can you hear us?" Mike said.

"Yes, I can. Much better." I explained everything I'd gleaned from Noah, adding that it was all on the record and would soon be public information. "We should write something. This is a fascinating story. I'm in a position to type up an article."

"Hmm, sounds like a brief," Mike said. "I think the morning cops reporter can handle it."

"A brief? It's a wild story. Even if it's accidental, have you ever heard of someone dying from an exploded leaf blower?"

"No," Mike admitted. "But I don't have a freelance budget, so it's going to have to wait until tomorrow. No one reads the website on a Saturday night anyway. It can wait, and we'll get better traffic tomorrow."

I was about to protest, but then I realized I was no longer a journalist, that it wasn't my newspaper, and that I had to get up at five thirty tomorrow morning to open the coffee shop. Not my circus, not my monkeys.

"Okay, your call. I'll talk with you two later. Dad, I'll see you tomorrow at noon when your shift starts."

Perkatory was technically Dad's—well, Mom had started it years ago, and it had been in both their names—but I was effectively running the place now that Dad was semi-retired and obviously a senior party animal. He was good about showing up for his shifts at the café, and he was an excellent dog sitter.

"Stanley and I will be there," Dad said, and we hung up.

* * *

At that point, did I go to bed? No.

Or did I forget about the death next door and do something productive, like bake treats for the upcoming week at the café? Also no.

Instead, I flopped on my bed with my laptop and scoured the internet, looking for information about Gus Bailey, my now deceased neighbor.

Immediately I learned from the *Devil's Beach Beacon* that Gus had owned—or maybe still owned, I couldn't tell—a local business, the *Royal Conquest*.

It was a well-known, black-hulled boat that looked like a pirate galleon and was docked at the marina not far from Perkatory. Every night at sunset, it was packed with tourists. The ship circled the sparkling blue waters of Devil's Beach, playing Jimmy Buffet tunes interspersed with cannon blasts. People who took the two-hour cruise were treated to an all-you-could drink open bar and a special Mardi Gras–type necklace with a medallion that read "BOOZE BEADS BOOTY."

Needless to say, it wasn't my cup of coffee. While I adored living on a beautiful tropical island in the Gulf of Mexico, I preferred activities that were less raucous. Like reading under the shade of an umbrella. Or drinking an iced coffee in the shade on my porch. Or taking Stanley to the dog park, the one with the big, shady oak trees.

As I was about to navigate over to the county court's website to see if Gus had any pending lawsuits—a common research tactic among reporters across Florida, since almost everyone in the state had some sort of brush with the legal system, whether it be a divorce, a civil lawsuit, or actual illegal activity—when there was a loud knock on my door.

I jumped up and ran out of my bedroom, through my living room, and to the front door. When I flung it open, Noah was on the other side.

"Hey there! You ready for that coffee?"

"Am I ever." He brushed past me.

I expected more officers to follow him, but since he was alone, I shut the door.

"Wait. You want some coffee?" I stared at him. Noah rarely, if ever, drank coffee. I'd only seen him drink one cup in the time I'd known him. His normal drink was hot water with lemon.

He threw his hands up in the air. "No. Yes. Maybe a half cup. Do you have decaf?"

"Whoa. If you want coffee, this must be pretty serious. Come on into the kitchen."

"Do you have, like, half decaf–half regular? I don't want to get too jittery."

I refrained from teasing him, since his face was pinched with worry. "Sure. I think I have a bag of decaf beans I can grind up. Sugar? Creamer?"

"Yeah, both." He sank into a stool at the high-top table in the kitchen as I bustled about. "Feels weird without Stanley here."

"It does. Dad's taking good care of him, though." I chattered on about my dad's apparent new love of electronic dance music, but Noah didn't laugh.

After carefully brewing and mixing his half-decaf coffee, I poured it into a to-go cup and set it in front of him. "You okay?"

He sighed as he took a sip. "That's pretty good, actually."

I smiled, triumphant. "Told you."

"This is going to be a difficult case. I can feel it."

I sat across from him and leaned over, resting my hand on his knee. "Why?"

"ATF is here."

"Oh goodness." I knew that the Bureau of Alcohol, Tobacco and Firearms got involved during unusual explosions, terrorist acts, and other interesting cases. "So they must be really worried that there's a defect in that leaf blower. They'll likely issue a recall, right?"

Noah shook his head. "No. It's not a flaw with the machine. They think it was tampered with. It was quite obvious by looking at the wiring and the fuel source, someone spliced it together to cause an explosion."

For the second time tonight, I was at a loss for words. "So. It's a . . ."

"Homicide? Yes. We're officially calling it that. Of course, we still have the autopsy, which Vern will do tomorrow."

"That's wild. Do you have any suspects? Who wanted him dead? He was the owner of a pirate tourist boat, I think. Doesn't seem like the kind of guy people would want dead."

Noah lifted the cup to his lips, took a sip, and then stared me straight in the eyes. "He recently sold the tourist boat business in the last couple months." He swallowed. "And I can think of one person who recently had a fight with him."

I frowned. "Who?"

"Erica."

My mouth opened, and a growl of outrage welled in my throat. "Erica isn't even on the island. She went over to Joey's, and they were headed to Orlando for the night."

"Are you certain of that? Have you heard from her? Has she texted you?"

"Of course I'm certain." I mean, she hadn't texted in hours but that was probably because she was having a blast at the water park. "Erica's not a murderer, Noah. Come on."

"Just so you know, we're going to investigate all possibilities." He drained his cup. "Thanks for this. You should try to get some sleep."

Instead of responding with something feisty, I was quiet as I walked him to the door. Then I ran for my phone to text Erica. I should've told her the news hours ago.

But she didn't text back. It was almost midnight, and it was likely she and Joey were shooting down a giant waterslide or dancing in a wading pool with glow sticks.

Envy for and fear of missing out on a carefree night at a water park hit me hard.

I tried to sleep but tossed and turned because of the muffled sounds of the police voices right outside my window.

Chapter Five

Morning broke, and with sleep still clawing at my eyes, I blinked and patted the other side of the bed. Noah, who had come in at two AM and crashed at my house for a couple of hours, was gone. No light illuminated the bathroom, and I couldn't hear any activity downstairs. For a second, I wondered why Stanley wasn't at my feet, but I remembered that he was with Dad.

It was five fifteen in the morning, and still dark.

With my body feeling worn and creaky, I padded to my bedroom window. It was on the second floor and overlooked Gus's property. I scanned the yard, hoping to spot Noah.

The hubbub of last night's police activity was gone, replaced by yellow crime scene tape across the driveway that flapped in the breeze. A lone police cruiser was parked in the driveway. It wasn't Noah's car, and I could make out the silhouette of a blocky, flat-topped, military-style haircut. No, that definitely wasn't Noah, who had unruly dark hair that grew fast and looked adorable when it was on the longish side.

From this vantage point, I could see exactly where Gus had died—in the swath of lawn in between our homes, but closer to his building. He'd taken his final breath mere feet from my kitchen on the first floor.

What a terrible tragedy. Even though I hadn't been friendly with Gus, his death shook me. And the situation could've been even worse—our houses could've gone up in flames—had the neighbors not been around to call authorities. Or if the explosion had been more powerful.

The normally vibrant green grass was blackened and singed, and even the cream-colored siding on his bungalow was tinged an ominous brown.

I checked my alarm clock. Crud. Already I was running a few minutes behind, so I showered quickly, then threw on a clean, long-sleeved, cream-colored Perkatory T-shirt; a pair of jeans; and my most comfy sneakers. Then I recalled that it was January and the forecast was for winter temperatures—well, winter for us— and I dug out my warmest jacket: an old, puffy army-green parka that was better suited for a ski slope.

Since it was Florida, I didn't care if I looked ridiculous in my winter clothing. Dressing weird in winter was almost a point of pride among locals.

As I ran out, I spotted a note on the kitchen counter.

Had to leave early to get my beach run in. I'll see you later at Perkatory. xo, Noah

At least that made me smile. Noah never missed a day of exercise, unlike me. I'd been trying to attend beach yoga, and bicycle more, but he was diligent about jogging five miles a day, bless his big, healthy heart.

Since I only lived a few blocks from the café on Main Street, I extracted my sky-blue beach cruiser from the garage—Erica had upholstery cloth spread everywhere—and prepared to bike the short distance. Okay, so that was what I meant by "bicycling more." It was a start.

I paused in my driveway while waiting for the garage door to close behind me.

The presence of the police car in the nearby driveway reminded me of Gus's death, and I shuddered as I pedaled away. The January air felt crisp and cool on my cheeks, and I reveled in the sensation. This was our week of winter here on our tropical Florida island, and if we blinked, we missed it. Although I wasn't a morning person, the hushed darkness was a calming presence as I pedaled beneath the street lamps.

Once I was inside my café, life felt far more normal. I actually sighed aloud with relief as I flipped on the yacht rock satellite radio station, the soothing sounds of Fleetwood Mac filling the air. I slipped off my puffer jacket, thankful that I'd worn a long-sleeved shirt today. It sure was chilly.

I felt even better as I ground a batch of house roast and put the coffee in the filter. While we sold a lot of cold brew, our other top seller was our regular, drip coffee. I hauled out the bucket of cold brew from the back room and poured myself a small cup. Last year, I'd had a rough patch with the cold brew and had struggled to get it to taste right. Ever since then, I sampled each batch.

No cream, no sugar, no flavor syrup. Today, it was delicious, smooth as silk. Good deal. In the warm months I'd drink the cold brew all day, but today, I helped myself to a cup of drip coffee, needing the warm hug that only a fresh cup of joe on a chilly day could provide.

While drinking that, I tidied the contents of the fridge. My baristas yesterday—Heidi and Barbara—had left the milk cartons haphazardly on the shelves. I preferred them lined up in a certain way for easy access, in order of popularity: cow, almond, oat, coconut. When I started at Perkatory about nine months ago, we didn't offer a variety of plant milk, mostly because I'm a coffee purist and felt that it should be dairy milk or, preferably, nothing in our drinks.

I'd come around to expanded offerings because of customer demand. More and more people asked for alternative milk, and I was on the verge of adding chia and cashew.

It was a few minutes to six, with a glimmer of sunrise in the sky, and I'd just finished organizing the syrups—hazelnut, vanilla, caramel—when there was a sharp rapping sound against the glass door. I hustled over and took a gulp of air when I saw who it was.

Erica?

"Don't you have your key?" I said as I unlocked the heavy wooden and glass door.

"I'm coming straight from Joey's and didn't bother stopping at home, so no." She breezed past me and slipped on an apron. I did the same. "Dang, it's chilly."

Erica wore a long-sleeved black turtleneck and a big, fuzzy scarf, along with faded black jeans and black leather combat boots.

"What are you doing here? Isn't today your day off? You're not supposed to be working." For a moment, I forgot what day it was. Last night I'd barely slept, and because of Gus's death, time was warped and malleable. "Today's Monday, right?"

She sighed and an exasperated look left two lines between her brows. "We didn't go to Orlando, so I figured I might as well work. Joey had car problems. So we hunkered down and watched a *Fast and Furious* marathon."

"I texted you several times last night." I felt almost guilty that I sounded accusatory, like a jilted lover.

"Yeah, my phone died. Forgot to charge it until this morning."

"Wow," I said, suddenly uneasy at the realization she had been on-island when Gus was killed. The conversation I'd had with Noah raced through my mind. "You won't believe what happened last night."

I was about to explain everything when three people, all local retail workers and Perkatory regulars, streamed in.

As usual for this hour, everyone seemed subdued and half asleep, and Erica and I snapped into action with soft smiles and soothing, low voices.

No one wanted upbeat, boisterous baristas at six in the morning.

It was hard not to notice that people were wearing their old winter clothes. In Florida, this was usually a hilarious sight, with outfits cobbled together from old wardrobes "up north." One guy had on two sweaters, shorts, and socks with his flip-flops. Another woman, who worked at an insurance company and was from Haiti originally, wore earmuffs and a puffer jacket similar to mine. A third person wore a black ski mask, and loudly announced that he was merely cold, not here to rob us. It turned out that it was John, the owner of Beach Boss, a touristy souvenir shop in the same building as Perkatory.

Everyone in line chuckled when he pulled off the mask.

"So what's up?" Erica asked after handing John his coffee.

"Gus is dead," I said in a hushed tone.

"No way. He went to the big leaf pile in the sky?" She snorted, obviously not believing me.

"Erica!" I shot her a nasty look. "Don't be so flippant. It's a suspicious death. It might be murder." I emphasized the last word in a dramatic sotto voce.

She screwed up her face. "Yikes. You're right, I'm sorry. He's really dead? How? Who killed him?"

I took a bracing inhale. "His leaf blower exploded."

Erica visibly blanched. "Oh my God. No. You're joking. Is it on the news and everything?"

"Good question. I reached for my phone to check the *Devil's Beach Beacon*.

"Yep, here it is." There was a short article about Gus's death. It was the second story on the homepage, right after an article about a man who thought he was reeling in a fish in the waters off Devil's Beach—but it turned out to be a gun weighted to a brick.

The entire story on Gus was no more than three hundred words, and the only person quoted was Noah. It read like a rewrite of a police news release. Tsk. If only Mike had let me write the story.

But no. I was no longer a reporter.

I flashed the screen to Erica, and she grabbed the cell out of my hand and read aloud:

We're treating this as a suspicious death," said Chief Noah Garcia. "It's not typical when a man dies from an exploding leaf blower."

"Hello, Captain Obvious," Erica added.

"I'd have used a different quote, if I'd written the story."

A tendon in Erica's neck went taut, and she handed the phone to me. I skimmed the article again and made another click with my tongue.

"The paper left out a lot of details—or didn't ask the right questions. I should mention this to Mike. Noah told me the

ATF is involved, and the blower was tampered with. Basically it exploded and killed Gus. They think. It's not a hundred percent, but somehow they know it wasn't operator error or some freak mechanical issue."

She rubbed the side of her face with her palm while looking slightly dazed. "Are there a lot of suspects?"

I shrugged. Should I tell Erica that Noah had mentioned her? Or had he been rambling while exhausted and stressed? "Not sure. Noah didn't list any—well, not exactly."

"What do you mean?"

I fidgeted with the frayed edge of my apron pocket. "Well . . ." I sighed.

"What? Tell me."

My eyes flitted around the nearly empty coffee shop. Was relaying the conversation I'd had with Noah a breach of trust? As I was about to open my mouth, the bells on the front door jingled, signaling a customer was entering the café.

"In a minute. Let's help this person first."

Erica let out a soft yet audible sigh. At that moment, a woman who worked at Sweet Thing, a saltwater taffy shop downtown, shuffled in wearing furry boots, plaid shorts, a parka, and sunglasses. She was one of our regulars who stopped in multiple times a day for coffee. Her name was Darla Ippolito, and I wasn't sure if she actually ate food, or only consumed caffeine.

Normally she wore her all-white work uniform or shorts and T-shirts. Today her outfit made Erica and me giggle.

"Sorry. I can't help it," Erica said, eyeing Darla's brown boots.

"I couldn't find my ski pants or my sneakers." she mumbled. "I didn't move to Florida for this cold weather. I'll take my usual, an iced espresso. No, wait. Hot coffee. A large regular with a shot of espresso. Hey, why's it so cold in here? Like a meat locker."

Erica began pouring her hot drink and said something about the coffee warming her up.

Darla scowled at me, and I held up both my hands. "Fine. Fine! I'll turn up the heat."

I scurried to the back room to notch up the thermostat, then texted Dad, asking him how Stanley had slept overnight. By the time I returned to the front, Erica had already served Darla, who was standing to the side of the counter, stirring her coffee.

At the sound of the jingle from the bells attached to the front door, I called out my automatic greeting. "Welcome to Perk . . . oh, hey Doug!"

Like Darla, Doug Rodgers was one of our uber-regulars. A Perkatory fanboy, if you will. He arrived by six thirty every morning and stayed through lunch, fueling himself with espresso, coffee, and whatever treats we had on hand. Sometimes he even ordered a giant pizza to be delivered for lunch, and shared slices with our staff. We weren't exactly sure what he did for a living, as he'd only answered our questions with nebulous phrases like "venture capital" and "digital nomad."

People like him were a solid quarter of the island's population, as far as I could tell, folks who'd decided to work from paradise instead of an office in a city. Couldn't blame them a bit.

Doug joked that Perkatory was his office, and we enjoyed him as a regular, since he was friendly, exceedingly polite and tipped phenomenally. Whenever we got new swag or merchandise—travel mugs, bags of limited edition whole beans, T-shirts—Doug would buy two, saying he would send one to out-of-state friends.

He'd worked from a corner table so often that we joked about affixing a brass plaque with his name to the wood.

Basically, he was our best customer. Normally, he'd bound in with a huge smile, his black messenger bag slung around his chest, wearing his cargo shorts and a crisp, plain white polo shirt. But today, he wasn't smiling. His face was long, his expression pinched.

"Everything okay, Doug?" Erica asked. She and Doug probably had the best relationship of us all, which was odd since he was usually so sunny, and she was her dark, punk rock self.

"I'm tired, is all," he said. "Had a rough night."

You and me both, I thought, as I wiped down the counter.

"Your usual?" Erica asked. Doug usually started his day with espresso.

"Naw. I need something stronger. What about a red-eye? I need to wake up."

"How about this? Lion's Roar. It's a new concoction that I wanted to try out. I named it myself."

Doug's eyebrows rose toward his hairline. "Sounds interesting. What's in it?"

"Mushrooms," I chimed in.

"Lion's mane mushrooms, to be exact. Plus coffee."

"That's disgusting," Darla piped up. The three of us turned our heads in her direction. I'd forgotten that she was still there.

Doug blinked for a second, then cracked a grin. "You always have the best suggestions, Erica. I'll take it."

"One Lion's Roar, coming right up." Erica busied herself at our La Marzocco machine. Doug and I gawked for a bit because Erica at work was like a ballet dancer on stage. Every motion was fluid and measured, and no time was wasted.

Erica took what looked like a vitamin bottle out of the pocket of her apron. "You sure you don't mind me trying this out?"

I shook my head. "Doug's the perfect test case. Aren't you, Doug?"

"Sure am. I'm game for anything."

She ground the espresso beans into the filter, carefully weighed that filter on a scale, then tamped the espresso holder by hand—basically pressing the ground beans into a uniform pod that would allow the water to flow through evenly. After that, she rinsed a glass with hot water, prepping it for the shot of espresso.

She inserted the filter into the espresso machine and tapped on a digital timer. Erica knew that the best shots of espresso were pulled in the twenty-five- to thirty-second range. Too little time, and the coffee would be weak. Too much, and it would be bitter.

"Perfecto," she said, when the shot came in at a perfect twenty-seven seconds. A lush aroma of coffee, with notes of cherry and chocolate, filled the air. I watched as she opened the bottle and stirred a teaspoon into the coffee.

"We're going to try this with honey, if that's okay?" she called out.

"Honey's good, honey," he responded.

I returned to the counter to chat with Doug. "I had the craziest night last night. My neighbor was found dead. Can you believe that?"

He blinked. "Whoa, nelly. You're kidding. I'm so sorry. You live over on the beach, right? With Peter, er, your dad?"

I shook my head. "No, I'm downtown here. It was my parents' house, the place I grew up in. But Dad and Mom moved to the beach right before she died, and Dad stayed there. When I moved home I went to the bungalow. I didn't know the neighbor well, but I couldn't sleep after the entire situation."

"Oh my. That's too bad, Lana." He coughed. "Sorry. Allergies are killing me this year."

Erica set the cup of turbo-charged 'shroom coffee on the counter. "Hope you enjoy. I think this will wake you up in no time."

"You're a lifesaver. I'll probably be back for a second." He took a whiff of the cup. "Interesting."

He took a small sip and nodded thoughtfully. "Wow, this is something. A little like . . ." he smacked his mouth. "Sweet earth."

"Is that an endorsement?" I asked with a wince.

"It is, actually. But I'll also take a triple espresso."

Erica clapped her hands together, gleeful. Doug thanked her and wandered over to his regular table and took out his laptop.

I turned to Erica. "Good lord. You're going to kill him with caffeine."

She waved me off. "He apparently has the CYP1A2 gene, which means he's a fast metabolizer of caffeine. He'll be fine."

"How do you know this?" Erica harbored the most bizarre details about people, I swear.

"Eh, we were talking about genetics one day. He invested in one of those companies where you spit in a cup and get your DNA tested."

"Okay, then."

"So back to Gus."

"Right. This is totally off the record—"

"Of course."

I pulled her behind the espresso machine because I didn't want any of the customers hearing that we were discussing murder. From past experience, I knew homicide was bad for business. "Noah kind of mentioned your name in relation to Gus. How you had that altercation with him yesterday morning."

Her eyes bugged out as she leaned toward me. "What do you mean, 'kind of'? He thinks *I* tampered with Gus's leaf blower and killed him?"

"No, he didn't say that. Not exactly."

"But he thinks I'm a suspect?" With jerky, quick motions, she began wiping down the espresso machine. "Do *you* think I killed Gus?"

"You? No. Oh my god. Never," I yelped, then quieted down. "You're a little eccentric and have a bit of a temper, but you'd never kill someone. You wouldn't even kill that gross flying cockroach that got into the kitchen the other day." Flying roaches were common in Florida, and Erica had taken great pains to trap it in a cup, then tote it outside so it could, in her words, "live its best life outdoors."

"So what's going to happen?" I could tell she was agitated by the way she ripped open a new bag of coffee instead of cutting it cleanly with a pair of scissors.

I shrugged. "Probably Noah will ask you where you were and what you were doing. No big deal. You've got an alibi in Joey."

She appeared to be lost in thought as she stared into the bag of beans for a couple of long and uncomfortable seconds.

"Erica? You were with Joey, right? Right?" I hissed while gently squeezing her shoulder.

She nodded and shook my hand away. "Totally. I hung out on his sofa all day. Watching *Fast and Furious* movies, like I told you. Yeah, I'm fine. A hundred percent."

A stream of customers came in, and Erica and I slipped into a companionable rhythm of taking orders, pulling shots, and mixing drinks. But I couldn't shake an uneasy feeling that she wasn't telling me something important.

Chapter Six

Hours later, Dad strolled in with a grin, wearing cargo pants, a black Pink Floyd T-shirt, mirrored aviator sunglasses and Stanley in a pooch pouch.

This was a tie-dye contraption that looked like a front backpack, the kind used for babies. Only this was specially designed for dogs. Stanley, who was on the smaller side for Shih Tzus, adored the contraption so much that Dad and I each had a pouch, so we didn't have to constantly adjust the straps. Mine was hot pink, though.

Stanley wiggled his little apricot-colored body when he spotted me and Erica. As a puppy, his fur was slightly darker, almost a black-tinged gold in spots. Now he was lighter and in bright sunlight, his fur looked like spun gold. There was no dog in the world cuter than Stanley, and although our origin story was tragic—his original owner, one of my baristas, was murdered—he was my heart dog. My soul pupper.

"Who's a good boy? You? Are you a good boy?" I said in a high-pitched baby voice, unzipping the pouch and freeing my dog so I could smooch him.

"Erica, I thought you were off today?" Dad said. "How long you staying?"

"Change of plans. I'm out when Barbara comes in." That was one of our other baristas, a woman close to Dad's age. She was also an artist who made wall hangings from scavenged beach detritus, and had recently expanded into making sea-themed jewelry.

"I'm going to wash up and put my apron on." Dad made his way around the counter and loped into the back room. "Stanley hasn't peed in a while."

"Thanks, Dad, for telling the entire café," I muttered, then turned to Erica. "You sure you don't mind staying until Barbara arrives? I need to get Stanley out of here."

Lately the town council and the health department had been cracking down on animals in eateries, and I didn't want to risk a violation.

"Don't sweat it, dude. I've got it under control with Peter."

Erica always had my back. "Thanks. And listen, don't even worry about that Gus situation, okay?"

"Nah, I won't."

She closed her mouth, then opened it again, but before any words came out, the music abruptly changed. One minute Don Henley was singing about the end of innocence, and the next there was a heavy bass beat, synthesized riffs, and what sounded like a guy grunting "oh yeah" over and over.

"What is that?" Erica whispered. "It sounds like someone's jackhammering inside my head."

"I feel like I'm in a cheap club in Miami." The song changed to a rhythmic beat, and out of the corner of my eye I saw Doug bob his head in time with the music. I turned my back to him and grimaced at Erica. "This is the kind of music Dad was listening to last night when I called him."

She visibly winced. "Might want to talk to him about that."

Nodding, I toted Stanley into the back room, praying that no one from the health department was in the café. Dad was washing his hands.

"Hey there, I have some wicked gossip for you." He lathered up. One thing Dad was diligent about was hygiene. And gossip.

"Uh, cool, but I need to ask you something. Did you change the satellite radio station?"

He turned the water off with his elbow and reached for a paper towel, his eyes glittering. "Yes, this is Diplo's Revolution. Don't you love it? I've been listening to this a lot lately. Don't you dig the beat?"

I stroked Stanley's fur. I very much did not dig the beat and found it headache inducing. But I was leaving, and if that was what Dad, Erica, and Barbara wanted to listen to, I guess it was okay. "Make sure the customers don't mind. They're usually pretty pleased with the yacht rock."

"Sure, sure. Now listen. About Gus."

I rifled through my backpack and found a leash for Stanley. "What about him?"

"Apparently, he and Honey had some troubles. They were separated. I told you that. But it turns out he had a girlfriend too."

I rolled my eyes. "What, he wanted someone even younger?" It was difficult to hide the snark, because I was a bit salty about older men who paired up with much younger women. My ex-husband—now a bigshot TV news reporter in Miami—had left me for a twenty-two year old.

"No, that's the thing. He left her for one of the women who works at the library. She's his age."

I clipped the leash onto Stanley's collar. When I stood, he immediately tried to climb my leg. "Well, that's a twist."

"Yep. And I'm hearing Honey isn't all that sad about Gus's death. Apparently she was skating by the beach today."

I scrunched up my nose. "How do you know those things?"

"Well, it's the leader of the crystal bowl group. You know, Abe?"

"Abe. No. Don't know him."

"He's a mystic. His wife, Ethel, is an astrologer."

"A mystic? Dad, come on. What even is that?" Sometimes Dad was a bit much, trusting in people I thought were total crackpots. As far as I knew, he wasn't giving them his life savings, but thankfully now that I was back on Devil's Beach, I could keep a close eye on the situation as Dad got older.

"A mystic's similar to a light worker."

I snorted. "Okay, whatever. That tells me nothing."

"Abe knows a lot about the people in the group. About their auras. He was something of a father figure to Honey."

"I'll bet he was." Sarcasm dripped from my tone. "Anyway. We're leaving so Stanley can do his business. We're going to take a little stroll to that new pet food store down the street, and then we'll be back for the bike." My bicycle had a deep basket in front for Stanley, and he loved riding with me.

"Sounds great, munchkin." Dad gave me a kiss on the cheek as he passed by, tickling me with his beard. Now that I thought about it, he looked a little like a thin Santa Claus. Or an extremely fit Jerry Garcia.

"Your beard's getting a little long," I called out. "And so is your hair. You look like a hippie."

"Make love, not war, man," he cried as he loped out.

* * *

I strolled out the back door of Perkatory, with Stanley on his leash, trotting alongside me. I wore a small, black leather backpack to carry some essentials: my phone, wallet, a bottle of water and some dog snacks. That last item I'd pilfered from Dad's tie-dye fanny pack that he'd stashed in the storage room.

Stanley paused to sniff a palm tree in the alley, and a chill went through me.

This was where Stanley's previous owner, a handsome Italian barista named Fabrizio, had been found dead—by me. That had led to the acquisition of my canine companion. I gently tugged at Stanley's leash, not wanting to spend too long at the spot. I'd disliked the alley ever since, and not just because I'd found Fab, who had been pushed off the roof of this very building.

It was because Fab's killer had almost forced me to jump from the rooftop myself. I had an intense fear of heights that hadn't improved since that incident.

Stanley was all too happy to sashay out of the alley and onto Main Street. It was his favorite walking path on the entire island, probably because he loved to stop at every patch of greenery and tropical flowers to mark his territory.

I didn't mind that the six-block-long downtown district took sometimes forty-five minutes to traverse with my dog, because it meant that I could peer into the windows of the cute businesses that lined the sidewalk. Main Street was adjacent to the beach. Locals tended to walk on the sidewalk near the shops, exercisers kept to the beach sidewalk, and tourists thronged both. The two-lane street that divided the shops from the beach was often filled with bicyclists, scooters, and recently, a guy with a python wrapped around his shoulders while navigating a hoverboard.

The scene was delightfully quirky, like Devil's Beach.

Today I noticed that Whim So Doodle, the craft store, had a new display. The theme was Valentine's Day, since it was only a few weeks away. Sparkly gold hearts, puffy white clouds made out of cotton batting, and pink papier-mache cupids crowded the window. I knew the store's owner and had heard she was holding crafting classes weekly.

For a second, I fantasized about making something cute for Noah. Then I wrinkled my nose. He was ten years older than me, for goodness sake. I was thirty-one, not seven. No, I needed something more sophisticated than a craft. He'd mentioned the Bahamas for the weekend, so maybe I'd get him . . . a book? An expensive pen? A new pair of swim trunks?

As I pondered this, Stanley pulled at the leash, wanting to sniff the next foliage spot. It was in front of the hardware store, and I waved at the clerk inside. I knew almost everyone who worked downtown, since most came to me for their caffeine fix.

My gaze shifted to the window, where there was a display of leaf blowers. It was an abrupt reminder of Gus and the entire situation with Erica.

"Eek," I said out loud, then turned to Stanley, who had his snout deep into a purple-and-yellow viola. "C'mon, buddy."

As he raised his head, I felt a rush of wind soar past me. It smelled faintly of coconut. Startled, I looked to my left and saw nothing. Then to my right.

It was a woman, roller-skating down the sidewalk, her long blonde hair flying in the wind. My eyes went wide, recalling Dad's words. Was that Gus's wife?

I watched as she stopped at the nearest corner and pressed the "Walk" button to cross. The pedestrian sign flashed almost immediately, and she gracefully rolled across the street, to the oceanside. A car beeped at her, and the driver, a man, waved and whistled.

The woman wove her way around a few packs of tourists. She took a hard right, which meant she was headed to the splash pad, a water attraction for little kids that was covered in asphalt and benches. Families loved it because it was a place to wash off sand from the beach and as a playground for kids.

Why was she going there? I'd passed signs that said "No Skateboarding" on the splash pad, because starting when I was a teen, a bunch of skate punks liked to terrorize downtown. That had to mean roller skating too, right? And why would someone want to roller-skate where there was water spurting from the ground, like mini Las Vegas–style fountains?

I swooped down and hoisted Stanley into my arms. He wouldn't walk as fast as I needed him to, not with his stubby legs.

Because he was all of nine pounds, I tucked him under my arm like a package, and making my way to the corner, crossed the street and power walked to the splash pad. Along the way, two teen girls ran past me.

"I can't believe we saw Honey in real life," one said breathlessly, as if she'd spotted a celebrity.

Excitement prickled at my scalp, similar to how I felt when I was chasing a big story back when I worked at the Miami newspaper. So it *was* Gus's wife. Why was she skating in public less than twenty-four hours after the man was killed?

Interesting.

I arrived at the entrance to the splash pad, slightly out of breath. There was a folding sign that said "SPLASH PAD CLOSED MONDAYS," which answered at least one of my questions.

Because I knew half the town, I didn't want to make it seem as though I was following Honey or, worse, desperate to gawk at her, so I set Stanley down and tried to pretend we happened to be strolling by. Dogs weren't allowed on the beach, but they were allowed on all the concrete paths near it, so we sauntered in and found an empty bench.

But I quickly deduced that it didn't matter what I was doing, because all eyes were on Honey. There had to be at least thirty people gathered in the circle, some sitting on benches, others on the ground. Most were young, in their teens. I even spotted Darla, our regular customer from Saltwater Taffy, sitting in her cobbled-together winter outfit, drinking coffee from a Perkatory cup.

I waved, but she must not have seen me, because she didn't wave back. Weird. My attention was immediately diverted to Honey, who commanded center stage in the middle of the pavement circle.

She slowly spun a few times, then came to a stop. "Who has a portable speaker?" Her voice was velvety and rich, and combined with her pretty, tanned face and long legs, it was no wonder that Gus had fallen hard for her. Most men, and many women, would too.

But her question struck me as weird. Who carried portable speakers with them?

"We do!" The two girls who'd passed me by squealed. "What do you want us to play?"

Maybe not that weird. Maybe I was old and out of touch with new technology.

"Pick a disco tune. Anything you want." Honey said, gathering her long hair into a messy bun with a pink scrunchie.

The girls, who had been born decades after the disco era, conferred and got busy. One hunched over a phone while the other took out a small, blue wireless speaker. About thirty seconds later, the funky strains of the seventies tune "Boogie Oogie Oogie" began.

Honey shimmied her hips, skated backward, and blew the girls a kiss. Then she literally boogied on wheels, and my jaw dropped. Even Stanley seemed transfixed by the dancing, undulating Honey Bailey. She wore old-school skates with white boots, the kind with four wheels. Those were silver and sparkly.

Her outfit consisted of hot-pink Lycra bike shorts, a matching bikini top, and a silver fanny pack around her waist. Light pink sunglasses topped the outfit off.

She was possibly the only person on the planet to make a fanny pack look cool, and for that alone, I was impressed.

This was Gus's estranged wife?

She skated in a circle, shimmying backward, doing little twisty motions with one foot in the air. She shook her hips. Snapped her fingers. Spun in circles. Swayed to the beat. Honey appeared impossibly hip, and I would be lying if I said I wasn't a bit envious.

I'd never seen anyone so graceful on roller skates, and the crowd obviously loved it. Most were taking photos or videos, while a few hooted, hollered, and clapped.

She ended her disco routine when the song did, by doing a lunge move and trailing her fingers along the ground. Everyone cheered.

"What talent," exclaimed an elderly woman sitting at a nearby bench.

Honey did a final spin and blew kisses. "Thank you, everyone. You make me feel so good. Something terrible happened yesterday, and having your support means so much. I love you all, and remember, if you're visiting, or if you're a local and want to take lessons, hit me up on my Instagram page."

She gave the name, involving the word *skate* and the number eight, and glided away to applause.

I remained speechless. As a third-generation Floridian, I was used to weird stuff in the Sunshine State. As a journalist in Miami, I'd covered all manner and sorts of oddities. People high on bath salts who attacked others at random. Serial killers. Gators in parking lots at gentlemen's clubs. Heck, even here on Devil's Beach we had the wild monkeys with herpes.

But this was among the top five strangest things I'd ever seen. A widow who put on a public roller-skating show a day after her estranged husband was murdered by an exploding leaf blower?

"My goodness," I said aloud—er, well, to Stanley.

"She's something else, isn't she?" A young guy strolling past heard me. "My girlfriend's taken lessons from her, and Honey is the real deal. She's a total Instagram star, and I can't believe she's right here on Devil's Beach."

"I can't either," I said, wanting to chat with someone, anyone. I squinted into the sun, looking at the guy with floppy brown hair, who seemed to be in his late teens. "So the lessons were good?"

"Yeah, my girlfriend could skate backward and everything after only two lessons. That was only a week ago."

"What's her story, anyway? Do you know? Honey, I mean?"

The guy shrugged. "Dunno. She's like around thirty. I think she's married to some old dude. Apparently he showed up at the lesson, but Honey told him to leave. My girlfriend said it was kind of awkward. But Honey's awesome. She's Insta famous."

I nodded slowly. "I see."

"Hey, I gotta run because I'm parked at a meter and didn't pay." The guy jogged off.

I plucked my phone out of my backpack and sent a quick text to Erica. If only she'd been here, I'd have loved to have gotten her snarky take on Honey.

Dude, you're not going to believe what I just saw.

* * *

"You mean she literally roller-discoed in front of the entire town?" Erica eyed me suspiciously, as if I was telling a tall tale.

We were in my living room, in our usual spots on the sofa. Stanley was asleep between us, on his back. Today's walk had been a lot for him, plus the stimulation of being around all those people at the splash pad.

It was five thirty, and we'd demolished a pizza that Erica had brought home from her boyfriend's restaurant.

"Yes. Look at her Instagram." I passed my phone to Erica.

She scrolled through it while I stroked Stanley's downy belly. When he slept on his back, he looked a little like a zombie, because he stretched both paws straight out from his body.

"You know what we need to do?" Erica handed the phone back to me.

"What?"

"Take lessons from her."

I curled my lip. "Why?"

"We might find something out about her and Gus."

"But . . ." My voice trailed off, and then it hit me. "You want us to sleuth."

She lifted a shoulder. "I personally don't like being a suspect in a murder case."

"Can't blame you there." I ran my tongue over my top teeth. "You don't trust Noah to do a thorough investigation?"

"It's not that. I'd prefer to find out some details on my own. That's probably my dislike of authority, though." She stretched, looking like a feline. "I figured you'd want to pitch an article to the *Beacon*, anyway."

Hmm. When I'd been laid off from the paper in Miami, I'd returned to Devil's Beach to run my family's café. Since then, I'd written a couple of freelance articles for the local paper, mostly since I knew the editor. The *Beacon* had been my first journalism gig as an intern back in high school.

"I guess I could see if Mike Heller wants an article." I swiped to my messenger app. "He did want me to look around last night. But he didn't seem that jazzed about a story."

"I'll bet he will be now that it's officially a homicide."

I texted him with my story about Honey and her earlier roller skating performance, including a photo I'd snapped while she was in mid-pirouette.

The dreaded three dots flashed on the screen, indicating that Mike was messaging back. But no message came, and the dots disappeared. Why wasn't he answering me back? Probably he didn't have the heart to tell me that he couldn't afford to pay a pittance for a freelance article.

Five minutes went by, and Erica and I changed the subject to Stanley's newfound love of baby carrots. I checked my phone again. No message from Mike.

I sighed and let my head flop back. Journalism was circling the toilet bowl of life. "I don't know about this."

"Whatever, baby. We're getting this cheddar."

"Cheddar?" I grimaced. Erica always had some new, hip phrase at the ready.

"This is an excuse to have an adventure. Plus it could get me off the hook. Please?" Erica looked at me with giant, doe-like eyes. "Pleeease?"

"Fine," I grumbled.

Erica picked up her own phone, tapped at the screen, and put it to her ear.

"Hello? Is this Honey? I wanted to find out about lessons." She paused, then a look of excitement spread on her face. "You have time tonight? Really? Can we rent skates?"

I looked up and stared at her with an open-mouth grimace. Roller-skating lessons? Tonight?

"An hour at the roller rink? Perfect. I'll be there. My name's Erica." She tapped at her phone screen. "There. We're all set."

"Erica. What? I'm not ready? I . . . I . . ." But I didn't have a decent excuse not to go, other than my sneaking suspicion that I'd break a bone roller skating. Especially since I hadn't actually roller-skated since I was about twelve. "I don't have a cute outfit. And I don't know if I want to go undercover with my reporting."

"We're not going undercover. We're taking a lesson. And it doesn't matter what you wear, but remember to bring socks. They have rental skates. C'mon, let's get ready."

She launched herself off the sofa, but the obvious lingered in my mind. Why was Honey giving lessons and skating around town without a care in the world so soon after her husband had been murdered?

Chapter Seven

The Hot Wheels Skate Shack was on the far east end of the island, right before the bridge to the mainland. It was tucked into the town's only industrial park, in a giant warehouse—so it definitely wasn't a shack at all. More like eighties warehouse chic.

I pulled into the parking lot and stopped at a space facing the dull beige building. I stared at it for a few seconds. This was absurd.

"Has this rink always been here?" Erica asked.

"No. I think it's somewhat new. When I was a kid, my mom and I would go to the mainland to skate. Starlight Skate, that was the name."

"Oh, so you've skated before?"

I got out of the car, and Erica followed. "For a couple of years. But the rink on the mainland closed down when I was a sophomore, or maybe a junior. Mostly I loved the music because they played the good stuff from the seventies."

A small lump formed in my throat. My childhood memories at the rink with my mom were among the best. She was a solid, graceful skater—nothing like Honey, but still good—and I loved watching her glide around, singing to Fleetwood Mac tunes. Now that I thought about it, skating to those songs with her was what had sparked my love of Stevie Nicks.

"I also used to skate with Gisela." I paused to adjust my backpack, which held two pairs of socks, wallet, phone, and mints.

"Your friend from high school who went missing?" Erica knew all about the saga of my teenage bestie.

I nodded and took off for the entrance. "I stopped skating after she disappeared."

Erica pulled open the door, and my heart sped up when I dragged a breath into my lungs. The place smelled exactly the same as the rink of my childhood, a unique odor of popcorn, wood floor cleaner, and shoe polish.

We were greeted by a bored-looking teenager behind a counter. She was sitting in front of rows of skates, her head buried in her phone. The skates were rentals, I guessed, since they had a camel-colored boot and were not the snazzy kind that I'd seen on Honey earlier.

Behind the counter was a menu board listing the price of rentals and various specialty skate times on different days of the week. Today was Monday, which meant it was private lesson day. Tuesday, Wednesday, and Thursday evenings were for adult skating, and Fridays and Saturdays were for kids only.

"Welcome to Hot Wheels. We're closed for private lessons tonight."

"That's exactly why we're here," Erica said, drumming her fingers on the counter. "We're meeting Honey."

The teen, who had a pierced eyebrow, nodded and gestured to a glass door. "Go ahead, then. She's got the far side of the rink tonight, along the back wall."

We thanked her and passed through the door. I expected to see the dazzling skating rink of my memories, all black light, dayglow planets, and shards of disco ball glitter. This was far less exciting, probably because the harsh fluorescent overhead lights were on, and everything seemed tired and cheap, especially the threadbare red carpet.

The rink was partitioned into three zones: two at the ends and one in the middle. A handful of people, mostly parents helping kids lace their skates, sat on the benches. One end was occupied by a tiny woman teaching two tweens, the middle by two men in rollerblades and with hockey sticks, and then there was a lone figure along the far wall.

"Is that Honey, in the bell-bottom jeans and seventies fringe top?" Erica whispered.

"Yup." We moved in her direction. She was doing a disco dance routine very similar to what I'd seen earlier.

"Holy cow. Is she cosplaying the seventies or what?" Erica asked.

"I think that's her thing. Her brand. She always dresses like that."

"Gotcha." Erica broke away from me and leaned over the rink rail.

"Hey there." Honey smiled and glided over. "Are you Erica?"

"I am. And this is my friend Lana. She's going to be the one taking the lessons."

I shot a panicked look at my friend. "But I thought—"

"Nah, I'd rather watch you. Maybe next time." Erica gave me a hard stare. She was probably trying to tell me something, but for the life of me, I couldn't deduce what.

"Awesome! What size are you? Did you bring socks? I'll get you some skates." Up close, Honey was even prettier. Her blonde hair was in a tight ponytail. She seemed so friendly. So helpful. Not at all like a killer.

"Uh, I'm a seven. And yeah, I brought socks."

"Perfect." She took a phone out of the back pocket of her tight jeans. "Hey. I need some sevens down here. Thanks. Only one pair."

She hung up and slipped the phone back in her pocket. "My name's Honey Bailey, and I'm a professional roller skater. I guess you probably found me from my Instagram. I charge twenty-five an hour for the first five hours of instruction, and then the price goes up. But we can get into all that later. It's groovy to meet you both."

She even talked like she was in the seventies. No wonder my dad was so fond of her. We shook hands, and her grip was featherlight.

"So, Lana, what's your skating experience? Why do you want to learn to skate?"

I tugged at my earlobe, increasingly uncomfortable with the situation. "I skated for a couple of years when I was a kid. At Starlight, which used to be on the mainland."

She nodded enthusiastically. "I've heard a lot of people talk about that place. Lots of memories there."

"I haven't skated since. But I really enjoyed it." At least that was the truth. Hopefully she wouldn't press me on her other question—why I wanted to skate as a thirty-one-year-old woman.

"Wonderful. So why take skating lessons now?"

Crud. I swallowed. "Well . . ."

Erica jumped in. "I'm her best friend, and Lana's been complaining that she needs to find an exercise that she loves. She's tried jogging, yoga, and kayaking. Hates them all. I told her that fitness needs to be fun."

"I didn't hate kayaking. I only disliked all that sun."

Honey let out a little laugh and ignored me, still focusing on Erica. "That's exactly my philosophy. I promote fun. I'm a fun ambassador."

I let that sink in for a half second, until the bored teen from the front shuffled over with the skates. "Which one of you needs these?"

"Me. Thanks." I accepted the skates.

Honey clapped her hands together. "While you put those on, I'll grab the consent forms from my bag." She glided away, to the other side of the rink, and Erica and I stepped back and sank onto a hard wooden bench.

I turned to Erica. "Why aren't you taking the lesson with me? Why are you leaving me alone with her?"

She spoke slowly, as if I was having trouble absorbing words and concepts. "So I can try to rustle up info from everyone else here while you chat her up. Divide and conquer. We can find out more this way."

It made some sense, but I didn't have to like it. Grumbling under my breath, I slipped my backpack off and rooted around for my socks. "This isn't the way I usually approach a reporting assignment."

"We're launching a casual inquiry. And, you were complaining last week about how fit Noah is and how you wanted to find something you could do for exercise and enjoy. So I wasn't fibbing. And you did say you hated kayaking, so don't lie."

She'd actually been listening to me when I went on my rant about how my boyfriend ran at least five miles daily, rain or shine. Without the benefit of caffeine.

I slipped on the socks, then tugged on the boot of the roller skate and laced it up. A snug fit, just as I remembered. As if it had a mind of its own, my foot glided back and forth on the floor.

By now, Honey was back on our side of the rink. She held out the form, and Erica took it from her.

I fished out a pen and quickly scrawled my signature on the paper. Honey waved at it. "Oh, leave that there, with your stuff. I'll grab it at the end."

"Well, have fun," Erica said in an uncharacteristically bubbly voice. "I'm off to get a soda pop. Later, alligator."

She wandered away, hands in the pockets of her black jeans. I turned to Honey and smiled.

"Since you've skated before, Lana, I like to start the lesson by seeing how you are on the rink. Come on in, and skate around this U-shape here." She made a curved motion with her finger, following the rink.

I took a deep breath and stood up. Part of me expected to splat on my butt almost immediately. After all, I was deeply inflexible when it came to yoga. But my balance on a paddleboard wasn't bad, and Mom had taught me to skate all those years ago.

I rolled easily over to the opening and, with great care, stepped onto the rink. Honey smiled encouragingly. I was now trapped here with her.

"It would be a lot easier if there was music," I murmured.

"Oh, I know. Wouldn't it? But the rink keeps the tunes off during lesson times. If you continue, we can do more during free skate, and that's when they play the good songs. I know the DJ personally, so we can get him to play whatever you want." She winked at me. "Now take a spin so I can see your form."

Staying close to the rail, I pushed off with my right foot. Something in my brain clicked, and my body almost instantly took over. Until now, I'd never believed in muscle memory. But

I easily skated around the end of the rink, slowed my roll, and stopped across from where I'd started.

Honey was still at the gate, and Erica was nowhere to be found. Part of me wanted my friend to see how well I was doing out here.

Honey gave me a thumbs-up. I skated back the way I came, feeling more confident by the second. As I approached her, I dragged my right wheels against the floor to come to a stop.

"Wonderful! Wow!" She seemed genuinely impressed. "You are so good! How long did you skate for? You have excellent form."

"I do?"

"Absolutely. You have a natural rhythm to your flow. I can tell it's going to be easy to take you to the next level. You do want to learn to disco skate, right? Because that's my specialty. Maybe you want to do your own Insta channel?"

Now that I was on wheels, the idea of skating for exercise and fun was indeed tempting. Showing off on social media definitely wasn't. "I dunno about that. Maybe I'll start with the fun fitness part."

"Killer," she said, and my scalp prickled, remembering why I was here.

"How did you get into skating?" I asked, figuring I'd start by asking her a simple question.

"Probably like you and all other kids. I went to the rink with my brother and his friends. I loved it and never stopped. Then I watched YouTube videos of rinks in the seventies, and I became obsessed with the aesthetic. Got an idea to film my own videos." She giggled and gestured to her macrame fringe top. "As you can see."

"Your Insta channel is amazing." I was being truthful and also wanted to ease into the conversation. The best way to do that was with a little flattery. My years of being a reporter had taught me that.

"Thanks. I started it three years ago. A friend of mine in Fort Lauderdale made a little video of me skating by the beach, and it kind of took off from there. Wild, right? I didn't expect to be famous or anything. I live to skate. But it's really opened a lot of doors."

"I'll bet it has."

"Last week, a documentary crew contacted me. They want to do a whole thirty-minute show on me. For Netflix." Her blue eyes widened.

"Whoa, that's amazing! Congrats." I paused while she murmured thanks. "When did you come to Devil's Beach?"

"Only a few months ago." She smoothed back an invisible lock of hair. "I moved here with my husband, who went to high school here. Well, my ex. It's complicated."

Gus was a Devil's Beach native? How had I—or Dad—not known him? I started to calculate ages and high school graduation dates in my head. He was younger than Dad but older than me. That was probably why neither of us knew him.

"Men always are." I swallowed. Now was the time to take the plunge. "Where does he work?"

"Uh, he owns a business here. Well. Did." She inhaled sharply. "He sold that a couple of months ago, and then, uh, . . . passed away."

I pressed my hand to my chest while gripping the railing. "Oh no. I'm so sorry. That's awful."

She nodded, and I noted that her eyes weren't even watery. My heart rattled in my ribcage.

"We were separated. We'd only been married a couple of years, and I was going to divorce him. But his death has really messed with my head."

"That's quite understandable. And he must've been young."

She stared at me for a beat. "Well, not really. He was older. Fifty-two. You might've read about it in the local paper today. There was a brief. His name was Gus Bailey. There was an accident at his house."

Oh dear. What to do now? If I didn't tell her I lived next door to Gus, what if she discovered that info later? Would we have a second skating lesson? Should I come clean and inform her I was rooting around for a story—one that no one at any news outlet had assigned or requested?

I decided to tell the truth while omitting the detail of how Erica and I were here on a fact-finding mission. With a genuine, sad expression, I said, "I know Gus. He was my next-door neighbor."

Her pink lips formed an O. "On Hibiscus Street?"

I nodded. "I'm in the bungalow with the begonia hedge. And the manatee mailbox. Well, that's not helpful, since everyone on the street has one. Well, everyone but Gus."

Probably I should shut up now.

Honey frowned. "Weird, you don't look familiar. I think I know the house, but I never saw you. I wasn't paying attention." Then she lifted a shoulder into a shrug. "Or maybe because I only lived in that house for a month, and then Gus and I separated. I moved to a place on the beach because I really love it here."

"I'm sure that's it." My tone was soothing and conspiratorial. "Plus I work a lot of weird hours. I manage Perkatory, the café. Anyway, I'm really sorry about his passing. Seemed very . . . unusual. Quite a shock to me and all the neighbors when the police came, since it's such a quiet street. He was certainly well-known in the neighborhood."

"Oh yeah, I've heard of that café. Never been in. I'll have to try it out. I usually go to Island Brewnette."

Gah. She wasn't taking my bait about Gus's odd death.

"I see." I tried to keep my voice neutral. Island Brewnette was the other coffee shop on the island, pretty much the polar opposite of Perkatory. It was minimalist, sleek, big-city hip. My shop was like a tropical cozy heaven with fluffy pillows and woodwork painted robin's egg blue. I'd have never pegged her for an Island Brewnette customer, not with her gauzy, 1970s style.

"Yeah, I go there because I get free coffee. I don't even really like the taste that much." She rolled her eyes. "It's super bitter, and I prefer sweet with, like, caramel. Or vanilla. I'm a vanilla girl."

"Free coffee?" I tilted my head. Mickey wasn't the kind of business owner to give anything free to anyone. Although Honey was so pretty, it wouldn't surprise me if she got a lot of perks everywhere she went.

"Oh yeah. The owner of the place and my husband—ex-husband—were kind of partners together. Or something. My husband sold a business to Mickey, I think. For a while met at Mickey's café."

I gnawed on my bottom lip. Mickey Dotson, the owner of Island Brewnette, was an irascible, difficult man. His daughter, Paige, had been my nemesis in high school. The fact that he was involved somehow with Gus didn't surprise me—but the fascinating tidbit did thrill me to my core. I couldn't wait to tell Erica and Dad.

"What kind of business?" I asked casually.

"Oh, you probably know it since you're a local. The pirate cruise ship."

"The one with the fake cannon fire?" The *Royal Conquest* had been a staple on Devil's Beach for years. With its red and black hull, tall masts, and majestic sails, it looked like an impressive Disney version of a pirate boat. The crew dressed the part, in puffy shirts and eye patches, and the attraction was known for its well-stocked bar.

When I was in high school, it had been owned by an out-of-town corporation that had similar boats in Clearwater and Daytona Beach—and I hadn't realized ownership had been transferred to Gus, or that he'd turned around and sold it to Mickey.

She nodded. "Gus owned it for several years, bought it before we met. When we moved here, he sold it to Mickey and some other guy. Maybe more than one guy. Honestly, I didn't pay much attention because my Insta was blowing up, and I was done with our marriage and his cheating."

"I see. I'm sorry," I said.

She gave a little shrug. "Between us?"

"Yeah?" I rolled a little in her direction. This was getting good. I felt exhilarated, like I had when I'd nailed a big interview for the Miami paper. Sometimes I missed journalism with a palpable ache, although the feeling had faded in recent months. Until this moment.

"I'm kind of glad he's dead. He was a total jerk to me. Had an affair almost the minute we arrived on Devil's Beach. Some woman from high school. A librarian. Can you imagine? Bridget something-or-other. I didn't ask or want to know her last name."

Whoa. So Dad's gossip was true. "That's terrible. How could he do such a thing? You seem so nice, and you're gorgeous."

"Thanks. Anyway, you didn't come to hear about my sad personal life." She let out a laugh, which sounded like wind chimes on a summer day.

Actually, I did, I almost said, but refrained. An awkward silence overtook us while on the other end of the rink, an instructor's yelled exhortation to "push with your legs" echoed in the air.

"Lana, can you skate backward? If you can, show me? Why don't we start there?"

"I think I tried once or twice when I was little." My mind spun at all the information she'd shared.

"Well, let's start there. Skating wipes reality away—you'll see."

She propelled herself backward into a spin and motioned with her hand for me to join her in the middle of the rink. For the next hour and a half, she kept me so busy with drills and instruction that I didn't have time to ask another question.

Chapter Eight

When the lesson ended, I thanked Honey as I sat and unlaced my skates. Part of me was hoping she wasn't a murderer, because I'd enjoyed my lesson so much. "That was actually super fun. I think I want to do this again."

"You can leave those here." She gestured at the skates. "You were excellent, Lana. I'd love to see you take follow-up lessons. You could do something with that talent of yours. You're a natural, I can tell."

Erica, who was standing next to me, elbowed my shoulder. "Look at you. See?"

"Do something?" I stood up with a confused expression. "Like what?"

"Instagram account, maybe doing tricks down at the beach. I was thinking about putting together a group performance of my best students."

I tried to imagine myself in tight jeans and a Stevie Nicks–style shirt, swaying and shimmying around town. It was difficult to picture, but the thought of Noah watching me show off like that made me grin. "We'll see. I'd definitely like to take another lesson. You're an awesome teacher."

It was true. She was. Honey seemed to have a well of patience in showing me how to skate backward. Which I'd somehow figured out during the lesson.

"How about next Monday?"

There was the issue of the article and of Erica's innocence. Would next week be too late? There were dozens of questions I still wanted to ask Honey. "Maybe later this week? I'm a little busy next Monday with work."

"Sure, sure. How about Thursday?"

"Excellent. Here?"

"No, let's skate in the real world. Meet me at the splash pad. We'll skate on the sidewalk by the beach. I'll bring skates for you. Unless you want to buy your own before then."

"I think I'll wait a little while before taking the plunge."

"Cool, cool. Do you know where the splash pad is?"

I saw you there earlier today, I almost said, but didn't. She'd probably think I was a weird stalker. I said I knew where it was and thanked her for the lesson.

Honey, Erica, and I all beamed as we said our goodbyes. As we walked out, Erica leaned into me. "I found out something wild."

I whispered my response. "I did too."

Once inside the car, Erica asked me to turn on the car, and crank the heat. "Don't turn on the air. Please. That place was freezing in there. It was like Antarctica."

I rubbed my arms, which were cool to the touch. "It was, wasn't it? So tell me what you found out."

"I chatted with the front desk girl."

"Wow, the bored-looking one? I would've never thought she'd talk."

"Existential angst. I know my people." Erica pushed her short black hair off her forehead, and it fell into a messy pompadour. "Apparently a week ago, Gus came in angry, demanding to see Honey. There was a very public argument, and Gus stormed out. The front desk chick said he looked violent."

"Whoa. But that's not a surprise 'cause he looked the same way on Sunday when you confronted him. What did they argue about?"

"Money. She felt that he should be giving her more. Apparently, she'd sent him an email asking for a bigger allowance. That's what she called it. An allowance, like a kid would with their dad."

"The front desk girl knew all that?"

"Yeah. Honey confided in her. Said her YouTube channel traffic took a dip, so she's not making as much. And she signed a prenup with Gus that said she'd get a certain amount of money if they separated or divorced, and he wasn't holding up his end of the bargain. He said she didn't make it to five years, under the terms of the prenup."

"Yikes. That's pretty incriminating."

"Yes indeedy, lemon squeezy. Apparently Honey is always good natured, but after that argument she was so angry that she cancelled all lessons that night. And she never does that, apparently. I tried to get more, but the girl got a text from her boyfriend. What did you find out?"

"Well, get this: Gus owns—or rather, owned—the pirate cruise ship in town. The *Royal Conquest*. He sold it a couple of months ago."

"Ooh." Erica turned in her seat to face me, and I did the same. "The red-hulled one, with the cannon blasts? The one where people get stinking drunk at sunset?"

I nodded. "And he sold it to none other than Mickey Dotson. Well, and some other people, but she didn't know their names. Mickey's been giving her free coffee at his café."

"Jerk. He probably flirts with her too. Hey, side note? What happened to his daughter? The one who was pregnant with Fab's baby?"

My history with the Dotson family was long and complicated. Right at the time my former barista, Fabrizio, was killed last year, his on-again, off-again girlfriend Paige Dotson found out she was pregnant with his kid.

"Haven't seen her in a while. I heard around town that she went to go live with her mother, Mickey's ex-wife, in Tampa somewhere."

"Ah. Well, maybe that's a good thing. Anyway. Do we think Mickey's a suspect in Gus's death?"

"I really dislike that man, but I don't think he'd kill anyone. Then again, I don't get the impression Honey would either. Most people don't seem like murderers to me."

"My sweet summer child, anyone could be a murderer." Erica laughed, and I did too. "Haven't you learned anything from all the true crime shows we've been watching?"

As I drove, Erica stared out the passenger window, a furrow in her brow. The inside of the car was silent for several minutes as we made our way down Main Street. "Who else disliked Gus?"

"Well, on our street, probably everyone. He moved in, fired up that leaf blower, and never stopped."

Erica snapped her fingers. "Perry and Jeri. What about them? Jeri looked pretty irate the other day."

"You think a retired lesbian couple in matching golf skorts intentionally tinkered with Gus's leaf blower so he would die?"

"You never know. We've been watching true crime shows on Investigation Discovery for three weeks now. It could be anyone. How can you be so naive?"

I sighed, unconvinced. By now we were at my house, and I felt a touch of rawness on my heels. I groaned as I got out of the car.

"I think those skates were too tight. I'm going to have blisters, I just know it."

*   *   *

After I put bandages on my heels, I lay in bed with Stanley at my side. Skating had been more physically taxing than I'd anticipated, but I felt spent in a good way. It had been a fruitful fact-finding mission, and Erica and I had several leads to follow up.

If we decided to look into Gus's death. I still wasn't convinced that we should, and even less so since Mike hadn't returned my text.

In the meantime, we had lots of potential research avenues on the internet, and it wouldn't be a bad idea to check out a few of them. For a second I pondered whether I should climb out of bed and go to Erica's room so we could do this together. Then I remembered that she'd said something about FaceTiming her mom in Seattle.

I tapped on my laptop, navigating to the *Royal Conquest* website. It showed the usual photos for a pirate-themed business: people drinking as they floated in the blue waters off Devil's Beach; dolphins; women in tight tank tops, throwing beads.

Goodness. I hoped those beads weren't ending up in the water. They'd almost certainly be terrible for the wildlife. Part of me wanted to tell Dad, but he had his hands full with the monkeys.

I poked around the website, trying to find further info about the owners.

Honey had said Gus sold the business to Mickey Dotson and another guy, but in the "About" section, all it said was that the ship was owned by a "local group of investors."

"That tells us nothing," I muttered to Stanley.

I navigated over to a notes file, the one I used when I was working for the newspaper. I tapped the return key a few times, then made a list:

SUSPECTS

1. Honey Bailey
2. Mickey Dotson
3. Unidentified business owner no. 2
4. Perry and Jeri
5. Bridget Something (library lady/lover)

When I got to the sixth line, I hesitated, thinking of Erica. Had I been a reporter—or a cop—I would have added her name to the list. But since I was her friend, it seemed almost blasphemous to consider.

My fingers hovered over the keys, unsure of what to type next. I looked over at Stanley, who was sleeping in his zombie pose. Belly up, paws straight in the air.

I sighed. "This is stupid, Stanley. I have no business looking into this, or writing a story."

I was too close to one of the suspects. The victim was my next-door neighbor. At any big-city paper, these two things would immediately disqualify me from doing an article. Things were a bit looser on Devil's Beach, though. Mike needed my expertise on this, and his staff were wide-eyed, recent journalism-school graduates.

My phone softly chirped with an incoming text, and Stanley opened his round brown eyes. Hoping it was Mike answering me about my story pitch, I lunged for the cell.

It was Noah.

Hey Cupcake. I'm finishing up at the station. You have anything to eat at your house?

I smiled. Noah rarely ate at work, especially when he was working on a big case, and was always ravenous at the end of a long day. A month ago, he and his officers were deep into a rash of car-break-ins—there had been dozens, including my Honda in the driveway while I'd been at Noah's one night—and I'd brought him dinner for a week straight so he'd eat something.

Yeah, I think we have some leftover pizza. Come on over.
Be there in five.

"Guess who's coming over?" I said to Stanley, who sprang into a sitting position and cocked his head. "Your favorite human. Noah."

He let out a soft wuff. I snapped the laptop shut, stood up and helped Stanley down to the floor. He stretched, like he always did after a nap. I checked my long-sleeved white T-shirt to make sure it had no stains, then inspected my gray sweatpants. A quick glance in the mirror was surprising: my wavy hair looked halfway decent, and all that skating exercise had left a healthy pink hue in my cheeks.

Good on all fronts.

By the time the dog and I made it out to the living room, there was a knock on the door. Stanley barked once, and Erica poked her head out of her bedroom.

"Are you expecting someone?" she asked, holding her phone in hand. Why did her face look so pinched and worried?

"Noah."

"Oh, okay. Tell him I said hi. I'm on the phone with Mom."

I nodded and went to the door. She knew Noah came over often to say hi, so why had she asked that question? Weird.

When I opened the door, I found my boyfriend standing there smiling, holding a bouquet of daisies in hand. He extended them to me and moved inside quickly because Stanley lunged, balancing on his back paws, with a manic expression on his adorable face.

"Aww, you are so sweet," I cried. "Thank you."

I kissed Noah, then shut and locked the door.

"Hey, buddy," he cooed. By now he'd taken Stanley into his arms, and my dog was trying to give his face a tongue bath.

"I'm going to put these in a vase and get you the pizza. Make yourself comfortable. Stanley, don't try to French-kiss him. Only I get to do that."

Noah chuckled and I went into the kitchen with a heart full of warm fuzzies. I'd never had a boyfriend who was as kind or gentlemanly as him.

The flowers went into a crystal vase that had been my Christmas gift to my mom when I was twelve, and I warmed up the pizza in the microwave.

"Here you go," I trilled as I walked into the living room with the plate and a napkin.

Noah kissed the top of Stanley's tawny head, making me melt, then prodded the dog to relocate to the floor. Stanley pranced his feet, hoping to snag a piece of pepperoni.

"No way, dude. Go to your pillow." I pointed at the dog bed near the recliner, then sat on the sofa next to Noah.

Stanley stared at me. I shook my head. When he realized I wasn't giving in, his round puppy eyes flitted to Noah, who was lifting a piece of pizza to his mouth.

"Dog bed. Now," I commanded.

Noah chewed, swallowed, and chuckled while Stanley slunk away. "You sound exactly like a mom."

A zing of awareness went through me. What was behind that observation? I was thirty-one and hadn't much thought about children. I'd assumed that someday, I'd have them. Noah was ten years older. My heart sped up.

"How was your day?" he asked. Typical man. He didn't even know the inner turmoil he'd caused with one tiny statement.

I exhaled. Now was not the time to spiral into an existential life crisis. Especially since I was facing an actual dilemma: whether I should tell my police chief boyfriend about my sleuthing activities. "Great. It was super busy at Perkatory in the morning—and oh, get this: Dad's now into electronic dance music."

In great detail, I told him about Dad and his newfound love of club music.

"That's odd, but I wouldn't expect anything less from Peter. And you told me about this earlier." He wiped his mouth with a napkin and put the empty plate on the table. "Some of those songs can be pretty good, though."

I wrinkled my nose and Noah grinned. He was so handsome, and my heart fluttered from his nearness. As it always did.

"Oh, let me get you some water." I jumped up and was dashing into the kitchen when I caught my heel on the ottoman. I swore out loud. "Sorry. Sorry. I have blisters on my feet."

While pouring Noah's favorite flavored ice water—fresh cucumber and lemon; I kept a pitcher of it in my fridge at all times—it occurred to me that I should probably come clean and tell Noah of the day's developments.

I hobbled into the living room and handed Noah the glass.

He thanked me and nodded at my feet as I sat next to him. "New shoes? Lemme see."

I folded my knees to tuck my feet under me, the wide bandages on the heels visible. "Sort of. Rental shoes."

Noah tilted his head. "Did you and Erica go bowling tonight?"

"No, roller skating."

Noah was mid-gulp, and he lowered the glass slowly, his dark eyes on me as he swallowed. "Roller skating. Hmm. I didn't realize you even knew how."

I twirled a lock of hair around my finger. "I used to skate all the time when I was little. Thought it would be nice to take lessons."

The side of his mouth quirked into a half smile. He knew where I was headed with this. "Lessons."

I nodded slowly. "There's a great teacher here on the island. She's Instagram famous and thinks I really have a future in the sport."

That might be exaggerating a little.

"You want to be a roller-skating Instagram star?"

He knew exactly why I'd taken the class and now was toying with me. So I'd play right back, because not only was I incapable of lying to anyone, but I had an inability to keep any secret from Noah Garcia and his searching, sexy, mahogany-colored eyes.

"Yeah, you know, dress in cute seventies and eighties outfits. Boogie down by the beach." I shimmied my upper body.

Laughing, he put the glass on the coffee table, then stretched out his arm, wrapping it around me and drawing my body close. "What am I going to do with you?"

"Come watch me skate?"

"I'd love to watch you skate." He kissed my temple. "What did Honey Bailey tell you?"

"Probably nothing that she hasn't already told you."

"Hmm."

I paused, hoping he'd share what she said when he questioned her. Because surely he already had. "She really is an excellent teacher. I'm going back on Thursday. We spent a lot of time on backward skating."

"I think that's . . ." His voice faltered. "That's wonderful. You've been talking about finding exercise that you love."

I softly rolled my eyes, because he sounded like Erica. "I mean, we did talk a little about Gus. How could we not?"

He let out a sigh. "Lana, I hope you're not investigating his death."

I shifted back a few inches, noting that his tone had gotten a touch more serious. "Would I do such a thing on my own?"

"Perhaps. If you were, say, writing an article. Or trying to prove that your best friend is innocent of murder."

"What are you talking about? She is innocent. And I might be writing a story. I've already texted Mike Heller."

He bit his lip, and I waited for him to speak. When he didn't, I softly pinched his thigh. There wasn't much to grab between my fingers because it was pure muscle, but I tried. "What? What are you about to say?"

"I hesitate to tell you this, but you've been pretty forthcoming with me about your, uh, investigative activities thus far, so I don't know if I should."

I eased out of his arms and lowered my brows. Whenever he talked in cop jargon, I knew he was serious. "Tell me what?"

"I figured you might do something like this given that Gus is—well, *was*—your neighbor. And since Erica's involved. I happened to run into Mike today at the sandwich shop, and your name came up."

"And?"

"And I politely asked him not to assign you a story. Or decline if you offered to write one."

"You did what?" My eyes shot wide open.

He lifted his hands. "Lana, you can't launch your own murder investigation. That's not how it works."

"You tried to silence the press?" So this was why Mike hadn't returned my text? I was incredulous. "There are many words for that, and none of them are kind."

"No. I didn't try to 'silence the press'—not at all. Mike Heller is free to write as many stories as he wants about Gus's homicide. Mike has plenty of reporters. I merely asked him not to encourage *you*."

My jaw dropped. Inside, a quiet rage bubbled. How dare he? Also, it was upsetting on a personal level—I considered Mike a friend. He'd been my first newspaper mentor, back when I was an intern at the *Beacon* in high school. He'd written a recommendation for my college application, and he'd been a professional reference when I applied at the paper in Miami all those years ago.

"Encourage me?" I had to remind myself not to shriek because Erica was either on the phone or sleeping, and I didn't want her intruding on my spat with Noah because she'd fiercely defend me. I didn't want more tension between Noah and Erica than there already was.

Noah pinched the bridge of his nose. "I shouldn't have said anything to you. Should've kept it between me and Mike."

"Well, if you think Mike will keep it secret, you're mistaken." I reached for my phone in a huff, hoping that Mike had somehow texted in the last half hour. "Like me, Mike is incapable of keeping information private, and he knows when a free press is being stifled. He knows when the Constitution is under attack."

"I don't think this has anything to do with the Constitution," Noah mumbled.

Ugh. No text from Mike. I threw the phone on the pillow next to me. "Noah, how could you?"

He let his head flop back on the cushion inhaled sharply. "I'm not trying to interfere with your journalism career. Or the newspaper. I swear. This case is complicated, and I know you're itching to find out more because of Erica."

"Well, duh! Gus is also my next-door neighbor, and I'd like to know whether I—and my neighbors, and Stanley, for God's sake—are in danger of being the next victim of a killer." My voice rose in pitch. "It's not as though police have given us any reason to feel secure."

He looked at me and blinked. It was a low blow, and I knew it. "Lana, you know that's not true. We've put out statements—"

I stood up and paced. "It is so unfair. So wrong. If we weren't dating, would you have made the request of Mike?"

He threaded his hands together and stared at them. "No. Probably not."

"Oh my word." I tried to count my breaths, in hopes of calming down. This was officially our first fight. I'd never been this angry with him.

"Lana, you were involved in the last two homicides on the island. First Fabrizio. You hadn't been out of journalism that long, and yeah, you did find him dead, and you did put two and two together about his lover pushing him off the roof. Okay. Then Raina."

Raina had been a yoga instructor who owned the studio next to Perkatory. A photographer at the paper had killed her in a hit-and-run crash, and I'd written a couple of stories about her death. And discovered that the paper's photographer was the killer.

I folded my arms and shot fire out of my eyes at Noah. "So basically, I'm doing your job, and you don't want me interfering this time because it will make you look bad."

"Lord help me," he whispered. "No. I don't want you involved because I don't know what we're dealing with in this case."

This piqued my interest, and I sat back onto the sofa. "Really? What do you mean by that? Don't you have any leads? Have you hit a dead end already? That can't be good. It's only been, what, twenty-four hours?"

"Well, Gus was . . . No. I'm not doing this, Lana. I'm not giving in to your subtle questioning. You're fishing for information. I'm not your investigative partner."

"We would make a good team, though. Except not now. Because I'm really angry."

He tried to tug me into a hug, but I resisted. "I knew you would be," he said, "but this Gus situation is delicate."

"Why?"

He lowered his voice. "Because Erica is very much a suspect, and Gus has been involved with some questionable people in his past, and I want you to be safe. Don't get me wrong. I like Erica. She's a great friend to you. But she has a bit of a temper, and I can't discount that during a murder investigation."

"Honestly. *Stop.* Yes, she's passionate about some things. Like coffee and food and whether men should wear flip-flops. She says no, I say yes. But she's not a murderer. She spent the afternoon in the garage fixing the upholstery on some of her boat cushions. I can show you the mess she left behind. It's still there." I couldn't believe he was accusing my best friend of killing Gus. Ridiculous.

"Are you sure? You said you, your dad, and Stanley left to go to your dad's house. Do you know what she did after that?"

I flapped my hand in the air. "She went to Joey's. They were supposed to go to Orlando but didn't because Joey's car broke down. Then they watched movies. They always watch movies together."

"And do she and Joey have alibis for the rest of the day?"

I stared at my boyfriend, hard. "Have you questioned her?"

"Not yet."

"Then until you do, and until you have something concrete, please refrain from accusing my best friend." I shot him a warning glare.

Both of us stayed like that for several long seconds, me glaring and him with those searching brown eyes fixed on me. Part of me wanted to bring up what I'd said the other night.

At some point, we're going to have to talk about us. Our relationship.

Now seemed like the worst time for that conversation, but the unspoken subtext hung in the air, as awkward as a cow on roller skates.

Finally, he sighed and hauled himself to his feet. "I'm going to call it a night. Let's chat tomorrow."

He mussed my hair and walked out without even saying goodbye. He also didn't rub his nose on the top of Stanley's head, which he usually did when he left my house. The pupper watched, forlorn, as Noah closed the door.

"Bye," I called out when the door shut behind him.

Seething, I picked up his plate and glass and stomped into the kitchen to wash up. Stanley followed me there and into my bedroom. I hoisted him onto the bed—I really needed to get those pet stairs because my mattress and box spring were so high—and I flopped onto the mattress.

I felt like crying out of frustration. Getting into a fight with Noah wasn't what I wanted. I really, really adored him and wanted our relationship to work. Truthfully, I was crazy about him and had never felt so intensely about a man. Maybe I even felt the L-word, although I hadn't said it yet. Neither had he.

Not even my ex-husband had inspired such strong emotions in me, and truthfully the force of my feelings for Noah was a tad scary. I still wasn't sure I should get so close to another person after getting my heart broken in Miami.

But Erica was my friend, and my loyalty to her was strong. And Noah shouldn't have interfered with my journalism—er, *attempted* journalism. I tossed and turned while thinking about the situation.

Sure, Erica did have a short fuse. But that didn't mean she was a murderer. But more than anything, I was angry at Noah for planting a seed of doubt about Erica in my mind.

Chapter Nine

Early the next morning, I moved around Perkatory with tender steps, wincing every time my feet hit the floor. Should've worn sandals or even flip-flops today. The skates had definitely been too snug with thick socks, and my heels were peeling and raw. They looked like ground hamburger.

Unsurprisingly, my mood was about the same. I couldn't stop thinking about the fight between Noah and me, and I'd texted him good morning despite the fact that I was still annoyed with him for going over my head and talking to Mike.

Noah seemed to be past our fight. He'd come in for his usual hot water with lemon, and with a wink had handed me a box of Band-Aids. Since the café was bustling with customers, Noah and I hadn't gotten a chance to talk much, and he'd left for the police station.

The bandages helped, but only a little. The skin on my heels was apparently as tender as a baby's—thanks to obsessive foot care routines and a love of flip-flops—and the roller skates had peeled several layers away.

While I tried to remember whether I'd stashed another pair of more forgiving shoes upstairs in the office, customers flowed in. Several asked about our drink of the month. During a lull, a mother–teen daughter duo, who looked identical with their black Afros and copper-colored skin, walked in and pointed at the sign.

"It's February the first. Are you continuing with the brewberry flavor? The sign says January. We've been here all week, and I'm not sure about ordering that berry flavor again. What do you think, Emmaline?"

The girl sighed dramatically. "I was hoping for something new. Let's go to Island Brewnette and try that."

I stopped myself from letting out a strangled groan. We'd been so busy focusing on Gus's murder that we hadn't set the drink of the month. While not a huge deal, it was a clue that I needed to get my act together, organization-wise. I didn't want to lose customers to that jerk Mickey Dotson.

Who probably had all sorts of info on Gus, since he'd bought the pirate ship from him. Why did a coffee shop owner buy a pirate ship, anyway?

"Apologies. That's my mistake," Erica said breezily, overhearing the duo's exchange, and rested her hand on the counter next to the register. "I forgot to update the sign. But lucky for you, I brought in the ingredients for the new drink, and you two will be the first to try it. But before I make it, I need to know: Are you both okay with double shots of espresso and a hint of citrus?"

The mother and daughter beamed. "Are we okay with it? We're more than okay. Make it triple shots."

"Sweet or no?" Erica asked.

"Sweet," they said in unison.

A saucy smirk spread on Erica's face, and she stepped away to root around in a plastic bag on a shelf. I went to her side and spoke in a low voice. "What are you making? That doesn't sound like the Lion drink."

She pulled out an orange and a vegetable peeler. I recognized it from my utensil drawer at home. "It's not. I'm trying out the citrus espresso we talked about on Sunday."

Gah. I'd forgotten all about that conversation. "Why aren't you continuing with the mushroom concoction?"

She wrinkled her nose. "I made it again for myself, and I feel like it needs to be tweaked. The earthy dirt taste was too strong."

"Doug enjoyed it."

"Yeah, true. But let's try this citrus out for a while. For today, at least."

Since there were no other customers, I watched Erica work her magic. First she shaved the peel off the orange in fat strips, distributing them into two medium-sized glass cups. Then she pulled six espressos in succession, three in each glass.

"Can you chill two shakers for me?" she asked.

"Absolutely." I still had no idea what she was doing. Would orange peels be enough to infuse the strong coffee with enough citrus flavor? Part of me worried that she hadn't made this yet for me so I could try it out and approve. Another part realized Erica had the best coffee palate I knew and that I should trust her judgment.

With a scoop, I shoved ice into two clean, stainless steel shakers. I swirled it around while Erica made the shots.

"I'm ready for the shaker," she said. The mother and daughter watched from the other side of the counter, rapt. "Can you set up two medium iced-coffee cups?"

I set the shakers next to her and got more ice for two glasses. She poured the espresso mixture into the shaker, peel and all, followed by a four-second squirt of simple syrup. With a motion that was worthy of something out of Coyote Ugly, she shook the contents near her right shoulder. Then her left. She timed her shakes to the beat of the song on the sound system: "I Can't Go for That (No Can Do)" by Hall and Oats.

Everyone grinned and we all did little boogie movements. It was one of those glorious moments at Perkatory where staff and customers were having a blast.

I set one glass filled with ice down. She stopped moving, uncapped the shaker top, and strained the espresso into the cup. The contents filled it perfectly with a deep, dark brown liquid. She reached for another strip of orange, twisted a few teeny drops of oil into the cup, then nestled the curlicue peel on top. A sharp smell of citrus cut through the aroma of coffee, and the two mingled in the air, mouthwatering and bright.

I grabbed one of the fat orange straws we usually gave to kids for their orange juice.

"Perfect," she whispered, then launched into making the second.

When she was finished, she handed both to the mother and daughter. "This is our monthly drink. It's called the Orange Blossom Special."

I held my breath while the two took their first sips.

"Oh my god, I never imagined those flavors would go together," the mom squealed.

"I was, like, so skeptical when she got out the orange, but it's amazing," said the daughter. "Thank you so much. We'll be back for another tomorrow. Or maybe later today."

As the pair wandered to a table, Darla, from the taffy shop, took her place at the counter and drummed on it with her knuckles.

Today she wore a similar outfit as she had yesterday, only with white track pants instead of shorts. It looked even odder, truthfully. "Hey, fellow scoundrels, I found my long pants, so I'm not as chilly today! Being cold really put me in a rotten mood yesterday. I'll have my usual iced coffee."

I poured her a cup. She paid and took a noisy sip through the straw. "That's some dang good coffee, Lana. Remember to come on in to the taffy place, and I'll give you a free pound."

"Thanks." I waved as she walked to a table. The idea of saltwater taffy made me vaguely sick. It had the consistency of bubblegum and a faint salty aftertaste that others normally couldn't detect, but I could.

I exhaled and relaxed as I turned to Erica. "Thanks for saving our bacon on that drink of the month. When did you come up with that recipe?"

Erica was at the espresso machine, pulling another shot. "Last night. I couldn't sleep, so at three AM I was in the kitchen, trying out various recipes. We had those oranges in the fridge. I'll buy more today."

I had a decent home espresso maker but hadn't heard its whirring and grinding sounds. Then again, I'd slept deeply, mired in vague, unmemorable bad dreams after my fight with Noah. "Wow, I didn't even wake up. Neither did Stanley."

"I tried to be quiet. I tested a drink with orange seltzer and orange extract, but neither were as good as using real oranges. Here, I'm going to make you one."

I wiped down the front counter while she concocted the drink. She set it down in front of me, a single shot in a smaller glass filled with ice. On mine she'd balanced orange peel on the rim of the glass.

Raising it to my mouth, I inhaled. It was a heady, rich mix of citrus and espresso. A dark, crisp fragrance that would almost be perfect for a men's cologne. I took a sip. Then another.

"Whoa, Erica. This is amazing." It was both light and complex, and most of all, refreshing. The citrus was subtle enough that it gave a momentary bright zing to the flavor of the espresso.

I downed the rest.

"I'm thinking about playing around with infusing a batch of cold brew with citrus." She stuck the peeled orange in the fridge. "Or doing a simple syrup involving the orange peels."

"Dunno—this is pretty perfect. And I love the name. Orange Blossom Special. How'd you come up with that?"

In a fake baritone, she began to sing a song. It was about going to Florida and losing the New York blues.

"It sounds vaguely familiar. Country and western?"

"It's my patron saint. The man in black."

"Johnny Cash?"

"Yep. It's about the real-life train that came to Florida in the 1920s. Connected New York to Miami."

"You did your homework."

"This is what happens when I have insomnia." Her smile was almost shy.

"Well, for this once, I'm glad you couldn't sleep. You did an incredible job with the February drink. Let me know what we'll need for the week and I'll buy or order it."

"Just oranges. That's all. We've got the simple syrup made already. I'll play around with the recipe some more. Although it would be great to find some actual orange blossoms to put on top of the drink."

This was probably a better bet than mushroom coffee, but I didn't want to say that aloud and hurt Erica's feelings. I liked to think of Perkatory as a cutting-edge café, but in reality, all people wanted was a good cup of joe and a selection of sweet, decadent drinks. Wasn't that how Starbucks had become popular?

More customers marched in, and Erica and I slipped into our familiar groove, with me at the register taking orders and her making drinks. When we were finished with that small crowd, two familiar faces walked in.

Perry and Jeri, my neighbors. They were wearing matching cheetah-print golf skorts and black sneakers. Jeri was in a black track jacket, which made her short silver hair and pale skin pop, and Perry wore a hot-pink, long-sleeved number, which suited her deep brown skin.

"Hey, neighbors," I called out.

"What's sizzlin'?" Erica asked.

"Perry here needed a caffeine fix," Jeri said.

"You've come to the right place. How about trying something new, with notes of oranges?" I asked.

Perry screwed up her face and shook her head. "Heck no. A regular, strong mocha cappuccino for me. To go, please."

Erica was about to turn to the espresso machine when Jeri waved her over. "We need to talk to you, missy. Come closer," she hissed. "Let Lana make the coffee."

Huh? That was weird. Why did they want to talk with Erica?

They were now a few feet away from me, and between the hum of conversation in the café, the sound of the espresso maker forcing water through the coffee grounds, and Fleetwood Mac on the sound system, I strained to pick out parts of their conversation, but could hear only isolated words.

It sounded something like this: ". . . Gus . . . death threat . . . shady business deals . . ."

I shifted in an attempt to hear more and glanced over as I frothed the milk. Erica shook her head, then shrugged. Perry asked a question, but since her voice was softer than Jeri's, I couldn't hear her words. Crud.

After sprinkling a light dusting of cocoa atop the cappuccino, I walked to the counter and presented it to Perry, who beamed and thanked me.

"So, yeah, if you think of anything, let us know, okay? We're curious cats," Jeri said to Erica.

She nodded. "Will do."

The pair ambled out of the café.

"What was that all about?" I asked Erica.

"They wanted to know more about my first altercation with Gus. Seems like they're trying to figure out who hated him in the neighborhood."

"I wonder if Jeri's going to use it in her true crime fiction class." I adjusted the strings on my apron.

Erica shrugged. "Who knows? Probably they're bored. Everyone's nosy and part of the gossip network in town. No one can resist dishing the dirt when someone's murdered."

It was true; people on Devil's Beach had a healthy love for discussing other people's business, especially if it involved something unsavory. It was best if I stayed out of it. I was busy, anyway, and needed to update the café's social media pages with the new drink of the month. But to do that, I needed a pretty photo of the cup of coffee.

As I pondered the feasibility of procuring orange blossoms, while sitting at a long, high-top counter near the window, I took out my to-do list from my apron pocket and jotted notes to myself.

This notebook was pale pink, with flowers and a quote from Frida Kahlo:

"I am here and I am just as strange as you."

I'd purchased it at the local bookstore, thinking it a fitting sentiment for my life on Devil's Beach. And Florida in general.

When I first started managing Perkatory, I'd kept a detailed calendar, with items written in different colored ink. As the months went on, I became more lax, and abandoned my calendar planner for a never-ending list that I carried everywhere.

I thumbed through the last couple of pages, hoping I'd crossed everything off from last week. A line I'd written caught my eye.

February 1: Trainer coming from Miami. Don't forget!!!

Despite the multiple exclamation marks and underlining the *don't forget* part, I'd obviously forgotten. No freaking way.

I gasped aloud. "Erica, we're in deep doo-doo," I called out.

She finished wiping the espresso steamer nozzle. "What's up?"

"The guy from Miami's coming today." I reached in my other pocket to thumb through my emails on my smartphone. My chest tightened. "In two hours."

Her brow fell into a frown. "What guy?"

"Remember? The trainer. From the coffee roaster place. He's going to be here all week."

She froze, hand in air. "I don't remember you telling me about that."

"I didn't?"

She waved the steamer rag. "Do we need a trainer?"

I looked around, baffled. In a second, life seemed to veer off-kilter. I thought I'd told Erica everything important about Perkatory. Dad had even joked that she was the manager, and I was the owner (even though, on paper, he was the owner). Maybe I'd mentioned it to Noah?

"They send someone once a year. To make sure we're getting the most out of the beans with our machine. To teach us some new drinks. Introduce us to new blends. Bring us up to speed on the latest in the coffee world."

Erica lifted her eyebrows and one shoulder in an insouciant shrug. "Not sure we need that here, but whatever."

"You don't, I don't, but Barbara and Heidi and Dad? They could use a refresher." Dad and Barbara were about the same age and were somewhat set in their ways when it came to coffee.

Heidi, our newest part-time employee, was going through a nasty divorce. She wasn't a bad barista—not by a long shot (no pun intended!)—but she didn't have Erica's innate sense of pulling the perfect espresso. At least not yet. It was something I was determined to teach her, and I was hoping the trainer from the roaster in Miami could help improve her skills.

"I suppose."

I glanced to Erica. "You don't sound convinced."

"I'm being inappropriately witchy. At my last barista job, these trainer guys would come in and try to teach us new tricks. Usually the staff was much more knowledgeable than they were, since we worked with the public and knew what it was like to work at a high-volume café. I know this machine like the back of my hand." She patted our La Marzocco, a piece of equipment that my mom had bought years before her death, when this was her shop.

"Well, try to endure, okay?"

"Sure." Erica could be so touchy sometimes.

A regular came in—the mayor—and Erica waited on him. Within seconds, the two of them were joking and laughing about the city council, of all things. I studied the exchange for a moment. The mayor was a straight-laced guy in his fifties who wore seersucker, and Erica was a post-punk who looked like an extra in a remake of *Blade Runner*. Somehow they got along famously. Erica tended to do that with the most unexpected of people. For all of her occasional prickliness, she was excellent with customers. That's all that mattered to me. Well, that and her espresso-making magic.

Doug, our other regular, approached from his usual table and joined the conversation. The three of them yukked it up, with the mayor regaling them over something hilarious about sewer rates.

I let them yak on while I slowly paced around Perkatory, straightening the sky-blue pillows on the sofa, pushing in chairs to the tables, arranging the shelf of Florida-themed coffee table books. I sank into the sofa and looked around my shop with a critical eye.

Did Perkatory need a deep cleaning? My staff and I did a pretty good job of scouring the place nightly. But somehow I wanted everything to be perfect for the guy from the roaster company. The more we seemed like we had our act together, the more we'd be offered special, rare blends of coffee. And maybe deeper discounts. Coffee prices had shot through the roof lately.

The roaster often played favorites—or at least it seemed that way in their monthly newsletter, which highlighted cafés around the region. Perkatory had never once been mentioned. My inner, mile-wide competitive streak meant that we had to impress the trainer coming to Devil's Beach, in exactly . . . an hour and a half.

I rubbed my eyes. The events of the past few days—Gus's death, the roller-skating session that left me with so many questions, and the blisters reminding me of my every step—had warped my sense of time. What day was it? I scrolled through my phone, trying to quell my anxiety with something Noah had taught me.

I pulled up a notes app on my phone. He'd told me about this technique once when I was worked up about a water pipe leak two months ago. I catastrophized the situation, thinking it would be the end of Perkatory. It hadn't been, and Noah had guided me through a meditation of sorts.

Gah. *Noah.* I longed to talk with him about my anxious thoughts, but I was still annoyed. And I sure didn't have time now to pester him. Also, he was likely busy with Gus's murder.

"When you get overwhelmed, cupcake, just write down three true things," he'd said.

I took a deep breath and searched my brain.

It's Tuesday.

I have a smart, engaged staff.

Gus, my next-door neighbor, is dead.

Okay, maybe those weren't all positive things, but they were undeniably true. The first I couldn't change. The second made me immensely happy. And the third . . .

As tragic and weird as his death was, it didn't concern me in this moment. As much as I wanted to write a newspaper story for the *Devil's Beach Beacon*, I couldn't, at least right at this moment. Thanks to my boyfriend. Gah. I had to set my questions aside. Not every murder on the island was my business, no matter how close I was to the case.

I could almost hear Noah's voice in my head. *"Clarity,"* he'd say in his rich voice. *"You need to gain clarity."*

The one thing I could do was to tidy up the café a little more prior to the trainer's arrival. Feeling emboldened, I climbed to my feet, smiled at a table filled with laughing tourists, and went behind the counter. First I'd pour myself a tall glass of cold brew and then get to work.

Erica was scowling at her phone and didn't look up when I approached.

"I'm going to straighten up back here, and the storage room too." I pointed over her shoulder.

She glanced up, her eyes wide with an emotion I'd never detected on her face before. "Uh, I was about to ask you if you could handle the counter. I need to go."

"Well . . ." I stuttered. Erica never asked to leave in the middle of a shift. If anything, she insisted on working longer. "We've got a lot going on today, and we'll be getting the after-school rush soon."

She gulped in a few breaths, and seemed uncharacteristically shaken. "Noah called. He wants to interview me about Gus's death. I have to be at the police station in a half hour; otherwise, he said he'd come here to escort me to the interrogation room."

Chapter Ten

Where were the extra to-go cups? A manic mood had washed over me, and I shuffled the two packs of biodegradable cups on a shelf under the espresso maker while scowling.

"Dad, for the love of god, can you please turn off that music?" I stood up, wincing from the throbbing blisters on my heels. The trainer from the coffee roaster company was due at any second, and all plans to change shoes had been scuttled. Hopefully the Band-Aids would hold for another couple of hours. I needed to get home and check on Stanley too. "What happened to the other three packs of cups?"

"Oh, I put them in the storage room. They're in a box with lids, plus some utensils. I wanted to consolidate."

"Good plan. Thanks. But, Dad, seriously, the music. We need to change it." I stared at him with a pleading look. When Erica left for the police station, I'd called Dad in early to work the counter while I tidied up. "This constant bass beat is making me nervous. Look, I think I might be breaking out in hives."

I pointed to a red patch on my forearm. I'd actually gotten it yesterday while skating, when I'd accidentally flailed my arm into the rail. But I was so desperate to change the music that I was willing to tell Dad a little white lie.

"Munchkin, don't sweat it. Everything's going to be fine. You don't need to be perfect for the guy from Miami, and Erica's having a friendly little chat with Noah. You'll see."

"I don't like any of it. This is the worst time for an outsider to come to the café, and I don't appreciate how Noah treated Erica. Telling her he'd escort her to the interrogation room. What's up with that?"

Dad scratched his beard. "If he thought she was a serious suspect or a menace to society, then he would have arrested her. And trust me, if Erica had killed someone, she wouldn't have hung around Devil's Beach. She's a smart cookie. She would have fled."

"True," I said with a sigh. "I wish Noah would've given me a heads-up."

Dad fiddled with his phone, and mercifully, the background music on the wireless speakers switched from Diplo—whoever he was—to the soothing strains of Earth, Wind and Fire. One crisis solved. The muscles in my neck loosened.

It was right around two in the afternoon, which meant it was the afternoon lull at Perkatory. The high school crowd would descend upon us soon.

Doug was in the corner, tapping away at his laptop and drinking his third, maybe fourth, iced coffee. A couple of women in yoga clothes and with shiny, straight hair sat at a table near the window. An elderly woman who was another regular sat reading a book and sipping a latte.

Everything's normal, I repeated to myself like a mantra.

But if it was, the logical part of my brain screamed, why had Erica been at the police station for more than an hour? My fingers itched to text her or Noah, but I refrained. This was serious business, her being questioned in connection with Gus's death.

The bells on the door jingled, and I braced myself for the trainer to walk in. I gripped a nearby chair, then tensed even further when I saw who it actually was.

Mike Heller, the editor of the *Devil's Beach Beacon*.

I wasn't sure whether to be angry, annoyed, or relieved. I tried to keep my face neutral, but said nothing.

"Mike," Dad cried from behind the counter, "how you doin', old man?"

I blinked as I watched them chuckle and guffaw about the party the other night. Apparently, they'd all ended up in Dad's pool, and I cringed, hoping it wasn't some sort of senior citizen skinny-dipping party, or that no one posted photos on Facebook. Since Dad had learned to use the social media site, his posts had become weirder and more popular among the over-sixty set on the island.

"What would you like to drink this afternoon? I've got an amazing small batch blend from Guatemala." Dad tapped on a cute display of ground coffee packs that I'd set out a half hour ago, hoping to show the trainer guy that I was showcasing his company's products.

Mike turned to me. "Peter, I'm well caffeinated today. I'm actually here to talk with Lana."

Dad pointed in my direction. I gave a weak wave. "Hey. How's it going?"

As Mike walked toward me, he put on that editor expression. I knew that look well, having worked with several irascible editors over the years. It was the one that said, *I know you tried hard with this story, but it's total junk, and you're going to have to rewrite the entire thing.*

Pasting on a smile, I gestured to an empty table. It was about four feet from Doug, who was absorbed in his computer and had his earbuds in.

I didn't have time for a tense chat with Mike. At any moment, the trainer from Miami would be here. Or Erica would walk in, eager to talk about her interview with Noah. Or Erica wouldn't walk in, and . . .

Mike pulled out a chair, and swept a hand over his bald brown head. "I'm sorry I didn't get back to you, kid."

"Yeah. Noah told me that he, uh, made a request of you."

"And I thought long and hard about it." He threaded his hands together. "I actually wasn't going to take his advice."

My eyes widened. "You weren't?"

He shook his head. "You know how I feel about the authorities telling me to do something. Even if it is your boyfriend, who happens to be the best chief Devil's Beach has ever had."

Finally, I grinned. "So does that mean you want me to write something? Where's your regular crime reporter?"

"That's the thing. I do want you to write something because our crime reporter's busy on a project. But you can't, so I'll have to pull him off that project."

"Why can't I write it?"

"You're too close to this one, Lana."

"Because I live next door to the victim? I barely knew him. I talked with him maybe three or four times. Waved hello. He didn't wave back, by the way."

"No, it's because your close friend is officially a suspect. It's a conflict of interest."

A chill flowed through me. "Erica? Is she actually a suspect?"

"I saw her at the police station a half hour ago, and Noah and a detective were questioning her in an interrogation room, so I'd say that she is."

I slumped in my chair. "She didn't kill him. I know she didn't. Erica isn't capable of that."

Mike nodded, a somber look etched on his face.

"And one more thing," I said, pointing in his direction. "You let me report a story about my dead barista last year. Wasn't that a conflict of interest?"

He clicked his tongue. "You'd recently moved back, didn't hire him, and weren't all that close to him. Plus that was a feature article. Totally different scenario than this current situation."

A cramp seized my jaw; I was grinding my molars. I nodded but still didn't agree with his decision. I wasn't the boss, though. I wasn't even a journalist anymore. At best, I was a community freelancer, and maybe not even that. Rats.

Mike eased out a sigh. "Anyway, part of the reason I came here was to tell you in person why I can't have you doing the article. The other part is to give you, and Erica, some friendly advice, since I know she's been staying with you while her boat's under repair."

"What's that?"

"I suggest the two of you retain an attorney."

"Wait—what? Now I'm a suspect too?" I gripped the edge of a table to steady myself.

"No, I don't think you are. But she's bunking with you, and the longer she does, the chances go up of you being a coconspirator."

I rolled my eyes. "Come on. You've been watching too much *Law and Order.* I'm not a coconspirator. Erica and I spend our time cooking and playing with Stanley and—"

I almost said "watching true crime TV shows," but stopped short, figuring that particular detail wouldn't put us in the best light.

"I'll think about getting a lawyer. And advise Erica that she might consider it too."

"She shouldn't even be talking to the cops like she is." Mike lowered his voice into a deep, serious baritone. His near-black eyes bored into me, as if trying to tell me a hidden message.

One that I couldn't decipher. Didn't have time. "Thanks for this. Listen, I'm super swamped because I have a trainer coming in today. I'll make sure I talk with Erica tonight, okay?"

"Good deal. And listen, if you do hear anything about Gus's murder, let me know, okay? I can't have you doing a story, but my crime reporter and I are happy to take tips." He winked and rose. "We're going to write a short story for tomorrow's paper, by the way. Noah's not giving up a lot of info, though."

I also stood, then nodded. My muscles had taken on a decidedly deflated feel. "I'll call you if I hear anything."

We said our goodbyes, and I was still a little bitter that Mike didn't want an article from me but would be fine with some unpaid reporting tips. Sadly, this was typical of the journalism industry, especially at smaller papers, which relied on low-paid labor. Being laid off from a larger paper and having nearly a year of a news-free life had made me see the industry in a clearer way.

I watched Mike stroll toward the door. Maybe I should forget about Gus's murder. But could I? Not with Erica as a suspect. I mulled this over for a second.

As Mike slipped out of Perkatory, he held the door for a familiar-looking man walking in. He was of average height and handsome in a saucy, casual way. He wore a guayabera—a shirt popular in Miami among Latino men—expensive-looking jeans, and interesting black sneakers. A dark goatee accentuated his golden-brown skin. I guessed he was around thirty, my age.

If I didn't know better I'd have thought he was Noah's foxy younger brother. But Noah only had a sister.

The man paused, rested his hands on his hips and looked around, grinning and nodding. Then he clapped his hands loudly, startling everyone in Perkatory. We all looked to him, alarmed, as the opening strains of Barry White's "Can't Get Enough of Your Love, Babe" was the only sound that rumbled through the café.

I blinked twice as the man and I locked eyes.

"Who's ready to make some great coffee?" He chortled and did a little salsa move with his arms and hips. "Let's get this party started!"

* * *

Julian Hernandez, the top coffee trainer of Magic City Roasters had several pros and cons, as I'd discover over the next hour.

Cons: He was excessively positive. Like unicorns farting rainbows and eternal sunshine. Everyone on staff would probably love this, especially Dad. Well, everyone but Erica, who would likely chafe against such platitudes.

Julian was also gorgeous as well as one of those rare men who seemed to be totally unaware of how beautiful he really was. This annoyed me for some reason, possibly because it reminded me of how my ex-husband used to be when he was a local TV news reporter. That all changed when he became a network news guy, though. Then he considered himself God's gift to women.

Additionally, Julian seemed to have a habit of focusing intently on whoever was talking, nodding seriously and saying *mm-hmm* every three seconds.

"He's a great listener," Dad whispered to me when Julian was in the bathroom.

I grunted in response. Someone who said *mm-hmm* that much probably wasn't listening at all. I knew this because I'd done several interviews as a reporter where I'd reflexively acknowledged what the other person was saying while my mind was on the next question. I'd done this most often with politicians who went off on tangents, hoping to change the subject and not answer tough questions.

Still, Julian had many pros. Well, two. One was that he loved coffee and knew his stuff. Possibly more than Erica. He had excellent ideas, like holding after-hours "cupping" parties, similar to a wine tasting, where we would sample different coffee blends.

"It's a way to expand one's palate. To get familiar with new blends. Even to compare brewing methods. It allows customers to feel like they're part of the process, from growing the bean to harvesting and roasting it, to drinking the finished product." He gestured to the cup of espresso before him on the counter.

The other thing that was undeniably great about Julian: he remembered my mother. His family owned Magic City Roasters, and he recalled mom being one of the company's first clients years and years ago, when she first opened Perkatory. Mom had been a coffee buyer prior to opening the café, and had purchased beans from Julian's family farm in South America.

"I was working sales back then, while I was at the University of Miami, getting a business degree," he said while reverently running a hand over the exterior of our espresso machine. "And your mom came in, and she was full of passion and fire. I loved her instantly. She had a deep respect for the coffee bean and for my family's heritage, farming coffee in Colombia."

Grief, fast and fierce, washed over me, and I looked to Dad for help. Somehow Julian had captured my mom in only a few sentences. But Dad's eyes were downcast to the floor and didn't meet my gaze.

I swallowed the lump in my throat. "She was one of a kind."

He hummed a mm-hmm. "I'm so glad you're continuing her dream, Lana. It's what she would've wanted. She talked about you so much." He paused, then chuckled. "She even once said that she'd love to set the two of us up."

My jaw dropped, and I looked again to Dad, who was inspecting a frayed hem of his apron. Fortunately, I was saved from a response because the front door opened with a sharp jangle of bells and a slam, and the three of us turned our heads.

Erica entered, swearing under her breath.

I held up my finger at Julian. "Please excuse me for a moment," I murmured with a smile, then spoke in a regular voice. "Dad, why don't you show Julian around, maybe have him get acquainted with the back of the house."

I rushed to Erica before she reached the counter, Dad, and Julian. My hand clamped around her elbow to propel her outside.

She squawked in protest. "What the—"

"Hush. Come outside for a second."

I pulled the door shut behind us and gestured for her to follow me down the block. Perkatory was not only owned by my family, but so was the entire building. It was a former hotel that spanned an entire block, and there was a yoga studio next door. Beyond that was a shop selling tourist souvenirs.

Erica and I stopped somewhere between the yoga studio and the tourist shop, the latter of which was doing booming business by the looks of people streaming inside. It was pleasantly warm outside, a perfect sunny January day in Florida. Chamber of Commerce weather.

She slumped against the building's brick exterior, looking miserable in her all-black, Goth outfit of a T-shirt, black shorts, black stockings, and her usual black combat boots.

"What happened?" I demanded. "Was Noah nice to you?"

"He was fine. He's a good guy. I know that." She pushed her glossy blue-black hair away from her forehead. "It's complicated."

"Why? What's complicated about it? Did you or did you not kill Gus? What's so difficult about that question?" My voice rose an octave, and a couple of tourists glanced at me in alarm. Crud.

Unfazed, Erica shook her head. "Do you think I murdered our next-door neighbor?"

"No, of course not," I snorted.

"I mean, he was a big jerk, but I didn't off him. But I also don't have a great alibi for the hours before he died."

"You were with Joey. Isn't he your alibi?"

She stared at the ground. When we heard the jingle of bells on Perkatory's front door, our heads swiveled instinctively. Doug and Darla were coming out of the café together. They appeared to be deep in conversation, but waved at us. We returned the gesture.

I stepped toward Erica. "Hey, you didn't answer me. You were with Joey, right?"

"Sort of."

"I don't like the sound of that."

"We planned to go to Orlando, but his car broke down, and I stayed at his house instead. Watching the *Fast and Furious* marathon on TV."

"Then what's the problem?"

She kicked an invisible rock with the toe of her black boot. "We had a fight and he left."

My heart skipped a beat. "How long were you at his house alone?"

"From about six p.m. until he came back at midnight. I didn't even try to call him during that time, let my phone run out of juice because I was so angry. Which is why I didn't get your texts. Then when he came back, we were too busy making up and I didn't pay any attention to my phone."

I gaped at Erica.

"I know. It looks bad. I stayed there because his cat needs medicine, and I didn't want to leave her alone. And I thought he'd be back sooner. I wanted to apologize. The other time we had a fight, he was gone for only a half hour."

"Where did he go? When did he return?" My mind spun with the implications of her words.

"He came back at midnight. He stayed at the restaurant and took a nap on the office couch." Joey owned The Square Grouper, a restaurant started by his late father, who was once a New York mafia guy.

Erica and Joey had been dating for about as long as Noah and I. It seemed as though their relationship was going well; she seemed to glow whenever they were together. They shared a wry sense of humor, a love of nautical tattoos, and complicated cocktail recipes. "Is everything okay now?"

She nodded. "Yeah. It was a stupid fight."

"What about? And did you tell Noah all this?" I pressed my back into the brick wall, mirroring my friend's posture. All I wanted was for her to open up a little more, so I could figure out where we needed to go from here. My mind flitted to Julian inside, and I stifled a groan. It was rude to leave him with Dad like that, but Erica was crying out for help.

"Yeah, I did. I don't think he believed me."

"Why wouldn't he?"

"Because my fight with Joey was so ridiculous."

"Ridiculous how?"

"After we realized the car had broken down, we decided to get takeout. I wanted a cheese board from Bacchus, that new Italian place. But he thinks cheese boards—charcuterie boards in general—are stupid and a waste of money. Those were his exact words."

I screwed up my face. "What kind of person thinks charcuterie boards are stupid? They're delicious."

Erica peeled herself off the wall and gestured loudly. "Right? They're little bites of heaven. But he insisted that they're a rip-off and not filling and mediocre. He said they're basically a spread of deli pepperoni, a wedge of brie, and a few cubes of sweaty cheddar with some tiny, absurd pickles. That's what he called them: *'tiny, absurd pickles.'*"

"I like Bacchus's tiny pickles, and they're called gherkins." I rubbed my temples, hoping that my gentle encouragement would boost Erica's mood.

"Well, I do too, so we had a pitched battle about cheese boards." She paused. "We made up, though. He returned at midnight with a charcuterie board he'd made himself and apologized. He groveled."

"Aww." I was genuinely touched by Joey's gesture. "Why didn't you tell me this earlier?"

"Because. We were so busy this morning and you were wrapped up in the details of Gus's murder and . . ." She blew out a breath. "Your life is so perfect, and I felt silly talking about our fight. Your relationship with Noah is so adult. It's like picture-perfect. Hashtag relationship goals."

My mouth flapped open and closed out of sheer shock. In the months since I'd met Erica, she'd proved herself fearless (except when it came to snakes; she hated those). Otherwise, she was a woman who didn't care what others thought, a cool lone wolf who'd somehow let me into her world.

I'd never known her to be envious of anyone—or anything. And the thought that someone as interesting and worldly as her would be jealous of me was ludicrous. Most days, I felt like I was barely staying afloat with money, time—and yeah, my relationship with Noah. Sure, he was older by ten years, but the guy hadn't even introduced me to his family. Occasionally it felt like we were in our early twenties.

There were times I wondered why Noah was with me when he could be with a woman who had her act together—not one who spent hours in bed reading true crime novels on her day off when she should be doing laundry.

"Stop. My life is not perfect, and you know it. Noah and I have our issues too."

"I know. But you seem so perfect together. Like you're headed somewhere."

"I dunno about that," I muttered. "Did Noah say anything about talking to Joey? He'll be able to vouch for the fact that you were at his house."

"Yeah, he said he'd get in touch with him. Might not be easy because Joey's out of town for part of this week."

I frowned. "Where is he?"

"He's at a big restaurant convention in Las Vegas."

"You should've gone with him. I'd have given you the time off, you know."

She gave me a lopsided smile. "I hate Vegas with a white-hot passion."

Erica never ceased to surprise me with her likes and dislikes. I'd have assumed she enjoyed the tacky glitz of Vegas. "I'm sure it will all work out. How did you and Noah end the conversation?"

"He told me I shouldn't leave the island."

"So he's actually investigating you?" This was a lot to take in. My best friend, an actual murder suspect? It seemed incomprehensible.

She scraped her hair back with her hands, then allowed it to fall over her pale face. "I guess. Especially since Noah found out about those anger management classes I had to take in Boston a few years ago."

My mouth opened, then closed. I'd vaguely known that detail about Erica because she'd mentioned it in passing a few months ago. I didn't wanted to pry, so I hadn't asked for the story. "Okay. We'll talk about this later, when we get home. Julian from the roaster in Miami is here, so we should focus on that right now."

"Yeah. Let's go. Everything's going to be okay."

I couldn't help but feel that she was trying to convince not only me but herself.

Chapter Eleven

As expected, Erica was skeptical of Julian. I could tell by the way her mouth slanted, how her eyes narrowed, how she tilted her head, especially when he said things like, "Positive mind. Positive vibes. Positive life."

Dad had nodded enthusiastically at this statement while I'd scratched my neck and managed a tight smile. What did positive vibes have to do with espresso? I finally came to the conclusion that without coffee, there would be many more negative vibes in the world, and accepted Julian's inspirational cliché at face value.

I'd barely listened to him talk, though, because I'd been lost in thought about Gus's murder. I needed to do something to prove Erica was innocent. But what?

Julian clapped his hands—he did this a lot, signaling a change in topic—and Dad, Erica, and I simultaneously straightened our backs and blinked rapidly. Since it was around four in the afternoon, we were all likely in a post-caffeine crash. I eyed the espresso machine longingly.

"What's next on the agenda?" I asked Julian. When we'd first arranged this visit two months ago, I'd envisioned leading several collaborative sessions with him and my baristas. But today I'd let him run the show because I was so preoccupied with Erica's situation and the murder.

"That's it for today, Lana. Since it was a bit of a drive here, I'm going to my hotel to relax and have dinner. I'll plan on being back here at nine tomorrow morning. Lana and I will go over inventory, and then I'll work behind the counter for a few hours. And we're closing early tomorrow for our staff meeting, correct?" Julian looked to me.

"Yes. Everyone's been notified to be here at three. We're still planning on a five-hour session, correct?"

"Give or take. These trainings usually take a little longer, but no one cares. It's like a party. We'll get pizza." He winked at me. Party or not, I was paying people for the training, and I would've preferred to have firm hours for my weekly staff budget.

Julian and Dad wandered off, with Dad telling him about the best places to eat and drink on the island. I overheard Dad mention the words *monkeys* and *protest*.

Oh lord.

I stood there with my hands on my hips, surveying the café. Doug and Darla strolled back in, and both ordered their regular coffee. They'd left a while ago, but it wasn't odd for either of them to come and go, and order multiple coffees a day. But they seemed awfully chummy. Were they dating? Where had they gone for a couple of hours? Had it even been a couple of hours? I pressed my hand to my forehead.

Darla pointed at Doug's hands. He was carrying a bag branded with the logo of her saltwater taffy shop. "This could've been yours," she said to me with a chortle.

"Oh, uh, yes. I'll be there soon." I briskly moved around them, planting myself behind the counter. By *soon*, I meant *never*. Or I guess I could accept some candy and give it to Dad. Was he eating sugar these days? I couldn't keep up.

Darla and Doug each went to their respective tables, and Doug unwrapped a candy and popped it in his mouth before extracting his laptop from his bag.

"Oh God," I whispered to Erica.

"What? Oh, the saltwater candy? Yeah, it's gross."

"No. Not that. I think Dad's telling Julian about the monkey movement." I gestured with my chin toward Dad and Julian near the window.

She waved her hand in the air. "Your father's obsessed. What are you doing now?"

I shrugged. "Going home."

"I think we should feed Stanley, then visit the library." The corner of her mouth quirked up.

"To talk with Gus's mistress?" Huh. That was an interesting idea.

"Exactly." She lifted an eyebrow. "Your cop boyfriend doesn't want you sleuthing around, though. Maybe I should do it alone."

I thought about all the times Erica had helped me out, both with the prior murder cases I'd written about and around the café. She'd filled in for any shift on short notice and went above and beyond to patiently teach the other baristas her tricks—and customers adored her.

"I'll come with. I don't care what Noah says. He's not the boss of me. Especially when my best friend and the most talented barista to ever exist on Devil's Beach is a suspect in a homicide. Oh, and get this: Mike came in while you were gone."

I was giving her a brief rundown of our conversation when a twenty-something woman, wearing sunglasses, a turquoise bikini top, and a matching pareu covering her lower half, swept in. She was accompanied by two other women her age, all clad in flowy, bright beach attire that would be best described as Stevie Nicks crossed with a macaw parrot.

I was a bit jealous of their style, to be honest.

"There she is," the woman cried, taking off her sunglasses and pointing in our direction. We were standing on the customer side of the counter and turned our heads and blinked. I noticed Dad and Julian, who were behind the counter and near the fridge, gaping at the trio.

The women rushed over to us. Well, to Erica. One of the women practically pushed me out of the way.

"You're Erica Penmark, correct?" the first woman asked.

"Uh, yeah," she said, hooking her thumb into the pocket of her black shorts. "What's up, buttercup?"

The woman giggled. "I knew she'd have a sense of humor. Didn't I tell you, Saundra? I knew she'd be cool as heck."

The other women nodded. "Can we get a photo with you? I can't believe we found you so easily!"

"Aww," I said, glee and triumph shooting through me. "Those Instagram videos of you are really paying off, Erica." I smiled at the women. "She was so reluctant when I first put them up. But that one of her making the lavender espresso has practically gone viral. Want me to take the photo?"

The woman thrust her phone into my hand and the trio crowded around Erica.

"See, you're getting famous for your latte art," I said with a proud grin.

"Coffee? No, we're not here for that. I mean, I'd love to have a cup brewed by her because it would be an honor," the woman chortled. "We heard about Erica on a true crime podcast. Anyone who stood up to a guy who uses a leaf blower ten times a day should be idolized. I hate leaf blowers. Heroes don't always wear capes." She elbowed Erica in the ribs and laughed.

I lowered the phone, panic welling in my chest. "Excuse me?"

"Please, take the photo," the woman said.

"Wait. Put the phone down. What?" Erica yelped. "What true crime podcast?"

The woman beamed. "It's called *Crime Time in Paradise*. Haven't you heard of it?"

Erica and I shook our heads in tandem. While I read and watch true crime, I hadn't yet delved into the wide world of true crime podcasts, mostly because I felt as though many of the hosts were rehashing—and monetizing—journalists' hard work.

"We're here on vacation, and we love it on Devil's Beach. One of the reasons we visited is because the hosts live here and are always talking about how weird it is. I never imagined they'd do a show in their own backyard, though. Literally, they devoted a half hour to a murder that was right across the street from them. It aired this afternoon!"

"Across the street?" Erica echoed.

I sputtered for a second, then managed to spit out some words. "Perry and Jeri?"

"That's them," the woman pointed at me. "The hosts. They are amazing ladies. Funny as heck."

"Perry and Jeri have a true crime podcast?" I looked to Erica helplessly. "I guess that's why they were in here asking you questions."

"What did they say about me?" Erica's voice came out as a growl. Her eyes flashed, and the only other time I'd seen that expression was when she had gone after Gus.

The woman twirled a strand of long hair around her finger. "Well, first they talked all about Gus. And how horrible he was in the neighborhood with his leaf blower. They've mentioned him a lot on their show in the past couple of months. Sometimes you can even hear him blowing while they're talking. We even drove past his house today—now that was creepy! I really hope Jeri turns this case into her first true crime novel."

There were true crime groupies cruising our street?

"Right. Get to the part about Erica," I prodded. Out of the corner of my eye, I saw Dad and Julian inching toward us. This was not what I wanted Julian to witness, and I tried to catch Dad's gaze. But he was intent on listening to what the woman was saying because he couldn't resist a tasty piece of gossip.

"So they described what happened on Sunday, how Gus was out there leaf blowing, and they said that another neighbor, Erica"—she put her hand on Erica's forearm—"came out and started yelling at Gus. Then they talked about the police coming and how they found Gus dead later."

"Did they say I was a suspect?" Erica wore a shell-shocked expression. I wasn't sure it was possible for her to be more goth-pale than she already was, but here we were.

The woman screwed up her face. "Well, not really. But she said that you were one of the last people to talk with Gus. So yeah, actually. You're kind of a suspect. I mean, that's what we all thought."

She turned to her friends, and they all nodded.

"But it's okay. Even if you killed him, it would be justifiable manslaughter, right?"

Fed up with the entire inane conversation, I thrust the woman's phone toward her. "No, it would not be all right. You can't go around killing people if you don't like the way someone does their yard work."

"I didn't kill anybody." Erica glared at the woman. Her expression was scary, what with the flared nostrils and flames practically shooting from her dark eyes.

The entire café came to a standstill, so only the strains of Steely Dan's "Dirty Work," hummed through the café. Dad, who couldn't listen to a song without singing along if he knew the lyrics, murmured a line. I'm sure he didn't even know he was singing along, but I glared at him.

"Dad," I hissed, "stop it."

"I've always liked this song. Sorry." He grinned at Julian, who glanced around uneasily. I'm sure he was questioning his decision to spend a few days in Devil's Beach.

Doug, from the corner, took out his earbuds. The women's jaws hung open.

Erica sniffled once, as if she was about to cry. This shocked me more than anything because I'd never seen her this . . . emotional? Tender? Worried? Biting her bottom lip, she shook her head and rounded the counter, walking quickly into the back toward the storage room.

Pressing my hands in a downward motion, I made the international symbol to calm down. "Look. Erica didn't kill Gus. She was a little forceful with him on Sunday, but only because he started leaf blowing early in the morning."

"It was really inappropriate at that hour," Dad chimed in.

I ignored him. "I appreciate that you ladies are fans of Perry and Jeri's true crime show—"

"Crime Time in Paradise," the woman cut in. "It's the number-one true crime podcast on Spotify."

How did I not know this? I really needed to spend more time with my neighbors. "Whatever. Perkatory is a business. So if you're here to get coffee, great. We'd love to make you anything you'd like. If not, I'm going to have to ask you to leave. I don't want my employee, my friend, more upset."

The woman pressed both hands to her chest. "I'm so sorry. Yes, we'll totally order drinks. Do you have something like a Frappuccino? I figured Erica knew about the podcast or that Perry and Jeri told her they were mentioning her. I don't know how their podcast works."

"I don't either," I said through gritted teeth. But we were going to find out.

*   *   *

"Erica, it's really not all that bad. You come off as pretty sane. I mean, there was a lot of conjecture in the show, and I think Perry shouldn't have speculated on Gus's marriage like she did. But overall, I think you're fine. It doesn't actually implicate you in a murder."

We were at my house and I pressed "stop" button on my podcast app, breaking off Jeri's plea to donate five bucks a month to the podcast. I had to give it to Perry and Jeri; they certainly put on a compelling show. If I were them I'd be a little more concerned about slandering Honey, since they all but accused her of being a gold digger and killing Gus for his money.

Erica didn't respond, so I blathered on. "I felt their allegations against Honey were a little out of line. I can't believe this is the top true crime podcast on Spotify, though."

She pushed out a breath. "It wasn't great, Lana. Basically they spent ten minutes on a blow-by-blow of what I said to Gus on

Sunday morning. How I yelled at him. How I called him a tool to his face. They basically quoted what I told them earlier today. I can only assume they came into Perkatory and then ran back to their home podcast studio to do the show."

Erica was in a far better mood now, which meant that she was back to being cynical and a bit glum instead of despondent and sniffly. I was used to this Erica, so I welcomed the shift in mood.

I cleared my throat. "But they didn't say *you* killed him."

"Is that supposed to be a hopeful, helpful point?"

"Yes," I said before taking a sip of some homemade iced-tea mixed with lemonade. "But geez, Gus does come off like a jerk. I didn't know that he'd threatened Perry with a pair of gardening shears. We actually got quite a bit of background information out of that show."

"I wonder if Noah's heard it yet."

"Good question. Want me to ask? I'm guessing not. He's not a fan of podcasts. I've been trying to get him to listen to one about dogs, but he won't. There's this one dog podcast that I love. It's where I got the idea of matching jammies for me and Stanley at Christmas."

Stanley, who was napping on his bed, lifted his head when I said his name. I blew him a kiss. He collapsed back into slumber.

Erica made a face. "Why wouldn't Noah listen?"

"He says he can't multitask. If he's going to listen, he'll have to sit and do only that. He can't have the show on in the background and manage other things."

"Typical man," she muttered.

I was typing a text to Noah when Erica flicked my knee, hard. "Ow. What was that for?"

"Don't tell him about the podcast yet."

"Why not?"

"Because we should check out some of the things Perry and Jeri mentioned on their show. Like Gus's library lover."

I scratched my ear. Erica had helped me look into two murders—first, my dead barista and then the dead yoga instructor. In both those instances, I poked around under the guise of doing news articles for the *Beacon*. Now, I didn't even have that going for me. But Erica needed help clearing her name, and I also had a vested interest because I didn't want random people in Perkatory cheering her on as the possible murderer of a serial leaf blower.

A sigh escaped from my mouth. "We're doing this, aren't we?"

"What? Sleuthing? Heck yeah. I'm mad now. Let's go to the library. I'll grab the pooch pouch so we can bring Stanley."

Chapter Twelve

The Devil's Beach Library was at the far south end of Main Street. Built in 1915, it was known as a "Carnegie Library," which meant that it had been built with philanthropist Andrew Carnegie's cash.

It was easily the prettiest building on the island and looked a little bit like a frosted cake. At least I'd always thought so as a girl. The exterior was a soft peach, with white supporting columns, deep cornices, and ornate sculptural flourishes. The roof was a red barrel style, and green palm trees flanked the entrance.

"This was my favorite place when I was a kid. Did I ever tell you that? Dad would take me here, and he'd wander off to read a book about politics or music, and I'd be left to my own devices. I usually ended up in the archaeology section. I was obsessed with mummies."

Erica stopped at the bottom of the steps leading into the grand building. "Do you think they're going to have a problem with the pupper?"

"I doubt it—it's Devil's Beach. As long as he's attached to you, he'll be fine. You know Bernadette, the police dispatcher, the one with the parrot?"

"Sure do. That bird has vocabulary of a trucker. I'm kind of jealous of it, being free with words like that."

"Well, she comes in here all the time with the bird. So we're not going to worry about Stanley."

I scooped Stanley up to wrangle him into the pooch pouch, which was strapped to Erica's torso. Stanley was being especially stubborn today because he wanted to walk, and probably roll on the lush green grass under the palm trees. When he discovered that I wanted to strap him to Erica, he started to wriggle, then went limp, like an overcooked noodle.

"Come on, buddy," I pleaded with him.

Finally he relented, and I struggled him into the pouch before Erica and I walked up the stairs and into the building. When we passed through the heavy wooden door, we were greeted by an older man, about my dad's age. He was sitting behind a desk, and his gaze went from me to Erica, to Stanley.

Erica and I froze.

"Cute dog you got there," he said.

"Thanks," I replied in a bright voice, then took Erica's arm and steered her left, into the children's room. We went to a far corner, where there was an empty, faded orange wingchair.

"Wow, they haven't gotten rid of this chair," I murmured, running my hand over the scratchy fabric. "I haven't been here since I came back home. I spent hours here, reading." I turned to the bookshelf nearby and scanned the stack, wondering if the archaeology books were still here.

"Focus," Erica hissed. "How are we going to know Gus's girl-friend? It's not like she's going to have a sign on her that says, 'I Broke Up the Dead Leaf-Blowing Dude's Marriage.'"

I rolled my eyes. "We're going to walk around, pick up a few books, and see who's working. It's not like there are hundreds of employees here. If we can't figure it out, we'll ask the guy at the front desk. Honey said the woman's name is Bridget. Wasn't sure of the last name."

We strolled around the children's section for a while but only found two kids coloring at a table.

"Don't they have children's librarians anymore?" I murmured.

"Budget cuts, probably," Erica retorted, ever the realist.

We exhausted the possibilities in that room almost immediately, so we went back into the lobby and lingered near a bulletin board, pointing at tacked-up flyers and pretending to discuss community yoga classes and book clubs.

"Look at this flyer. Dog training," Erica said, putting a protective hand on Stanley. He was wide awake, his espresso-colored eyes darting everywhere. I could tell that he longed to get out of the harness and probably accost every human in the library with tongue kisses, but he was swaddled so tightly that he couldn't squirm.

"No chance. We tried puppy kindergarten, remember?" My mind flashed back to Stanley and I getting our Good Canine Citizen Certificate, although I had the feeling they handed out those awards to everyone, since Stanley was still incapable of basic commands like "stay" or "sit."

The two of us shuffled into the main adult room, which was an airy, high-ceilinged space painted in a tasteful pale yellow, with exposed white beams. I inhaled the paper-and-ink smell, which brought me immediately back to my childhood, walking in while holding Dad's hand.

My gaze landed on the reference desk, which was empty. "Jeez. Where are all the staff?"

"Just because she works here doesn't mean she's working today." Erica wandered off, toward the fiction.

We wove our way through two tall stacks, and when we rounded the third, Erica stopped abruptly. This caused me to crash into her.

"Wha—"

A woman was at the end of the aisle, next to a cart of books. She looked to be in her forties, brunette and trim, with a smattering of freckles across her cheeks.

"Be cool," Erica whispered, and we slowly sauntered toward the woman. "That might be her."

"I'm really looking for some . . ." Erica raised her voice, allowing her fingers to trail over the books at hip level. "Nora Roberts. I'm in the mood for romance. How about you?"

The woman looked up. "This is science fiction," she said with a helpful smile and sweeping gesture with her hand. "Romance is on the other side of the room. Near the door to the special collections. Aww, look at the cute little puppy."

Stanley, sensing that someone wanted to give him attention, attempted a heroic wiggle.

Erica and I paused. We were on the other side of the cart, a couple of feet away. My eyes were drawn to the badge on the woman's chest:

"Devil's Beach Library—Bridget Weber"

"Thank you. We'll check that out." My fingers dug into Erica's arm, and we retreated, crossing the room and hiding behind a tall bookcase in back. From our vantage point, we could peek around the corner and see the back side of Bridget's head.

"That's her," I whispered. "What should we do?"

Erica peered around the stack while holding onto Stanley with one hand. After surveying the situation for a few seconds, she turned back to me. "We could go back and strike up a conversation."

"Or maybe only one of us should. It would be a lot less intimidating. I think you should go and ask her more questions. Stanley will be an icebreaker. She'll almost certainly want to pet him. Did you see how she looked at him? Most people can't resist touching his fur."

"True. But what am I going to say? 'Hey, I'm a suspect in your lover's murder? What's up?'"

I licked my lips. Admittedly, our plan wasn't well thought out. "Good point. Maybe I should go and do my reporting thing."

"But you're not reporting."

"I'll make friendly small talk."

"Oh, right. Perfect. Let me look to see if she's still there." She leaned around the corner, then quickly ducked back when Stanley let out a muffled wuff. "Crap. Crap. Crap."

"What?"

"Crouch down." She kept her hand on Stanley's face while she crouched.

"Why?" I was about to peek around the bookcase when she grasped at my arm.

"Lana," she hissed. "Get down here."

I lowered into a crouch, which made my raw, blistered heels feel even worse. "What's going on?"

She tried to mouth something to me, and I shook my head. "I don't understand."

Stanley wriggled and squirmed like a recently caught fish. "Noah just walked in."

My eyes went wide. Eep. This wasn't good. "Did Stanley see him?" I whispered in her ear.

She nodded, wincing.

We both knew this was terrible. Whenever Stanley saw Noah, he went into a frenzy. After all, Noah was his favorite human. And although my dog fell short of obedience skills, he had a nose that was more like a bloodhound's than a Shih Tzu's.

Even now, his little snout was tilted in the air. "Stanley can smell Noah," I muttered in my lowest voice.

"Oh he can, can he?"

At the sound of that deep baritone, Erica and I looked up from our crouching position. We obviously looked ridiculous. Stanley barked once, loudly. From the looks of the frenzy in his eyes and the tongue that lolled out of his mouth, he was overjoyed.

I, on the other hand, was mortified.

"Hey there, Noah," Erica said in a shocked voice. "What brings you here?"

"The question is, what brings the three of you here?" He hooked his thumb into his police belt.

I reached for a Nora Roberts book and showed him the cover. "Checking out a romance. You know. Getting in the mood for Valentine's Day and all."

I winked and Noah let out a snicker.

Erica and I stood, and Stanley strained against the confines of the pooch pouch. Mercifully, Noah extended a hand to stroke his head, and the dog calmed.

"Lana, can I speak with you in private for a second?"

I reluctantly looked to Erica and nodded. "I'll meet you in the lobby."

She and Stanley loped off, and I prayed that she'd try to get a word in with Bridget on her way out.

Noah fixed his dark gaze on me. Normally I thought this expression was smoldering and sensual. Today it was steely and reproachful. "What are you really doing here?"

I put my index finger on his chest. We were alone in the back of the room, and I figured it might be best to flirt my way out of this situation. "I told you. Getting in the mood for Valentine's Day. Checking out a romance or two. Supporting the local library."

"You usually buy books on Kindle," he said.

"My, my, you're so observant of my habits."

"And I bought you a one-hundred-dollar gift card to the local bookstore for Christmas."

"That, you did. It was an excellent gift." I swallowed and batted my eyelashes. "So excellent that I've used it all up. Today I was looking for something specific. Something . . . spicier."

He rolled his eyes and clasped both of my elbows in his big hands. "Lana. Cut the sex-kitten act. You were here to talk with Bridget, weren't you?"

"I didn't know that talking with a librarian was a crime. What are you doing here anyway?"

"I have an appointment to talk with that particular librarian. It's part of my job." His response was pointed and on the edge of being terse.

"Oh, great! Well, I guess I'll be going then. Have to check out my book. Good luck with your interview." I waved the book in the air, figuring it was best if I didn't confirm or deny my intent to speak with Bridget.

He leaned down and kissed me on the cheek. As usual, his spicy masculine scent made me swoon a little. "I can't resist you, Lana. Even when you're being difficult. Want to hang out tonight? Do something to take our minds off murder?"

I paused before answering. Normally, I loved spending time with Noah, but I didn't want to fight about a homicide investigation or about my friend's innocence. If we were going on a date, we'd have to do something other than talk.

An idea came to me.

"How would you feel about roller skating?" I asked.

Chapter Thirteen

Whipping myself into a spin as the strains of Kool and the Gang blasted over the sound system, I let out a full-throated laugh.

"This is so fun," I cried, then skated over to Noah. Whooshing around the rink made me feel totally free and alive. Even my blisters weren't bothering me, probably because I'd fortified them with giant bandages, worn thicker socks, and rented skates a half size bigger.

He was clutching the rail, watching me. "I didn't anticipate you were a roller derby queen. I'm impressed, cupcake."

I gracefully came to a stop, my face flushed with excitement and pride that, finally, there was a physical fitness skill I was better at than Noah. "Come on, you haven't even gone all the way around the rink yet. Look, I'll teach you what to do. Start out like this." I bent my knees slightly.

"I'm not that graceful." His eyes went to a group of women on skates, who whizzed past us. They had matching pale blue shirts, and I suspected they were actually part of a team.

The idea of roller derby intrigued me, but first I needed to get Noah rolling. My eighth-grade fantasies of holding hands while skating with my boyfriend were still strong in my subconscious.

"You are extremely graceful, Noah. I've seen you on paddleboards, kayaks, and canoes. You can do this. Here's what I remember from my lessons when I was a kid. Point your toes out, and imagine you're walking like a duck. Learn to walk on the skates first, then learn to glide."

He winced, then laughed. When he attempted my instructions, he looked more like a wooden Frankenstein and clutched the rail.

"I might stay here and watch you. That's way more fun."

"Let me take another spin, and we'll pause for a drink. Okay?" Gingerly, I kissed him on the cheek, and he chuckled.

"Go, go. I love watching you." He waved me off.

I skated away backward, blowing him a kiss. Then I flipped around and glided, with long strokes of my legs, around the rink. For a few minutes, as my forward motion blew back my hair, I forgot about everything. Gus's homicide, my recent fights with Noah, Erica's troubles, Perkatory . . . they all trailed behind me as I enjoyed my little taste of freedom.

A black light plunged the rink into a funky hue, and the disco ball illuminated, sending a thousand splinters of shimmering light onto the polished floor. The song "Disco Inferno" blasted over the speakers, and the crowd on the floor erupted in cheers. I let out an excited whoop.

I whizzed past Noah, who looked a bit alarmed at the fervor that swept through the rink. "One more lap, babe," I shouted.

"I'll be in the snack bar," he called out.

I gave him a thumbs-up. For the next three minutes, I skate-boogied next to the members of the roller derby team. They were amazing, skating backward and doing limbo moves and gliding on one foot. Maybe someday I'd be as good.

At one point, one of the derby team and I did a hip bump to the beat, then high-fived each other. It might have been the single coolest moment of my life, and I hoped Noah caught it.

After the song was finished, the DJ announced that it was time for a break so the rink floor could be swept clean. I rolled my way to the nearest exit, still high on adrenaline and my new-found hipster status. Maybe I *would* start that Instagram channel after all.

Noah was in the snack bar, sitting at a table. Two bottles of Coca-Cola were in front of him, and he slid one toward me. His roller skates sat by his feet, which were clad in only his blue socks. I plopped down in the hard plastic chair across from him.

"Thanks for this." I gulped my soda, slightly out of breath.

"You were really great out there, Lana. I was watching you. So impressive. How'd you learn to skate like that? You never told me you had this talent."

I lifted a shoulder. "I used to go to the rink on the mainland, as a kid with my mom. Took lessons and everything."

"Why'd you stop?"

"That's a good question." I took another sip. "I guess because I started high school . . ."

For a moment, I was lost in thought. "No, that's not true. I went skating in high school too. Freshman year, with Gisela."

Noah perked up and leaned in. "Your friend who went missing?"

I nodded. Noah and I hadn't been together long when I'd told him about Gisela. She'd moved to the island with her parents our freshman year. The two of us had been inseparable. At the end of that school year, we'd gone to a party together, then walked home since we lived close to each other. That night, sometime after the moment we said goodbye, she'd disappeared. No one ever found her body or any evidence that she was either dead or alive.

She'd vanished, and that one detail had changed my life forever. It was what made me get into journalism and crime reporting.

"Yeah. Gisela." My voice turned quiet. "She loved to skate."

Suddenly it all came back. How we'd put on glitter eyeshadow and soda-flavored lip gloss, and beg my mom to drive us to the rink on Friday nights so we could scope out cute guys. We'd goofed around while skating, singing to tunes from the eighties and nineties, and sat in a snack bar much like this one, drinking weak coffee, talking about our hopes and dreams.

"Sorry. I know that's a difficult subject. Didn't mean to bring it up," Noah said in a somber tone.

I inhaled and nodded, a feeling of fierceness welling inside me. It was time to lay some of my feelings on the line for Noah. A realization about Gisela formed in my brain. "You know, I think that's why I'm so intent on proving Erica's innocence in this situation with Gus."

"Why?" His brows knit together. "I'm not following."

I looked down and ran my foot across the floor, feeling the wheels under my toes. "Because I couldn't help Gisela. You don't know how powerless I felt when she went missing. There was nothing I could do other than tell the police about our last conversation."

Noah nodded, a serious expression on his face. "Go on."

"I felt like an awful friend. I couldn't protect her. Couldn't keep her safe. I felt like a failure." I swallowed and paused, trying not to burst into tears right here at the Hot Wheels Skate Shack.

Noah opened his mouth as if to speak, but words tumbled out of my mouth. "Maybe that's why I haven't made many friends until now. Probably that's what a therapist would say anyway. Dad's insinuated as much, but I've always chalked his interpretation up to his new age philosophy. But maybe there's something there. I've always kept people—well, female friends—at arm's length. Because I don't want to lose them like I did Gisela."

"It's something to consider, I guess." He stared into his soda and rattled the ice in the cup.

"With Erica, I want to protect her. I know she's a badass and all, but there's something vulnerable inside of her as well. I feel like she needs me to help her. In general, and in this whole mess with Gus. My gut tells me she didn't—*couldn't*—have killed him." I shook my head, rattled. "I can't believe she would be so unhinged by a guy blowing leaves that she'd tweak a machine to explode and kill him."

Noah rubbed his neck. "It sure does seem difficult to believe. I wouldn't have pegged Erica as a murderer, but I've been surprised before. Still, some things don't add up."

"See?" I cried. "You agree with me. There must be other suspects. Other possibilities."

He clenched his teeth together and shook his head. "Gus was involved in a lot of shady business dealings. Let's leave it at that."

My heart started to pound. Was that a clue? It had to be. Should I probe more and try to pump Noah for more information so Erica and I could rest easier about her alleged involvement?

"So, does that mean—"

Noah took my hand and shook his head. "I'm not saying anything more. Look"—he gestured with his nose to the rink—"why don't you go take a few more laps. I think it's good for you."

I studied the skaters flocking to the oval-shaped rink as the strains of Donna Summer's "Hot Stuff" blasted in the air. A memory of me and Gisela cracking up while skating to this song came to mind.

I nodded at Noah. "I'll be back in a while."

"Take your time, cupcake. I'll be here answering some emails." He pointed at his phone.

I squeezed his hand, got up, and rolled away. These laps were for Gisela.

*   *   *

A couple of hours later, after Noah declared that I had an innate talent for roller skating, and following a sweet goodnight kiss on my porch steps, I walked into my house. Once again, my leg muscles ached, but in a productive, triumphant way.

Maybe skating was in my future—my elusive hobby. Everyone else, it seemed, had their own stress relief outlet. Dad had dozens of hobbies, and they'd grown in number every year since Mom had died. His yoga, his crystal bowl meditation, and his Reiki. Plus the monkey activism.

Erica had her sailboat and her craft cocktails. Noah had running and had also recently gotten into elaborate Lego sculptures.

I had work, reading, and baking. Two of the three were solitary pursuits, and none involved stepping outside of my comfort zones of home and Perkatory. But a new world had opened up. Dozens of cute roller-skating outfits cruised through my brain, and I hummed one of the disco tunes I'd heard earlier as I walked into the house.

I knelt to greet Stanley, who was ecstatic to see me. He let out a sharp bark and I shushed him. It was around ten PM, and I wasn't sure if Erica was sleeping.

"Who's a good boy? You? Does my good boy want a pupper snack?" I squeezed his fluffy, tawny body into mine and hoisted him up. I heard a door open.

"Lana? Is that you?" Erica's throaty voice soared through the air, from the direction of the guest bedroom.

"Yep, I'm back from skating. Everything okay?" Stanley wriggled to be released, and I set him down. He bounded toward Erica's room, probably thinking she was summoning him to playtime.

I called his name, and to my surprise, he turned and ran to me. His recall wasn't the best, so this seemed like a minor victory.

"Want a treat, buddy?" He pranced on his feet. I grabbed a stack of mail off the hall table.

"Erica?" I called out.

"Yeah, everything's great, I'm half asleep and headed to bed. I'm on the early shift tomorrow."

Of course, I knew this since I'd set the schedule for Perkatory. "Good deal. Night."

Her door snicked shut, and Stanley and I went into the kitchen. I deposited the mail on the counter and grabbed a snack for Stanley and a glass of water for me. Funny, despite all of the exercise tonight, I wasn't sleepy. Part of me wished Noah had accepted my invitation to watch a movie, but he'd said he had an early meeting and wanted to get home.

I wondered if he actually didn't want to sleep under the same roof as Erica, but pushed the thought out of my mind. Could it be that my best friend and my father were driving my boyfriend away? No, that was ridiculous. Noah was mature enough to tell me if that was the case.

Then I turned my attention to the stack of envelopes, flyers, and folders on the counter. For the past couple of weeks I'd taken the mail from the hall and left it on the kitchen counter. I figured that all the important items were sent to the café, but at the sight of the small mountain, I let out a sigh.

"I should really look through this," I murmured to Stanley, who was gnawing on a Pup-Peroni stick. He ignored me.

Grabbing the stack, I sank into the chair at my high-top kitchen table and began sorting.

More than half were flyers, ads, and political mailers. Those all went to my right, in a recycle pile. There were also a couple of bills, and a fancy invite to a new beach bar opening. I set those to my left, thinking that Noah might want to go to the beach bar party.

There was one fundraising letter addressed to my mother, which made me a bit sad to see, and a postcard for a medical marijuana collective in Tampa addressed to Dad. I put the former in the recycling pile, and the latter in the keep stack.

I rifled through the rest, which seemed to be all junk mail. But a thick, cream-colored, linen envelope caught my eye.

The letter, which had the return address of a law firm on the mainland, was addressed to Gus Bailey.

"Oh dear," I sighed.

This had happened to us once before, right after he moved in. When I'd brought him his mail, he'd practically grabbed it out of my hand and grunted a thanks—then slammed the door in my face.

"What's this?" I whispered, bringing the envelope closer to my face so I could inspect the postmark. It was dated last week, when he had still been alive. Eep. I probably should've gone through this stack earlier.

Feeling guilty, I rifled through the rest of the stack. There were two other official-looking letters addressed to Gus, both items I'd neglected to give to him.

My heart began to hammer against my ribcage and I reached for my cell. Noah would probably want to take a look at these. But instead of picking up my cell, I ran my index finger over the front of the envelope, over Gus's name, which was in a serious-looking font in heavy black type.

What if these letters contained some sort of clue to Gus's death? What if they exonerated Erica?

Opening someone else's mail would be illegal, even if that someone was dead. And Noah—well, he'd be disappointed at best and ballistic at worst.

What if I claimed to have accidentally opened the letter? Pretended that I'd assumed it was for me and ripped the flap? Would Noah believe that?

I eyed my teakettle on the stove, wondering about the old-fashioned idea of using steam to loosen the glue, then flipped the letter over, running the pad of my finger over the closed flap.

For a while I sat in silence, wondering if I should wake Erica up to steam the envelopes open. No. I needed more self-control than that. Opening someone else's mail shouldn't be done on a whim.

I scooped up the three envelopes and took them in my room, setting them on my bureau. They stayed there all night while I eventually drifted off to sleep.

Chapter Fourteen

M y eyes peeled open fifteen minutes before my alarm went off. Stanley was snoozing next to me, and I had a fuzzy memory of him leaping out of bed around five and hearing Erica open the door in the backyard so the dog could do his early-morning business.

I petted his soft fur for a while, and my mind immediately snapped back to what I'd been thinking about when I fell asleep.

The letters.

I tore the blanket away. It was almost seven in the morning, I had to be at Perkatory in two hours to meet Julian, and I was alone in the house.

It was a perfect time to steam those envelopes open. But why? What would I gain? *Possibly the truth.* Or maybe nothing, and draw a heap of scorn from Noah if he found out.

I shut my eyes, hoping sleep would take me away for another thirty minutes. My mind wouldn't allow that, and I thought about a conversation I'd had once back in high school with Dad, right in this very room. (I'd redecorated when I moved back and had removed the N'Sync posters, replacing them with tasteful art by a Haitian-American painter friend.)

Back when I was sixteen, I hadn't been sure what I wanted to do with my life. Being a journalist spoke to my soul, but even back then, I knew it was a precarious career choice.

"Maybe I should be a therapist," I'd said to my father.

"Lana, you're the most curious person I know. And you're like me. You love to talk about the things you've discovered, and you need to get to the bottom of mysteries. Do you really think you can keep secrets as a therapist? Or ignore your desire to get to the truth?"

Dad had been right then and was still right now. Maybe some folks could set aside a mystery. I wasn't one of those people.

Grabbing the letters from the bureau, I marched into the kitchen and fired up the kettle, still feeling a little uneasy about taking the plunge into committing a possible criminal offense. This was obviously a serious matter, since I was tackling this even before drinking my morning coffee. Still, I could multitask and boil water for my French press coffee and to steam to open the letters.

When the kettle began to boil, I selected the letter with the oldest postmark, dated two weeks ago. My curiosity clearly hadn't extended to my own correspondence; otherwise, I'd have noticed that this letter had been misdelivered long before Gus's death. For a second a pang of guilt throbbed in my stomach.

What if I'd spotted the letter when it was put in my mailbox and given it to Gus? Was there a chance that he'd still be alive? I knew that sometimes, people's lives hinged on seemingly trivial events and choices. What if this letter contained something so important that it would have altered the course of events, and Gus would somehow not have fired up his leaf blower on a random Sunday evening?

No, I couldn't think that way. This wasn't about me, and I wasn't responsible for his death because I'd been irresponsible with the mail.

I held the letter over the spout, trying to angle the seal over the steam. Unfortunately, my fingers were in the way.

"Yow!" I cried, dropping the letter onto the counter.

A better idea would be to use tongs, and so I grabbed them from a utensil holder.

"There we go," I whispered as I moved the letter slowly through the stream of steam. I backed off an inch or two because I feared the paper would get a bit soggy.

After about a minute, the flap was loose and puckered. I set the letter down on the counter and with my thumb and index finger, gingerly peeled it apart, trying not to rip the paper. When it was fully open, I let out a long breath and slid the paper out. It was on the same heavy, linen paper, and I unfolded it carefully.

It was a legal notice of some sort. Since I'd covered crime in Miami for the newspaper, I'd seen hundreds of similar documents. The text was terse, notifying Mr. Gus Bailey of an upcoming hearing in a civil case at the courthouse on the mainland.

The hearing was scheduled for tomorrow. I let out a grunt of impatience. Surely it would be canceled because of Gus's death? I reached for my old reporter's notebook and a pen—I still kept them in the kitchen, to jot down my grocery list—and scrawled a few details.

First, the case number. Then, the entity suing Gus: The *Royal Conquest*, doing business as *Royal Conquest Maritime LLC*.

Huh. Weird. Wasn't that Gus's former business? Were the people he sold to now suing him? My mind raced. Was Mickey Dotson suing him? I tapped the pen against my lips. I needed to check out the ship's LLC, and find out who, other than Mickey, was involved.

I refolded the paper and slipped it back into the envelope. Fortunately, the adhesive was still a bit moist from the steam, and I pressed down with my fingers. It looked a little puckered, but not too bad.

The kettle was still shooting out steam, and I quickly opened the second envelope. One was a legal notice from a divorce attorney representing Honey. It was addressed to Gus's attorney, and this was a copy of a letter. That much was obvious. I scanned the legalese and deciphered that it was a request for financial documents, and from the wording of the attorney, it seemed like this was a second, possibly third, demand.

Your client has not been forthcoming with this information, the lawyer wrote.

Well, now I had Honey's lawyer's name as well. I stuffed the paper back inside the envelope and successfully sealed it shut.

The third envelope was a little trickier. Possibly it had stickier glue, or a lower quality paper, because I had to hold it up to the kettle for much longer. The result was a soggy envelope, and I swore as I pried it open.

This, too, was from a law firm, notifying Gus of his bill for services rendered in federal court. "Bankruptcy," I murmured.

So Gus was going through a divorce, was being sued by some business associates, and had filed for bankruptcy. He had three different attorneys representing him on three cases—and those were the ones I knew about. That was a lot of money in legal fees, I guessed.

A fuller picture of the man next door emerged, and I mulled this over while I made a pot of French Press. I needed the robust, strong brew to start this day. Crud. If only I could focus on reporting today . . .

No, that wasn't an appropriate line of thought. I wasn't a journalist any longer. This wasn't a news article. I had other obligations, important ones.

I drank my coffee and scanned the headlines of the *Devil's Beach Beacon* on my phone. There was an update on the monkeys (state wildlife officials were coming later this week to discuss the situation with local officials), a piece about a guy who'd stolen a car from a dealership (only to try to sell said car back to the same dealership), and then a story out of Orlando about a woman who'd trapped a gator in a recycling bin by enticing him with a grocery store sub sandwich.

The latter was what passed as a feel-good story in Florida, since the woman didn't kill the alligator.

Oddly, there were no articles about Gus or his murder, which made me wonder even more about the situation. My mind raced in a million directions.

Gah. I didn't have time for this. Today was a big day with Julian, and then the all-staff meeting. I needed to get a move on so I could arrive at Perkatory before he did. Yesterday's scene with Erica and the true crime–loving tourists probably didn't leave the best impression, and I wanted to make up for that.

I showered and decided to dress up a bit, hoping a cute outfit would somehow make me feel less scattered.

I settled on skinny black jeans, a tight, long-sleeved white T-shirt, a long cream-and-white cardigan, a tan scarf, and—in a moment of inspiration—a pair of weathered yet cool cowboy boots. Rarely was it ever this chilly in Florida, and I figured the boots would be a nice touch for the day.

Plus, they were comfy, especially when paired with socks and a new set of bandages over the blisters.

It took me a few minutes to switch purses—my black leather wouldn't go with the brown boots, so I found a more appropriate bag—and stuffed the letters inside, thinking I'd run them over to Noah later, during my lunch break. After I kissed Stanley good-bye, I was off. Dad was scheduled to check in on Stanley in a few hours.

Today I decided to walk the few blocks to Perkatory, since the morning was so sunny and cool. Yes, this was perfect. Being outside, soaking in the sunshine and the blue sky and the vibrant green of the palm trees, was a balm for my soul. Plus the blissfully crisp and dry air. Today was a beach day for northerners, but to me, it felt like winter. My boots made a satisfying strike against the sidewalk cement, and the only thing that marred my seven-minute walk was the wail of an ambulance in the distance.

That was the only downside to living so close to town; the EMS/fire department was quite active and noisy, what with the island's many drunk tourists, inexperienced boaters, and daredevils who rented those electric scooters and didn't wear helmets.

As I approached Main Street, I waved at the woman across the street—Janey, a waitress from Bay-Bay's.

She was putting out the sidewalk sign advertising the specials of the day. The restaurant had the best seafood in town, much of it caught in local waters in the Gulf of Mexico.

It was definitely a day for grouper chowder from Bay-Bay's. That was what we all needed. Once we were done with training, I'd take the staff for dinner and drinks. An evening of bonding.

We'd show Julian a good time on Devil's Beach. No pizza—just local, delicious seafood.

It was so much nicer to think about that than homicide. Erica and I could deal with Gus later. Surely an arrest wasn't imminent—Noah would most certainly wait for the autopsy, which would likely take a day or two more.

I turned onto Main and walked past Beach Boss, the tourist souvenir shop that was one of the three businesses in the bottom of my family's building. A few people streamed out and stood on the sidewalk, gawking in the direction of my café. I spotted the owner of Dante's Inferno, the hot yoga studio in between Beach Boss and Perkatory, standing on the sidewalk. His name was Kai Lahtinen, and he rushed toward me.

"Lana, what's going on?" A line of worry was etched between his brows.

I slowed to a stop. My gaze snagged at a vehicle parked at the far corner, in front of the Perkatory door. It was an ambulance.

"Your guess is as good as mine," I said slowly.

Leaving Kai standing in the middle of the sidewalk, I pushed through the growing crowd and pulled open the Perkatory door. The first thing I noticed was that it was eerily quiet. No music, no happy chattering customers.

The second thing I noticed was that everyone in the place was standing in a circle, obviously gaping at something in the middle of the room. Doug, our regular, glanced at me, and beckoned. He gently put his hand on my shoulder and pulled me into the circle.

"What's happening here?" I whispered to him. Before he could answer, I spotted Julian lying on the floor, near a table pushed aside at a weird angle. A chair was on its side, and a puddle of iced coffee spread across the tile toward Julian's motionless hand.

Two EMTs knelt on the floor next to him.

"Julian," I cried, going to him. His olive-hued skin looked oddly pale, and he didn't turn his head or acknowledge my presence. His eyes were closed, and I whispered his name again. No response.

I turned to the nearest EMT. "What's going on? He doesn't look good at all." Was it a heart attack? A stroke? Did Julian have a medical condition? I searched my brain, trying to remember if his emails had mentioned any problems. No, in fact, he'd recently said he'd participated in a 5K run in Miami.

"Please stand back, ma'am," one of the EMTs said. "He's breathing and we're stabilizing him."

I felt like I'd been kicked in the stomach. My eyes flitted around the room. Our regular, Darla was here, and we locked eyes. She bit her lip, and I grimaced; then she pressed her hands together in prayer. I mirrored her gesture, then scanned the café, searching for Erica. I spotted her leaning against the counter, looking wide-eyed and as stunned as I felt. I made my way to her.

"He . . . he . . . oh my goodness." She clapped her hand over her mouth.

I dragged her behind the counter, away from the fray. "What? Why didn't you call me? Is he okay?"

She shook her head. "I didn't have time. It all happened so fast, like literally fifteen minutes ago. He came in early and said he wanted to check his emails and do some work at a table. He asked for something different, handed me his own travel mug because he's all about recycling. He even said it was clean, and that I didn't need to rinse it out. We talked about the mushroom coffee, and he wanted to try one, so I made the Lion's Roar. Fifteen, maybe twenty minutes later, he fell over and clutched his throat. Spilled the coffee everywhere. He also made a terrible retching noise, which totally freaked everyone out. I thought it was maybe a seizure. I don't know. I called 911 immediately."

My neck began to sweat. "Did he say anything to you? Is he allergic to something? I don't understand."

"I don't either, Lana." Her voice cracked.

Like zombies, we wandered away from the counter in time to see two burly EMTs put Julian on a stretcher. Everyone watched in silence as they carried him out, and when the door banged behind them, I studied the ten or so customers left in the place.

Most were regulars, like Doug and Darla. A few were older folks who were my dad's age. They'd been on Devil's Beach long enough to know that odd things, difficult things, occasionally happened. The tourists, however, were hoping for a problem-free, idyllic experience.

Erica scurried over to right the toppled chair. I clapped my hands together and eyed the pool of coffee on the gray cement floor. Crud. That was a liability lawsuit waiting to happen. "Okay, friends, I'm going to clean up the coffee here, so please be mindful of where you step, because it's slippery. But in the meantime, your next drink is on us."

Several people lined up at the counter, and I breathed a little sigh of relief as I grabbed an orange caution cone and the mop. As Erica worked quickly to make drinks, I mopped up, instructing everyone nearby to steer clear. It paid to give people two, sometimes three, warnings on stuff like this.

I lived in fear of a slip-and-fall lawsuit, so I stood by the wet spot on the floor while it dried, making small talk with Doug.

"I wonder what happened to him," I mused.

He lifted a shoulder. "Dunno. I was here working when he sat down. Then I went into the restroom. When I got back, he was on the floor. It was super odd. Maybe he had heart trouble."

"Maybe," I murmured. "He's pretty young, though. I don't think he's even forty."

"It can happen to young people," Doug said in a chatty tone, then launched into a story about his buddy in Silicon Valley who'd had a heart attack at thirty-five.

I listened to him for a while, until the door burst open, and Dad busted in, a wild look on his face. Oh, boy.

"Excuse me," I said to Doug, pointing at Dad. Doug grinned and nodded, because he knew how Dad was.

"Munchkin," Dad cried. "What's the deal? I got a call from two people saying there was a mass casualty event."

A few tourists looked up and blinked. Jeez, the gossips in this town were obviously starved for excitement.

I cleared my throat and pulled him toward the window, where a bank of stools sat against a weathered wood counter. No one was sitting nearby.

"Shh," I hissed. "Your sources are terrible. There was no mass casualty incident. One person had a medical issue, and he's fine. Everything's fine." I wasn't entirely sure Julian was fine, but I hoped that by saying it aloud, he would be.

"Oh." Dad looked a little crestfallen and stroked his goatee. "Was it anyone we knew?"

I pulled at my ear. "Julian. It was Julian from Miami."

His mouth formed a perfect O, framed by his gray, furry goatee. In truth, he looked a bit like Stanley. I almost giggled, but didn't because of the seriousness of the situation, and instead explained everything Erica told me.

Dad leaned in, and his scent of patchouli and peanut butter washed over me. "It's awful that Julian's first visit to Devil's Beach ends up with a trip to the hospital. Let's hope it isn't anything serious. Maybe he had an angina attack."

Did angina attacks leave someone with a gray pallor, unable to talk? Unlikely. I took a long, fortifying breath, hoping like an optimist that the worst was behind us.

Chapter Fifteen

S poiler alert: The worst wasn't behind us, not by a long espresso shot.

Two hours later, as Dad, Erica and I waited on customers and gossiped about Gus—I explained in detail all about the content of the letters—Noah walked in.

"Hey," I said brightly. "I was going to come see you, but we had a little incident here earlier, and things are just now calming down. I have something for you."

His face was stony and serious. "Can we go upstairs to the office?"

A cold chill went through me. "Uh, okay. You sure you don't want a cup of your usual lemon water, and we can sit down here?"

"No, I need to speak with you in private." He took off his police hat.

Mumbling, "Sure, okay—let's go then," I led him into the corridor to the bathrooms and the back staircase, forgetting all about the letters because of his unsmiling expression. We climbed the stairs in silence, and I was reminded of another time we'd done this—when my barista, who'd lived in an apartment on the top floor, was murdered.

I had the same ominous feeling now.

Unlocking the door to my office, I flipped on the light. When my mom had opened the café years ago, she'd declared this her inner sanctum, and it was a hippie, bohemian girl zone, with framed posters of Stevie Nicks and local art hanging haphazardly on the walls. I gestured to the threadbare tan sofa in the corner, and Noah eased down, moving aside a pillow with the word "Groovy" embroidered on it.

I plopped down in the worn black office chair and swiveled to face him. "What's up? Why the long face?"

He sighed and fidgeted with his hat, a sure sign that he was nervous and about to tell me something terrible. "I won't sugarcoat it." He paused.

"Please. Don't. I'm not a big fan of sugar anyway. What's going on? I can't stand the suspense."

He looked me squarely in the eyes. Noah sure could turn on the stern cop look when he wanted, and I immediately began to feel guilty for steaming those letters open. When he was in detective mode, his expression had a way of leaching guilt from everyone in his orbit.

"Julian, your coffee trainer from Miami, was admitted to the hospital here on the island. Doctors called us because he showed signs of being poisoned."

I clutched my scarf. "What? Is he okay?"

"As okay as anyone who ingested poison can be." Noah ran a hand through his hair. "He's in serious but stable condition because fortunately he didn't drink much. Doctors believe they can treat him here on island, but they haven't ruled out airlifting him to the mainland."

I blinked several times, stunned. "Is he conscious? Talking? Will there be any lasting damage? How did that happen? What kind of poison?"

"Is he conscious? Yes. Talking? A little, but I'm letting him rest until tomorrow before we interview him. Lasting damage? Perhaps, to his liver."

"What kind of poison?" I asked again.

"We're doing a test on the residual liquid in his mug. It spilled when he fell over. I've put in a rush order. And it's too early to tell if there's lasting damage. How did it happen? Where did it happen? Well, that's why I'm here."

I leaned back into the office chair, stunned. Julian was poisoned at Perkatory? No. That couldn't be right. "Are you accusing me—"

"No. I'm not accusing anyone. But I want to know exactly what went on here this morning. What did you see and hear, and who was in the coffee shop at the time this happened. You need to tell me everything, Lana."

I knew by the way he said my name—and that he hadn't called me cupcake—that this was a grave situation.

"I wasn't here yet. I came in a little later because . . ." My voice trailed off, guilt filling my chest because I'd been home, illegally opening a dead man's mail. "Because I scheduled a late staff meeting with Julian. I was supposed to meet him here at nine, and we were going to go over inventory and his roaster's upcoming product catalog for the year."

"So who was here?"

"Erica."

His jaw ticked, a movement that flashed past in a millisecond.

"Noah, come on. Erica had nothing to do with this," I said sharply. "Don't even go there."

He sighed and lowered his head for a second. When he raised it, his eyes were softer, less cop-like. "Cupcake, don't you think it's a little odd that she served his drink? And the whole Gus thing . . ."

"There is no 'Gus thing.' And why would she slip poison into Julian's drink? She met the guy yesterday. I've known Erica for months, and never once has she randomly poisoned anyone."

"You told me that she resented Julian's presence here."

I rolled my eyes. "Sure, she was a tiny bit annoyed because she thinks she's the best barista around. Which she is. She doesn't like authority or people telling her what to do when it comes to work. But that doesn't mean she would intentionally poison a total stranger while he drank his morning coffee. Goodness, Noah. You must really dislike Erica if you think that poorly of her."

"I don't dislike her, and I don't think poorly of her. I like her. But I also have to put my personal feelings aside when I'm investigating an attempted homicide."

I gasped. "Is that what this is? An attempted homicide investigation?"

He didn't answer.

"Is this a formal interview?" My pitch bordered on shrill. "Am I a suspect?"

"No," he said quietly.

I spent the next thirty seconds trying to regulate my heartbeat by breathing slowly. Noah sat slumped against the back of the sofa. Truthfully, he looked as miserable as I felt.

"What are you going to do now?"

"Talk with Erica. Try to chat with people who were here when it happened. Would you mind if I stayed up here to have the conversations?"

"I guess not." I swallowed hard.

Noah thanked me and I stood. "I'll send her up. Don't be surprised if she doesn't have info, though. She said it all happened in a few seconds."

He reached for my hand and squeezed my fingers. I didn't squeeze back. "It's going to be okay, Lana. We'll get through this."

I nodded but wasn't sure if I believed him.

He stood and stared down at me, his eyes every bit as serious as before. "Oh, and one more thing."

"Yeah?"

"You're going to need to stop serving, probably for the rest of today and maybe tomorrow. People can stay—*need* to stay—if they were here when Julian collapsed. I'm getting a few officers here to conduct interviews."

"Stop serving . . . what, exactly?"

"Food. Drinks."

My mouth hung open. "Why?"

Noah looked at me with an incredulous expression. "Because if there's a contaminant in your café, we don't want to poison anyone else."

All of the air escaped my lungs, and for a second, I couldn't breathe. We'd given freebies to customers right after Julian collapsed. I told this to Noah, and he pinched the bridge of his nose while shutting his eyes.

"I'm sorry," I whispered.

"Shut down right away."

"Right. Yes. Of course. Um. Can we still serve bottled drinks?" We had some bottled cold coffee sold by Julian's roasting company. Those had been sealed elsewhere, and not by us. I explained this to Noah.

He considered this for a minute, his brows knitted. "Sealed, bottled water is okay. Nothing else, though."

I flew down the stairs, panic rising in my chest. Two things were obvious: Perkatory was out an entire day of sales, and my best friend was now a suspect in two crimes.

* * *

"I think she should have someone with her. It's a mistake to talk to any law enforcement officer without representation. I even offered to call my buddy. He's the best criminal defense lawyer in Southwest Florida." Dad shook his head. He acted like Erica was making the biggest mistake of her life by going upstairs to talk with Noah.

"Dad, stop. She's an adult. She's innocent, and Noah is her friend. And my boyfriend. She doesn't need a criminal defense attorney. And I thought your friend was a personal injury guy, the one on the cheesy TV commercials."

Erica had been upstairs with Noah for an hour now. We'd stopped serving, telling people the espresso maker was down, that only bottled water was available—and we were giving it away free. Several people took us up on the offer and continued to work, read, and chill in the café while they waited to speak with one of the officers, who had arrived and set up shop at two tables at the front.

Dad had changed the tunes to some electronic trance garbage. My anxiety over Julian's poisoning was ratcheting up with every synthesized beat.

"Noah's still a cop," Dad grumbled, ignoring my jab about his attorney friend. "You can't ever be too trusting of authority."

"Dad," I cried, slamming an empty stainless steel espresso pitcher on the counter. "That's my boyfriend we're talking about. What if we were to—I dunno—get married?"

Fat chance of that, since Noah hadn't even introduced me to his family. And I wasn't sure if I even wanted to be married a second time. Plus I had my doubts whether we'd survive this current situation. But still.

Dad scratched his goatee. "I've wondered about that. Guess I secretly hoped that Noah would retire early and become a fishing guide or something. Don't get me wrong—I really like him. He's a good guy, and I think he's a great partner for you. So much more respectful than your ex."

"You don't say," I snorted. Noah and my ex-husband, Miles, were as different as chalk and cheese.

"But he's still a cop. Question authority, Lana. And try to talk him into an offshore guide job. Noah's a great fisherman, you know. He's like a fish whisperer. Has he showed you his tarpon photos? I love that he catches and releases fish."

I rolled my eyes. My father had the strangest notions, I swear. "Okay, let's drop this conversation. We need to figure out what we're going to do."

"First, I think you need to take another run at Gus's lover at the library."

"No, I meant with Julian." Exasperation laced my tone. Crap. I still had to give Noah those letters meant for Gus.

"Oh. Him. Sure, we should all go visit him at the hospital. We could close early tonight and all of us—you, me, Erica, Barbara, and Heidi—should show up in his room. That would boost his spirits."

I imagined all of us trooping into the hospital, looking like we'd climbed out of a clown car. "Maybe I'll visit him. Alone."

Before Dad could respond, our attention was directed to the other side of the café, where Erica and Noah had emerged. Both had grim, stony expressions on their faces. They paused in the doorway, and Erica pointed to the counter where I was standing, then power-walked over to me, with her head down.

"I have something for Noah," I murmured out loud. I knelt to open a lower cupboard so I could retrieve the letters from my purse.

"Can you grab my bag too?" Erica's tone was strained, and when I looked up, she was standing over me.

"Sure." I handed her black backpack to her, and she took out the bottle of mushroom powder I'd seen her use the other day to make the Lion's Roar coffee concoction.

Oh. Dear.

I rose, wanting to ask a million questions, but she went over to Noah and handed him the bottle. He shot her a tight smile, and by now, Dad had joined our group at the counter.

"What's the good word, Noah? How are things at the cop shop? You any closer to resolving the monkey situation? I hope you know that we're having a primate protest later this week."

For a brief second I scrunched my eyes shut. Why couldn't Dad have talked about the weather or offered him a bottle of water? Couldn't we go five minutes without controversy? We were dealing with serious stuff here.

Erica came next to me while I inspected the letters. Only one looked a little warped, which could easily be blamed on the United States Post Office.

"Hey, Noah wants to chat with the customers who were here at the time Julian collapsed. Do you remember who all was here?" she asked.

I peeked over the espresso maker and scanned the four tables filled with people. Most looked like tourists in beach attire, people

I didn't know. Darla was here, though, scrolling through her phone, looking unperturbed. "Was John from Beach Boss here? I don't remember seeing him when I walked in. Everything was a blur from the second I saw Julian on the floor."

"No, he just came in. I saw him come through the door while you were upstairs with Noah. Unless he was here earlier too. He comes in several times a day for shots of espresso. Heck, I don't know." Erica chewed on her bottom lip. "Doug was here when it happened, right?"

I craned my neck to look at his usual table. "He was, but he's gone now. I don't see his computer over there. He probably went somewhere for lunch, I wasn't keeping track. I think Darla was here too. How'd it go with Noah? Was he kind in his questioning? I was so worried about you."

"Not terrible, I guess."

"But not great?"

She lifted her shoulders. "The reality is, I served Julian a drink, and fifteen minutes later he was on the floor, almost dead. From poisoning, according to what Noah said."

I held up a finger. "Let's talk about this in a little while. I've got some thoughts."

Of course, I didn't have thoughts, but I needed to get these letters out of my possession because they felt like they were metaphorically burning a hole in my hand. I went over to where Noah and Dad were talking.

Of course Dad was still hammering on the primate issue, explaining to Noah how primates use olfactory cues.

"Primates are smart. They sniff each other's urine—did you know that?" Dad pantomimed a sniffing motion with his nose, as if he was rooting around like a pig.

Noah tilted his head and winced. "I don't think I did."

"News you can use," I trilled, putting my hand on Noah's forearm. "Sorry to interrupt, but I need to give something important to Noah. It's about Gus."

I stared at Dad, hard, hoping he wouldn't spill the beans about how I'd steamed my way into the letters.

"Oh, right, right. You two have stuff to discuss. I'm going to tidy up. See you around, Noah." Dad sped off.

Noah turned to face me. "Sorry," I whispered.

He waved a hand dismissively. "No, I'm sorry about Erica. She was incredibly forthcoming during our talk."

Well, duh. Of course she was, because she was innocent. But I didn't show any snark.

"I'm glad." I licked my lips, not wanting to fight with him about my friend's innocence. "Anyway, on another matter. I went through a stack of mail this morning and found a few items that had been misdelivered to me at home. They're Gus's letters. This happened a month or so ago as well."

He accepted the letters and shuffled through them, pausing at the wrinkled one and flipping it over to inspect the back. One of his dark eyebrows quirked up. "Misdelivered."

Surely he suspected I'd tampered with the mail. "Exactly. And you know how I'm not great with opening the mail at home. Mostly because of Mom."

"Huh?"

"I don't like seeing her name on junk mail, but I keep getting catalogs and such. So I try to ignore it. That's why I didn't see Gus's mail until today—uh, last night." I pointed at the three envelopes in his hand.

"Gotcha. Well, thanks for this." He slapped the envelopes gently against his thigh. "Let's talk later, okay? Make sure you stay closed for the rest of the day."

"Do you think we'll be able to open back up tomorrow?"

He bit his lip. "I hope so, Lana. My crime scene folks are on their way to grab some samples. Especially of this." He held up the bottle that said "Lion's Mane Mushroom Complex—Add to hot water for antioxidant goodness!"

My eyes widened and I nodded. "Gotcha."

I knew my expression looked wild and panicked, and expected him to kiss me on the mouth, cheek, or forehead like he always did. But today, he pointed to a table. "I'll be over there, waiting for my techs and officers. Then I'll take off."

"Sure, sure."

My stomach plummeted as I watched him walk away to the corner of the room. What did it mean for our relationship if we couldn't weather stress together?

I trudged back to Dad and Erica at the counter. It was only eleven in the morning but felt like nine at night. Both Erica and I looked defeated, but Dad was bopping along to the techno music with an excited look on his face while touching the crystal on a string around his neck.

"I should get home to check on Stanley unless you want to do it, Dad," I said. "But I'm going to have to be here all day while the crime scene techs take samples."

We all watched as three uniformed officers walked in and went to Noah's table.

"Wait—I think I have a plan for this entire mess," Dad said.

"Shush, not so loud." I subtly gestured toward Noah, who was sitting at the table, holding the bottle of mushroom mix and trying to read the label. He held the bottle at arm's length, then brought it closer to his face. He probably needed reading glasses, but now wasn't the time for me to make that observation aloud.

"What's the plan?" I asked Dad, exchanging a glance with Erica. We both knew this could be something smart—or something wacky. It could also involve monkeys. "Lay it on us, but don't be loud."

"Lana, you stay here and wait for the crime scene techs. Erica, you go home and look into all of the suspects online, since you're good with computers."

She nodded at Dad. "I'll also take Stanley around the block."

I sent her a grateful smile. "Thanks."

Dad continued in a semi-whisper. "I'll call the afternoon baristas and tell them they have the day off. Then I'll visit Julian, pump the hospital employees for info, and contact some sources about Gus. Lana, after you're done with the techs, you still can't reopen until you get the all clear from Noah. So that's when you take another run at Bridget in the library. That way, we cover all our bases in both mysteries. Then we'll reconvene at home—er, Lana's home—to compare notes."

Erica visibly exhaled. "That actually sounds pretty reasonable."

I had to admit that it did.

Dad clapped his hands and got the attention of the handful of people who were still in the café.

"Folks, I'm sorry, but we have to close down for the afternoon because of an emergency. If you stop by the counter before you leave, we'll give you a gift card for a free coffee for your next visit. We really appreciate your business and apologize for the inconvenience. Make sure you check with the officers and see if it's okay for you to leave after answering their questions." He pointed toward Noah and the table of police.

Dad grinned, and for once, I was thankful for his goofy, forthright nature.

"Thanks," I whispered to him. "You're a lifesaver."

"I'm always here for you, munchkin. Remember, this is only a minor blip in the whole scheme of things."

I wished I could believe him on that, but as I saw Erica slouch out of the place, devoid of her usual swagger, I had my doubts.

Chapter Sixteen

The crime scene techs didn't take as long as I thought they might. They'd left with samples of all of our products in small plastic cups, from the cold brew to the hazelnut flavoring, to the iced green tea in a pitcher.

Noah left, then texted me with instructions on how to handle the food and drink in the wake of this alleged poisoning. Anything that had been open and sampled by the techs had be thrown out, so I started on that task, hauling bagfuls of half-empty bottles out to the dumpster while tallying the amount of each wasted item in my mind.

Julian's poisoning was going to cost us a pretty penny—not to mention the potential damage to our reputation. Business had been decent lately, with all the winter tourists, and Perkatory had a little cash cushion. But we were a food business and some weeks ran on a razor-thin margin. These busy months were supposed to sustain us for the lean ones.

Back inside, alone, I scrubbed the espresso maker for an hour, ran all of the dishes through the washer twice, then paused to scan the *Devil's Beach Beacon*, wondering if a story had been posted about Julian. It hadn't, and I exhaled in relief, then yawned. Without thinking, I opened a fresh bag of coffee and ground some beans into the espresso filter.

Was it safe?

I stood by the espresso maker, my hand gripping the filter filled with ground beans. If I didn't think it was safe, how could I reopen tomorrow and serve customers (if Noah allowed it, that is). If I didn't think it was safe, it would mean that I thought my best friend had poisoned a man.

"This is absurd," I whispered to myself. "Erica didn't poison anyone."

The machine was clean, and the beans were new. Even if she had poisoned someone—which I didn't think she had—there would be no traces in this particular clean cup. And since no one else had been sickened, it's not as though there was arsenic in the machine. Probably.

I pulled the espresso and tossed it down my throat, not pausing to savor the crema or the chocolatey aftertaste. It was easy to believe there was no poison at Perkatory, and it felt like time for some sleuthing, so I put a sign on the door that said "Closed for Training" and locked up.

Hopefully the entire island wouldn't automatically jump to conclusions and think we were shut down by the health department for being overrun by roaches. That might be as bad as poison.

I kept my head down and power-walked on the beach side of Main Street so I wouldn't run into anyone I knew. By three thirty I was at the library and expected it to be overrun with high school students, since this was where I used to study when I was a teenager.

Apparently things had changed, because it was nearly empty, save for an elderly, bald man in the periodical section, sitting in a gray leather chair and flipping through the pages of *Popular Mechanics*.

"Hey again," the guy at the counter said, greeting me. It was the same person who had been behind the information desk the other day.

"Hello there," I said, looking around for Bridget. "Doesn't anyone use the library anymore? This place used to be packed when I was in high school."

He made a face. "Not like they used to, that's for sure. Our busy days are the weekends, though. I mean, that's what I hear. I'm a weekday staffer, myself."

I let out a little hum, still scanning the place for Bridget. *Weekends*. Gus had died on a Sunday. I wondered if she had been here that day. It was time to take a gamble. I pretended to inspect a flyer for a metaphysical-themed book club, then set it down when I saw that Dad was leading the group.

"Come to think of it, I was here last Sunday." I smiled at the guy as I fibbed. "A really nice woman helped me with a book, and I was hoping she was here today. Didn't catch her name. Dark hair, pretty, wearing flower-print pants. A little older than me . . ." I let my voice fade away, hoping he'd fill in the blanks.

"That sounds like Bridget. She knows every book in this place because she's been here the longest. But"—he shuffled a stack of papers—"she wasn't working Sunday. You sure it wasn't the other day? I saw you two talking."

So she hadn't been here. Where had she been? Maybe tampering with Gus's leaf blower? I snapped my fingers. "That must've been it. I lose track of time."

"She's here today, if you want to talk with her. I think she's working on a new display in the children's room."

"Cool, thanks," I said casually, giving a little wave. I started to mosey off.

"Wait," he called out.

I turned. "Yes?"

He held up a piece of paper. "I forgot. Bridget *was* working this past Sunday. She filled in for someone who was sick."

"Oh. Okay. Thanks." Well, there went my initial theory. My mind spinning, I made my way over to the children's room.

I located Bridget in the kids' room, assembling an impressive book display about dinosaurs. She was balancing a foot-long brontosaurus skeleton atop a stack.

"Wow, that looks good," I said.

She gasped, dropping the dinosaur. It fell to the linoleum floor and its long neck snapped in two.

"Oh God, I'm sorry," I cried, scrambling to retrieve the body, which had skittered across the floor. Well, this was a terrible beginning to a conversation.

I handed her the headless dinosaur, and she snapped the head back onto the body. "Good as new," she said.

"I'm really sorry. I thought you saw me."

"I did, sort of. But my reaction to things has lag time, and I startle easily. I'm sorry." Her smile was infectious. "No need to apologize. How can I help you? Are you looking for a book for your child?"

I stammered for a second, realizing this was the first time in my life that I was pegged for someone's parent. Suddenly the realization that I was no longer in my twenties hit me with full force. *Focus, Lana, focus.*

"No. I'm not. I actually wanted to chat with you. You're Bridget, right?"

She nodded, her giant brown eyes growing a bit wide. "Are you with the lawyer's office?"

I hesitated, wondering if I should lie. That would go against all of my journalism training. Probably Dad or Erica would've rolled with her question and said yes, but I didn't have it in me to mislead anyone. This situation called for brutal honesty.

Also, why would she assume I was with a lawyer's office? What was that about? "No, I'm not. I live here on Devil's Beach. My name's Lana Lewis. I own Perkatory, the café on the other end of Main Street."

A look of confusion crossed her face. "Okay? I don't drink coffee. I'm a tea person."

I set that piece of information aside and leaned on the kid-sized bookshelf, which came up to chest level on me. "I'm Gus's next-door neighbor."

She opened her mouth as if to speak, but only her bottom lip trembled.

"I'm sorry for your loss," I said in a gentle tone, then went out on a limb with my next statement. "You must've cared about him deeply."

"Thank you," she whispered. "How . . . did you know about us?"

I swallowed hard. This wasn't a question I'd anticipated. Probably for the best if I didn't bring up Honey. "Heard some rumors around town."

"That wench," she hissed. "I can't stand her."

I blinked in confusion, pretending I didn't know whom she was referring to. "Excuse me?"

"His ex-wife. Honey. Worst decision he ever made. She's told everyone about how I broke them up, which isn't true. Gus and I knew each other for years, and the time was never right for us to be together. Until it was. He and Honey were having problems, and he asked her to leave. Only then did I get involved with him." She touched a ring on her finger, a diamond. It was on the third finger of her right hand, and I wondered if it had been a gift from Gus.

"I see." So had Honey been lying about their breakup? Huh.

"Why do you want to talk to me?" For the first time since I'd approached, she eyed me suspiciously.

I cleared my throat. As a reporter, I'd often tried to make people feel as comfortable as possible with a mixture of small talk, flattery, and softball questions. Sometimes, however, I knew I'd only have one shot at asking a difficult question. My instinct told me that this was one of those times.

"Who do you think killed Gus?" I blurted out.

She rubbed her glossy red lips together. "I don't know." She drew out each word, as if dragging it through quicksand. This was my cue to continue probing.

"I'm sure you're curious about why I'm asking."

She nodded. Her eyes brimmed with tears, and my heart tugged a little.

What I said next would be a gamble, but in this instance, honesty was probably the best policy. It didn't seem like Bridget was a suspect in Gus's death. Unless she'd hired someone to tamper with his leaf blower, she wouldn't have had time herself to turn it into a death machine.

"My friend is a suspect in his death, and I know she's innocent." All the cards were on the table—or rather, the bookshelf.

Her eyes widened, and I continued. "My friend is definitely one hundred percent innocent. Her name's Erica. She was with me the other day."

"The one with the dog strapped to her chest?"

I nodded.

"Why is she a suspect?"

"Gus and Erica had an argument the morning he died."

She rolled her eyes. "About his leaf blowing?"

"Yes. That."

"He called me right after the police were called that day, and told me all about the altercation. I told him to cool it with the blower. All the neighbors hated him. That couple across the street, the woman in back of him—they all complained. Left him notes on his car windshield." She sniffled and let out a little laugh-sob. "It was the only thing we ever fought about."

"The leaf blowing?"

She nodded. "We fought about it a few weeks before he died. When I told him to only blow every few days so he wouldn't upset the neighbors, he accused me of not being on his side. I figured it was common courtesy. Why would you want to make everyone around you angry? But Gus had a particular way of doing things. He came off as nasty to some people, but he was really a sweetie. He couldn't help his leaf blowing. It calmed him down, and it didn't sound as loud to him because he was deaf in one ear."

"I didn't know that."

"Yeah, he had a benign tumor in high school. That's when we met. I was his tutor." She smiled a little, and her shoulders loosened. This was my chance to chat her up. "Funny thing is, he said he'd never owned a blower until he moved back to Devil's Beach. He'd always hired a landscaper before moving here."

"Oh. You've really known him a long time."

"Since we were kids. We never were brave enough in high school to tell each other how we felt. I went away to college in Georgia, and he went into the Army. By the time he got out, I was in a relationship, and when I broke up with that guy, Gus was in a relationship, and it went like that for years. Then he and Honey moved here, and I ran into him on the beach one day. He was walking alone, and I was alone, and it was like—wham! All the feelings came rushing back."

"Wow. Even though he was—"

"Even though he was married. Of course, what man wouldn't want Honey. Have you seen her?"

I nodded.

"Then you know what I mean. She's gorgeous and young. But he realized it was a mistake even before they moved here. She had her little Instagram influencer business and was basically a child. He was trying to get out of the relationship even before he ran into me."

I leaned in, lowering my voice. "Do you think she killed him?"

She sucked on her teeth and shook her head. "As much as I dislike her, no. I don't think she did. For one thing, I don't believe she has the smarts to tinker with a leaf blower. She's too self-absorbed to get her hands dirty. Although she was quite angry when he wrote her out of his will and stopped giving her cash."

"I can imagine." Honey was quickly moving up the suspect list in my mind.

"He did that after they formally separated. And he stopped paying her alimony. I was like, alimony for what? They only were together a few years, and she makes a lot of money roller skating, if you can believe it. If anything, she should've given him money."

"Hmm," I said noncommittally, trying not to pass judgment either way. "Was he having financial problems?"

She raked in a breath. "I only knew about the situation with Honey because she waltzed in here one day and demanded I talk with him about giving her the alimony. Can you believe that?"

"Sounds bold."

She snorted. "More like delusional. But to answer your question, I don't know. He tried to shield me from all of his problems. He called me his princess and said I shouldn't worry about anything. Gus was my protector."

An awkward, difficult pause ensued. She stared mournfully at the shelf, and my eyes followed her gaze. There was a book in full view titled *Ham Helsing*, and it was apparently about a vampire pig. I wanted to giggle but refrained.

"Who do you think killed him?" I asked in my most gentle voice.

Her eyes snapped back to mine. "The cop asked the same thing the other day. I truly don't think it was Honey."

"What did you tell Noah—er, the cop?"

"I told him that Gus had a lot of business ventures. He rarely talked about them. But I suspect it was tied to that." She snuffled.

"I'm sorry to bring all this up." I paused for a respectable amount of time. "He owned the pirate cruise ship at one time, right?"

She nodded. "I only found that out after he died."

How odd. The two had been friends most of their lives, and yet she knew so little about him. He'd been willing to leave his wife for Bridget, but not tell her about his businesses? "Do you know a man named Mickey Dotson?"

"He's the guy who owns that café, right? Wait—you own a café too. Are you partners?"

I vigorously shook my head. "He owns Island Brewnette. I own Perkatory."

A frown crossed her face. "Oh. I knew Mickey owned something coffee related. I get my tea from that shop at the mall on the mainland. Why do you ask about him?"

"Gus sold a business to him. The pirate cruise ship."

"I knew he sold the ship, but I didn't know to whom. I don't get involved with business stuff. Don't have a brain for it."

I mulled this for a second, wondering if she was being evasive or outright lying. It didn't seem like either, but one could never tell. "Can you think of anyone else he was involved with, business-wise? Or do you know any of the other businesses he owned or sold over the years? You're a smart woman. I'm sure you'd have picked up on something unusual—"

She let out a soft laugh. "That's almost exactly what that cop said."

I stifled a snicker at the idea that Noah and I asked similar questions in a similar way. "Did you notice anything unusual in your time with him?"

"We mostly met at my house. Sometimes we'd go out of town." She exhaled loudly. "Although now that I think about it . . ."

"What?" I leaned in, eager.

"After Honey moved out, I was over at his house one morning. Gus was doing his usual leaf-blowing thing, and his cell kept ringing over and over again. At first I assumed it was his ex-wife, but I checked the screen."

"Oh yeah?"

"It said Yates on the screen. That was the name. Yates."

I hummed an encouragement to go on.

"I asked him about it, wondering if that was Honey's maiden name. We got into a big fight, and he accused me of being jealous. I mean, I was. I get like that, you know. Women's intuition."

I nodded my support and sympathy, knowing that I'd probably feel the same if some woman were repeatedly texting Noah.

"Over the next few days, this Yates person kept calling and calling, and he refused to answer. So you know what I did?"

"What?"

"I snooped in Gus's phone, looking for texts. I'm not proud of it, but I've been burned before by guys, you know?"

I held up a hand. "I hear you. My ex was a cheater, and I might've looked at his phone a time or two."

She put the back of her knuckles to her mouth and looked around for a second, then removed her hand. "I took a screenshot of what I found."

My eyes widened and head tilted, like Stanley's did when I asked if he wanted a treat. "Oh, really?"

When she reached into her back pocket, my heart sped up. She spent a solid fifteen seconds swiping and muttering to herself, things like *no, not that,* and *hang on.* "Here."

She showed me the screen. "Gus's texts are in green. Yates's are in gray."

Yates: *You're too much of a coward to fight us in court.*
Gus: *Leave me alone.*
Yates: *You're not going to get away with this. You sold us a failing business.*
Gus: *I gave you all the information I had. It's not my fault that you and that other bonehead can't keep a business afloat. I had no problem turning a profit.*

Yates: *We're going to prove you cooked the books.*
    You'll see.
Gus: *Prove this, scum.*

Here he included an emoji of a middle finger, which I thought was a particularly hilarious and juvenile thing for a grown man to do.

Yates: *You'd better watch your back, Gus. We've got*
    our eye on you and Honey.

Gus responded with a long string of colorful and foul language.

"Whoa," I whispered. "Do you know if he reported that to authorities? That's quite threatening."

She shook her head. "I doubt it. Gus wasn't a fan of police."

Weird. "I wonder why?"

"His brother is in prison up in New York. Gus felt he was innocent and was railroaded by cops and prosecutors."

"Oh. What's he in for?" My mind was tumbling like a clothes dryer with all the possible questions.

She waved her hand dismissively. "Something white collar. Securities fraud? Embezzlement?"

"Huh. So when did you see those text messages?"

She squinted at the screen. "Looks like about ten days ago. I peeked at Gus's phone when he was in the shower."

"Not long before he died. Did you tell him that you'd seen the messages?"

She shook her head.

"Would you mind if I got a photo of that text thread?"

"Why?"

"For our own, er, investigation."

She stared at her phone for a while. "I guess not, but I don't want you sharing them with police."

Who was I to argue with her request? I didn't wait for her to change her mind, and yanking my phone out of my bag, I quickly snapped a photo of her screen. A sense of triumph and relief washed over me when I slid my phone back into my purse.

"You didn't show those to the police?" I asked, incredulous and wanting to make sure my hunch was correct.

She shook her head, then her eyes flitted to the entrance to the children's room. A woman holding hands with two little kids walked in. "Hello, welcome," she called out in a cheerful voice.

"How come?" I asked.

"Gus once told me never to cooperate with cops. I thought it was because of his brother. But now I wonder if it was because he was involved with something shady. Honestly, I don't want to be part of anything sketchy. I don't want any dangerous people to think I ratted them out. Gus is dead, and there's nothing I can do about it. An arrest of some sketchy person won't bring Gus back." She reached out and squeezed my arm. "You seem like a nice person, though, and I'm sorry your friend's a suspect. I don't think someone mad at him for leaf blowing actually killed him. I hope your friend's name is cleared. Does that make sense?"

I nodded as I absorbed all this new information. "Definitely."

"Will you keep me posted about what happens?"

"I promise I will. Thanks for all this."

I gave her a genuine smile and beat it out of the library, wondering who Yates was and whether Noah had him on his suspect list.

Chapter Seventeen

I power-walked home, or tried to. My normally ten-minute journey was waylaid by employees of the downtown stores saying hi, friends of Dad's who'd known me since I was knee high to a grasshopper, or tourists who wanted directions. It seemed like everyone wanted to soak up the dry, barely warm sunshine, and everyone had a smile on their face.

Two people from the flower shop, who knew where I lived, asked about Gus but had no gossip to offer; they were hoping I knew something. Obviously I wasn't about to share what I'd learned from Honey, so I shook my head sympathetically. The flower shop employees looked crestfallen, as if I'd let them down. I suspected what they were thinking: *"She's not as plugged in as her father."*

Which wasn't true, I thought as I politely extricated myself from the conversation.

Then I ran into yet another person I knew, and sighed mightily to myself, channeling Stanley when he's exasperated from my incessant kisses.

It was Shawn Simms, the owner of a watersports company. He was coming out of the bank, waving and calling my name. Crud.

I was in a hurry and didn't have time to chat, but couldn't ignore him either. He jogged down the steps in my direction, and I plastered on a tight smile.

"When are you going to take me up on my free jet-ski ride?" Shawn had the eager expression of a golden retriever, and the same color hair. He regarded me with a giant, goofy grin while wearing a dark blue hoodie, board shorts, and orange flip-flops.

I smiled. *Never,* I wanted to say, but that didn't seem polite. Shawn had been a suspect in the murder of a yoga teacher on the island six months ago, but I'd helped clear his name. In return, he insisted on giving me a free, unlimited day of Jet Skiing—an activity I had no interest in. "I'm not sure. Maybe when it gets warmer."

I pretended to shiver from the cool air, which of course felt incredibly glorious. Then a thought came to me. Shawn's business was located at the marina in town, not far from the pirate ship. My reporter's instinct kicked in. Duh. I should've called Shawn a couple of days ago.

"Hey, you know that pirate ship? The booze cruise? The one that's docked near your business?"

"Yeah, what about it? You know I hate that thing. It plays the worst music, and those tourists get hammered and leave trash everywhere." He made a sour face. Like many of the locals, the public carousing of the island's visitors got on his nerves. "And the owner's a piece of work. Well, the old owner."

"Oh yeah?" A tingle of excitement ran up my arms, and I wished I could take notes.

He scrunched his nose. "The employees also try to snag the tourists from other businesses. Well, they used to, under the old owner. It's gotten a little better, I guess."

"The old owner? Who's that?"

"Some guy, I'm not sure his name."

"Gus?"

"Yeah, maybe. I ran into one of the workers at the Dirty Dolphin one night. That worker quit, but he told me the owner demanded they try to lure tourists from all the other marina businesses. One of their tactics was even to give brochures and deals for the pirate cruise to tourists standing in line for other businesses."

"Wow. That's really strange. So the old owner was cutthroat?"

"Totally," Shawn said in a tone that perfectly mimicked Jeff Spicoli from *Fast Times at Ridgemont High*, but in an unironic way. "He paid the workers like crap too. Apparently they all got raises when the new owners took over."

"Do you know who those new owners are?"

Shawn squinted at me. "You doing an article? What's going on?"

"Maybe," I hedged. "I'm looking into something."

"I heard Mickey Dotson's one of the owners. An investor."

"Who else?"

He shrugged. "Dunno. I see Mickey there a lot, doing maintenance on the boat."

"I know him, but I didn't realize Mickey knew anything about boats." *He barely knows anything about coffee either.* "What kind of maintenance?"

"Cleaning, organizing. Oh, he was working on the engine one day. Asked me if I had a certain kind of wrench."

"Wow, that's a pretty big boat to do maintenance on. I've always known Mickey as a shop owner. He owned a hotdog stand before Island Brewnette."

"I guess he's kind of a Renaissance guy. He told me that he used to own a big landscaping company years ago on the mainland. They mowed lawns and planted trees and stuff."

My jaw dropped. Mickey had owned a landscaping company? Mowed lawns? Bells, whistles, and air horns went off in my head. I regained my composure and responded with a smart-sounding "Well, that's interesting."

Shawn nodded. "That guy's done a lot. He's kind of cool. Doesn't like you much, though."

My expression turned into a grimace. "The feeling's mutual."

"I told him you were hella cool. Anyway, I gotta run. Yoga's starting soon. I'm teaching at Dante's Inferno now. You should come by. Or let me take you on a jet-ski trip around the island." He winked.

Hot yoga and Jet Skis were the last things I desired, but I nodded with a thoughtful expression. "I'll think about it. See you around."

We waved goodbye, and I darted down the next cross street, not wanting to get sidetracked by running into anyone else on Main. There was too much to share with Erica and Dad at this point, and I was beginning to think Mickey, my archnemesis, might be the person to concentrate on in our informal and totally clandestine investigation.

* * *

When I arrived home, Erica and Stanley were already in the living room. They were snuggled together on the sofa, a plush fleece blanket over both of them.

"Look what I whipped up," she said, pointing at the coffee table. A charcuterie board was perfectly arranged with cold cuts, cheese wedges, dried apricots, and crackers. A bottle of Spanish cabernet sat next to it, open and with two glasses at the ready.

"It's probably ready to pour. I was letting it breathe. At this point, drinking is our best option." She gestured at the bottle.

Seemed like an excellent plan to me, especially after this crazy day. I poured a glass, handed it to her, then helped myself to some red liquid. "Wow, when did you have time to do all this?"

Then I glanced at my watch. "Holy Pup-Peroni. It's been almost three hours. It's five o'clock."

"Which is why I opened the bottle of wine. It's five o'clock somewhere, and definitely here on Devil's Beach. Time to have a drink." She leaned forward and grabbed a cracker, and I swore the shadows under her eyes had gotten darker since I'd seen her last.

Had she been crying? I squinted at her and was about to ask, when she continued talking.

"I've gotten so much done. You're not going to believe what I found online. And your dad's also here."

"Sweet. I unearthed some interesting stuff too." I snatched a piece of pepperoni and a cracker and sank next to Stanley, who was nestled in the red blanket. "Hello, buddy. Oh yeah, where is Dad?"

"He's in the garage, looking for something."

"Any word about Julian?"

Erica winced. "Apparently, he's talking. Your dad wouldn't say much more than that."

A crash from the direction of the garage echoed through the house, and I looked in the direction of the loud noise. "What's he in there for, anyway?"

"Not sure. He said he wanted to find something to write on."

I took a sip of my wine. It slid down my throat, warm and tangy. "He knows I keep the empty notebooks in the kitchen. Can't he use one of those?"

At that moment, Dad came lumbering in, carrying a giant, old whiteboard that had been Mom's. She'd used it years ago—decades, even—to chart where she was traveling to as a green coffee buyer. During my middle school years, it was how I kept track of where she was. Heck, I hadn't even known we still had the thing. It was one of many mysterious family items buried in the bowels of my messy garage.

Stanley perked up from under the blanket, eyeing the whiteboard warily.

"Hey, Dad. You're scaring the dog," I said. "What's that for?"

Dad set it on the arms of my upholstered recliner. "It's to help our investigation."

I rubbed my eyes, wondering why he had to complicate matters. Erica and I locked gazes and stifled laughter.

"Okay," Dad said, uncapping an erasable marker. "Who wants to go first?"

"Why don't you go, since you have the floor." I waved my hand in his direction.

He cleared his throat, like he was about to give an important speech. "I have good news about Julian. He's talking and alert. It looks like his liver is out of the danger zone."

Erica let out a breath. "Thank God," she whispered. She looked exceptionally exhausted and seemed unusually quiet. Normally, she was all about the quips and one-liners, but not today.

"Did he say anything about what happened to him?" I asked.

Dad fidgeted with the marker, accidentally getting it on his finger. "He said he ordered the mushroom coffee, went to the table, and started drinking it while checking his emails. Said it was delicious, so good on you, Erica." He pointed the marker at her.

She blew out a breath. "Good, but deadly—that's me."

"Then he went to the bathroom, and when he came back, he drank a few more sips. He felt a terrible burning in his throat, and that's all he remembered until he got to the hospital. He looks awful, like he was hit by a train. I feel bad for the poor guy. He's going to be in the hospital for several more days, and he's talking to his insurance company about airlifting him to Miami."

I let my head fall back and groaned. "I'm thankful he's going to be okay, but this is so, so bad. He's never going to want to work with us again. My source for amazing coffee is gone. Is he angry with us? Please say he isn't."

Dad stroked his goatee thoughtfully. "Well, I don't think he's well enough to be angry. He doesn't have the energy for that. So, not yet."

Probably I should start looking for a new coffee supplier tomorrow. "That's not great news," I said. "Anything else? Did you pump your hospital source for any other pertinent info about Julian or Gus?"

Dad shook his head. "My murse friend wasn't working."

"Murse?" Erica and I said in tandem.

"Male nurse. There's a gentleman at the hospital who's part of the crystal bowl meditation. I have a message in to him. Henry. Works in the ER."

"Great. Well, while we wait for Henry, let's move on. Erica said she found out some interesting tidbits online."

Dad started to write on the board, the marker making a squeaky noise that caused Stanley to hop up onto all fours and bark once.

"Wait—no," I called out as I leaned forward and took a couple of dried apricots from the platter. "Why are you writing Julian's name down?"

"I dunno," Dad said. "Because we're investigating."

Stanley began to paw at the blanket and sofa, as if he was either making a nest or trying to cover up an invisible hole with invisible dirt. We all ignored him despite the fact that his antics looked adorable.

"No, we're not investigating that, Dad. Julian's situation has nothing to do with Gus. It's totally random that he ingested poison. He did ask Erica to use his own cup, and we don't know where that cup had been or what he'd been doing with it prior to Perkatory. We don't know if he has enemies or if he's involved in shady stuff in Miami. This has nothing to do with us. Let's stay focused on the task at hand."

I popped the dried fruit into my mouth. My dad often had great ideas, but sometimes too many of them. It was my job to make sure he remained focused.

Dad pointed the marker at me. "Good point. Okay, Erica. What did you find out?"

She set the wineglass on the coffee table and scrubbed her face with her hands. "Okay. This is a lot. Bear with me."

She picked up the glass again, took a big slug, then put it back down. "I looked into the people who bought the pirate ship from Gus."

"Excellent!" My tone was filled with false cheer because I'd never seen Erica so scattered or upset. Frankly, it unsettled me. Erica was one of two people in my life who was always calm, confident, and collected. Noah was the other. "Who are they?"

She reached for a notepad, which was on the end table near her, and opened the cover. "As we know, Mickey Dotson was only one of the people who bought The *Royal Conquest*. Another is the guy I've been dating for six months."

"Wait. What?" I yelped. "Joey?"

She nodded. "Yes indeed. Joseph Rizzo."

"Did you know this?" Dad asked, his voice hushed.

"No." Erica flipped to the next page in the notebook. "He told me he was thinking about investing in some local businesses, but I thought it had to do with a food truck, because he'd been looking at the financials of a truck called Nacho Daddy. And that made sense, since he owns the restaurant, and he loves nachos. I never had any idea he was interested in a tourist pirate ship."

"How did you find this out?" said Dad, who carefully wrote *JOEY* in big block letters on the whiteboard. My heart went out to Erica; I knew she'd been in bad relationships prior to coming to Devil's Beach, and that Joey was the nicest guy she'd dated in years.

What if he turned out to be a killer? "Oh dear," I whispered.

"I went to the state department's business and professional regulation website to look at the corporate officers and the LLC paperwork, like Lana showed me."

I secretly smiled. I'd taught her how to check that website months ago, when we were being nosy and searching for information about a strange, new clothing store in town. We'd been convinced it was a Mafia front and had spun all sorts of scenarios during a few early morning conversations at Perkatory. Finally, I'd showed her how to look up a business registered with the state, something I'd done regularly as a reporter. The clothing store, as it turned out, was actually owned by an elderly Italian lady who also made great cannoli—and not the Gambino crime family.

"Did you call Joey and ask him about this?"

"Tried. He's still in Vegas for that food convention."

"Convenient," I muttered.

"Do you think . . .?" her voice trailed off.

"I don't know. It seems weird. But the timeline doesn't add up, does it? When did you get to his house that day?"

"I left here around . . ." She grabbed her phone and tapped on the screen. "Two in the afternoon. See? I texted Joey at that time to say I was coming over, and he texted back. So we were together from two until we had that fight and he left. That was around six."

"Gus was killed in that time frame." I finger-combed one of Stanley's ears.

"That doesn't give him a lot of time to tamper with a leaf blower. Plus, wouldn't Gus have heard him going into the garage?" Dad asked.

"I think he keeps the leaf blower in the shed, not the garage. I saw him taking it out one day. Still, it doesn't seem to add up. I wonder what Gus did all day. Was he here?" I mused aloud.

Erica lifted her hands in the air. "I don't remember if I even saw his car in the driveway when I left."

"I thought he kept the car in the garage," I said. "Did you see anything else in the paperwork?"

"There was the name of a registered agent. Didn't you say that's often the lawyer?" she asked.

"It often is, but it can also be a corporate director or a CPA," Dad chimed in. "Who is it? I might know them if they're local."

She flipped to a second page. "Okay, so the registered agent is a person named D. R. Yates."

"Yates!" I jumped up, startling Stanley.

Dad scribbled the name down on the board, next to Joey's. "You know Yates?"

"Yes. Well, no. Not exactly. His name came up while I was talking to Bridget. Erica, do you have anything more?"

She shook her head. "After I saw Joey's name, I lost the will to go on. That's when I made the cheese board. I think cheese, wine, and coffee are all I have left. Clearly my choices in men suck."

"Maybe there's a perfectly reasonable explanation." Even I didn't believe my words, but what else could I say to her?

She waved a cracker at me. "Tell us about Yates."

While pacing the living room, I gave them a long, detailed rundown of my conversation at the library. Dad wrote Honey's and Bridget's names on the board.

"And so she showed me these texts and let me take a photo of her phone screen. But she hasn't told Noah or any of the detectives about these messages."

I showed the screen to Dad.

"I can't see it, don't have my glasses," he said.

"They're on your head," I pointed out.

"Oh. Right." He slid them on his nose and peered at the screen. "Still too small for me."

I brought the phone to Erica and handed it to her.

"She didn't tell Noah? What a dumbass."

"Seems weird, right?" I asked.

Her head flopped back as she groaned. "Maybe if Noah knew about this, I wouldn't be a suspect."

I sank back onto the sofa near Stanley, who was snoring like a tiny chainsaw. "That's what we need to figure out. Should we tell Noah what we know?"

"Well, what do we know? Who are our suspects?" Dad tapped the board with his fingers.

"Honey, Bridget, Mickey, Joey, and Yates," I recited. "Although in my mind, Bridget and Joey are iffy because of the timeline."

"Anyone else?" Dad asked.

"Jeri and Perry from across the street," Erica answered.

"That's another good possibility. They probably hated Gus more than anyone. Well, at least Jeri did." I gave Dad a recap of the true crime podcast.

"We don't know where they were that Sunday afternoon," Erica said.

"There's a way to find out," I said.

"What?" Dad asked.

"Talk to them. We can ask. We should chat them up anyway because maybe they've gotten tips after their podcast."

Dad, Erica, and I looked at one another. "What day is it?" Dad asked. Sometimes he was a little fuzzy on time, given his weed-smoking habit.

"Wednesday," Erica and I said in tandem.

"Want to have a barbecue?"

"It's five thirty and we've killed almost half a bottle of wine and gorged ourself on cheese and crackers," I pointed out.

"So? I can go buy some veggie burgers and fire up the grill."

"What does this have to do with Jeri and Perry?" Erica asked, confused.

Dad walked over to the window and peered through the blinds. "There's Jeri now, pulling some weeds. Seems like this is a good night to invite the neighbors over for a cookout."

Chapter Eighteen

I didn't think Dad's half-cocked plan would pan out, and wondered how he'd pull this off. He marched outside and approached Jeri, who was bagging up some lawn clippings. Erica and I—with Stanley in my arms—watched from the open door as he gestured toward my house, and Jeri nodded and beamed.

The two of them looked at us and waved.

"Fire up the grill," Dad hollered, and Erica gave him a thumbs-up. Then he chugged off to the store in his Prius.

"I guess we should make some side dishes," Erica said. "I'll assemble another cheese plate."

"Let me start the charcoal outside, and then I'll get to work on a green salad."

My thoughts and emotions were all over the place as I filled our old-school BBQ kettle grill on my back porch with briquettes. While giving the charcoal a good squirt of lighter fluid, I faced Gus's house.

His death had really mucked things up for a lot of people, most of all him. What was his story?

Who had really killed him, and why? He'd made no shortage of enemies in his brief time on Devil's Beach. And who knew what he'd done, whom he'd angered, prior to moving here. The fact that his brother had been involved in shady dealings also raised more red flags than a matador.

Although whoever had killed Gus had known of his leaf-blowing habits, which seemed to be unique to this place. Bridget had said he'd never owned a blower until he'd bought the house next door.

I reached for the grill lighter and clicked its trigger. There was a *foom* sound, and the blue flame danced across the charcoal. I watched as the fluid burned off, and the coals simmered with heat.

It was time to return to the kitchen. Stanley greeted me at the back door on prancing feet, sensing that something exciting was underway. He watched from the kitchen door as Erica and I circled around each other, gathering our mise en place, as she liked to call it.

I was chopping a red onion and trying not to tear up when she turned to me, knife in hand. "I can't believe Joey would kill Gus. Why would he? That doesn't make sense. There has to be some kind of explanation. I can't even believe he invested in a pirate ship without telling me."

"I don't think he would kill anyone either. He's the kindest, most gentle guy I know. Even more gentle than Noah, and that's saying something."

"Yeah, remember the dolphin?" Erica asked.

I nodded. Joey and I had gone on Erica's boat for an afternoon sail to a nearby sandbar one morning. We'd come across a dolphin tangled in a fishing net, and Joey had jumped in the water and carefully cut the net away with a knife.

"We need to figure out why Gus was being sued by the new owners of the boat. When does Joey get back?" I scraped the onions into a bowl.

"Tomorrow."

"Perfect. We can talk to him then. Well, you can. We could also try to look up the case, but from my experience, the online records aren't great, so we might have to go to the mainland and visit the clerk's office in person. And there is that hearing." I sighed. We still had the matter of Julian in the hospital and the fallout from that. What if word got around that he'd been poisoned at Perkatory?

Could we even open tomorrow?

Crud. I'd forgotten all about that particular worry during the flurry of fact finding with Dad and Erica. As I chopped, I worried my bottom lip between my teeth. I'd have to chat with Noah and get the all clear to open.

"Maybe you can go to the court tomorrow while I ask Joey?" Erica said hopefully.

I nodded. "Maybe. We'll work it out somehow. I'm kind of thinking we should talk to Joey together, in case . . ."

"In case what? In case he's a murderer?"

I stopped chopping and faced Erica. "We can't be too careful."

She fell silent again as she arranged a row of capicola flowers on the charcuterie board. "I'll be okay talking to him alone. Figures that I meet a decent person and he turns out to be a murderer."

"We don't have any proof he's a killer. So quit it. There are a lot of suspects, and honestly, the fact that Mickey Dotson once owned a landscaping business seems like the most incriminating evidence of all, don't you think?"

"How are we going to find out where he was on Sunday?"

I chopped a few olives, then remembered that Dad hated them. "Dunno. Let's get through tonight and see about Perry and Jeri's alibi."

"Are you going to tell Noah about all this?"

I washed my hands, then blotted my eyes with a napkin. "Don't know that either. I should. Really, it's bad that I'm keeping any of this from him. Here I am demanding honesty from him when I'm skulking around, steaming open letters, and launching my own investigation."

"In all fairness, I could see where he'd be annoyed by us sleuthing. And as you know, I'm not exactly on his side at the moment, since I'm one of his prime suspects."

I put my hand on my hip and nodded. "You're right. I should tell him about what I've found. I feel a little bad about breaking Bridget's trust, but it's not as though this is for a story. Maybe I won't say I got the text from her. Can I do that?"

"You can do anything you want, Lana."

"I feel like I need to. For you. We've got to clear your name. That's top priority now."

She continued arranging the cold cuts in perfect meat roses, her lips thin and tense.

While I reached for the spinach, dried cranberries, and bacon bits, I pondered the situation. Had I been a reporter, my promise to Bridget would have been ironclad. I never revealed an off-the-record, or background, source.

Was this different? The information she'd given me might lead to exonerating my best friend. Yeah, I had to tell him. No question.

"I'll be right back," I mumbled, wandering into the living room for my cell. Noah and I had left things on a tense note earlier, and

I desperately wanted to apologize for acting like a child. I needed to be more mature in this relationship, starting now.

I fired off a quick text to Noah: *Hey there. We're doing a cookout tonight with Dad and some of the neighbors. Come on by when you're done with work. I promise Dad won't bring up the monkeys. He's making veggie burgers, and I'm throwing together my special spinach salad. Erica's doing a killer charcuterie board.*

I followed it up with a smiley face emoji but winced at my own choice of words.

Sounds good, cupcake. Save me some, I haven't eaten a vegetable in days. I'll probably be there later rather than earlier. Things are hopping on Devil's Beach.

Don't I know it. Looking forward to seeing you, I typed quickly.

XOXO, he texted back.

A small wave of happiness washed over me. He wasn't angry; this wasn't the end. I could still come clean about everything I'd discovered and maybe salvage our relationship.

But first, the barbecue.

I eyed the whiteboard marked with Dad's blocky handwriting. Probably best if I moved that to the garage so Jeri and Perry didn't see their names in the suspect column.

*   *   *

Two and a half hours later, Dad, Erica, and I sat around our large picnic table in the backyard, along with Jeri and Perry. Our evening's conversation had consisted of talking about everything but the large, angry elephant that loomed only a few feet away: the murder of Gus, next-door.

We discussed the city council; the cool weather; and, of course, the monkey saga on the island. Dad filled us in on all the details, about how there would be a protest against the Fish and Wildlife Commission later this week.

"Can't wait for that," I said.

"Lana, you should join us," he replied, excited.

"Gotta work. Perkatory." I stifled a groan, thinking about how customers were going to take the news from today's poisoning. Gah. For tonight, I just needed to focus. And maybe pump Noah for information later on.

The five of us had a nice meal, with Dad grilling the veggie burgers, everyone raving about my spinach salad, and Stanley hovering nearby, begging for pieces of cheese or cold cuts from the charcuterie plate.

For dessert, Erica brought out a bowl of sliced fresh Florida strawberries and a can of whipped cream.

It was dark now, and the air had taken on a cool moistness, a feeling on my skin that always brought me back to childhood winters here on the island. Tonight, we were all bundled in jackets and heavy sweaters. We'd discussed going indoors but had decided not to; it was so rare for it to be this crisp that we wanted to soak it up and enjoy not sweating to death while outdoors.

Overhead, strings of globe lights illuminated the darkness, giving the porch a cozy vibe. I loved my backyard, and tonight everything looked picture-perfect. We'd even gotten out the tablecloth and place mats Mom had bought years ago in Cuernavaca, Mexico, and more than once I saw Dad run his finger over the pattern and look wistfully at the colors.

As we all took turns spooning strawberries into bowls and squirting the whipped cream on top, Dad stroked his goatee.

"I still can't get over what happened next door. I wonder who killed the guy."

I shook my head and murmured a "me neither," and Erica made a tsking sound with her tongue.

"Couldn't have happened to a better man," Jeri said. "I hated him from the moment I met him. Arrogant, entitled—you name the terrible adjective, and it described him. You know, when we did the show on him and his death, and we mentioned the leaf-blowing, you wouldn't believe how many people identified with hating their neighbors over that one thing."

Dad snorted a giggle, and Jeri and Perry did too. He sure had a way of making people feel at ease by mirroring their emotions. "Jeez, Jeri, tell us how you really feel. You haven't shared those thoughts with the cops, have you?"

Perry rolled her big brown eyes. "She did. And I told her she was going to end up being a prime suspect."

Jeri cackled and waved her hand in the air. "Pfft. We have an iron-clad alibi. In the form of mullet."

Erica raised an eyebrow. "The fish or the hairstyle?"

I squirted whipped cream into my bowl. "You know, I was going to ask you two about that. Were you here on Sunday afternoon? Did you hear or see anything weird at Gus's after we had that neighborhood argument?"

Jeri pointed at my bowl. "Where are your strawberries?"

"Oh." My face flared suddenly. "I actually hate them."

"Who hates strawberries?" Perry eyed me warily, as if I'd admitted to a crime against humanity.

Dad smacked his forehead. "Lana, dang. I forgot. I'm so sorry." He turned to Perry. "She's never liked them. Even as a kid. Thinks they're slimy. Someone even gave her a Strawberry Shortcake doll as a girl, and she drowned it in the ocean."

"That doll was creepy." I licked a spoonful of cream.

Jeri chuckled. "Maybe we should be asking you about where you were on the afternoon of Gus's murder."

"I was with my boyfriend, the police chief." I smirked. "And don't worry about it, Dad. You always forget. Whipped cream all by itself is a favorite of mine anyway." I scooped up a second cloud of the fluffy white substance and licked it clean. "So."

There was an awkward pause, and then Jeri snapped her fingers. "Right. You asked about Sunday. From twelve to about seven that night we left the island and went to the mainland. The situation with Gus happened not long after we returned home. We went to that mullet festival. We volunteer there every year."

"Oh, the one with the smoked mullet dip contest? I heard about that and wanted to go. Darn." Erica said. "I love smoked mullet."

The conversation drifted to the intricacies of a smoked fish recipe, and indeed, Jeri and Perry were both judges for the competition. Flashing their phones, they showed us photos of themselves on the festival's Facebook page. Which meant they did have a solid alibi for that day.

We could cross them off our list. Unless they had somehow tampered with the leaf blower immediately after our neighborhood altercation . . .

Stanley, who was lying flat on his stomach with his legs splayed like a frog, jumped to his feet and let out two sharp barks. He ran to the back door and barked again.

I rose from my chair. "I'll bet Noah's here. Stanley always has a sixth sense when he's about to arrive. I think he can hear him get in his car at the police station five blocks away."

Stanley and I went back into the house, and sure enough, someone was knocking at the door. The dog ran ahead, barking his little fluffy head off.

"Coming," I called out.

I flung open the door with a smile, which grew larger when I saw Noah. He stepped inside and swept me up into a tight hug as the door shut behind him.

"Hi, cupcake," he whispered in my ear. "Sorry about earlier. Didn't mean to be so gruff. It hurts me to see you stressed out like that. It also pained me to ask you to shut down Perkatory."

I ran my hands over his back, feeling the muscles underneath his shirt. His tender words and deep embrace made my heart skip a beat. "It's okay. Tough day, right?"

"Probably about as tough as yours."

I sighed contentedly in his arms. He fluttered kisses on my neck. Stanley let out a low growl.

We stayed like that for a long minute, with Stanley climbing our legs, hating that he was being left out of all the affection. Noah brushed a kiss on my lips and looked down.

"Someone's jealous," I said.

He bent to pick up the dog, who squirmed in a frenzy of excitement now that his favorite person was paying attention to him. "Come here, you little monster."

I watched the two of them nuzzle each other. It was a blessing that Noah loved my dog as much as I did; my ex-husband hated animals, which is why I'd never gotten a pet in my previous home in Miami.

"You hungry?" I asked.

"Starving. Where is everyone?"

"Dad and Erica are on the porch. Jeri and Perry came over too."

Noah set Stanley down, and the dog trotted off. "That's interesting. I didn't know you were so close with the neighbors."

"Dad invited them," I said breezily.

He followed me outside, and everyone stopped talking the minute they saw Noah. A beat of discomfort hung in the air, and the only audible sound was the crickets. Goodness. What had they been discussing?

"Hey, Noah!" Dad finally cried, standing up and shaking his hand. The two launched into a chat about the weather, and I directed Noah to sit in my chair while I went inside to get a sixth folding chair in the garage—aka, the junk room.

"I'll grab it," Noah protested.

Eek. I didn't want him to see the whiteboard and our list of suspects. "No, you eat. Sit. You're tired."

Dad hustled to prepare Noah a burger. When I emerged from the garage, Erica was standing in the hall. "Hey, I'm beat. Heading to bed."

I set the chair against the wall. "Aww, so soon? It's only nine."

She nodded, and I wondered if she simply didn't want to be around Noah. I couldn't argue with her about wanting to hit the sack. My entire body felt heavy, but that could also be because I'd eaten a loaded veggie burger and several handfuls of chips.

"Get some rest, okay? We'll try to keep it down. I won't let Dad blast the techno music."

That won me a grin. "Nighty night."

Stanley tottered after Erica, and she glanced at me before shutting her door. "I guess he's sleeping with me tonight."

"Perfectly okay with me," I called out.

When I got back outside with the chair, Jeri and Perry were on their feet.

"Hey, thanks for your hospitality," Jeri said. "Great burgers, Peter and Lana. We'll return the favor soon."

"Oh! You're leaving?"

Dad shoved a handful of chips on Noah's plate. "You know, I think I'll head home, too. Give you two some privacy. Jeri and Perry, I'll walk out with you."

We all hugged and kissed goodbye, and Noah and I were left at the table alone.

"Was it something I said?" Noah asked in between giant bites of the burger. "Was my small talk about the weather offensive?"

"No," I said, exhaling heavily. "They probably think we want to be alone or something."

"Or something."

I watched him chew his veggie burger and shove a few chips in his mouth.

Gah. In an instant, the tension between us was back. I couldn't handle this. It was time to clear the air.

"Noah, we need to have a talk."

He popped the final bite of burger in his mouth and lifted a dark eyebrow. "A talk is usually bad news."

"I'll wait until you're done eating."

He swallowed. "Thanks."

He cleaned his plate of the chips, and I served him a bowl of strawberries in silence, then handed him the whipped cream. He shook his head.

"I thought you didn't like strawberries?" he asked.

"Still don't. Dad forgot, though, and bought a bunch."

"So you didn't have dessert?"

"I had a bowl of whipped cream."

A small, foxy grin emerged, and my desire to have any sort of confrontation with him crumbled at the edges. When he finished, he nudged the bowl away.

"Okay, shoot."

The temperature outside seemed to have dropped ten degrees in the last half hour. "How about . . ."

He took my hand. "How about we go into your bedroom and watch a movie to take our mind off everything?"

His eyes were big and dark and alluring. My mouth went dry at the thought of spending the next several hours in his arms, but I had to stay strong.

"How about you make two of those rum hot toddies and I'll clean up, and then we'll reconvene on the sofa?"

He pretended to ponder for a second. "I can live with that. Is the rum still in the cabinet next to the fridge?"

I finally smiled. "It is."

We both did our respective tasks in companionable silence. I loaded the dishwasher while he boiled hot water, honey, a couple slices of lemon, and two cinnamon sticks, and then combined all that with shots of rum. He'd made this once before, about two weeks ago, when we'd had a cold snap, saying it was one of his mom's recipes.

I loved not only the taste but the aroma, and had been thinking about how to replicate the drink for Perkatory, minus the booze.

He brought both mugs of hot liquid into the living room, which was illuminated only by one small lamp, making everything look snuggly and intimate. I accepted the mug, and he sat next to me.

"It's probably too hot to sip, but cheers." We touched mugs. "So what do you want to talk about?"

I raised the mug to my nose, smelling the heady, spicy liquid. Then I set it on the coffee table. "Okay, I have a lot of questions. And some stuff to tell you. Which do you want first?"

"I guess . . . the questions."

"Okay. Here goes. Why are you so reluctant to introduce me to your parents?"

"Oh. *Oh*." He let out a little laugh. "Wow. I thought you were going to ask something totally different."

"You did?"

"Yeah, like about Gus or Julian."

"I'm not done yet."

His smile was lopsided. "I didn't think so."

"I've been wondering why you're so cagey about me and your family. There has to be an explanation. Either our relationship isn't as serious as I thought, or . . ."

He swept a lock of my hair out of my face, tucking it behind my ear. "I'm very serious about you, Lana." His tone was gentle, almost reverent. "I do want you to meet my mom."

"Then what? You don't want her to meet my dad? I know your family has a long history in law enforcement, and my dad is an old pot-smoking hippie. But I can ask Dad to be on his best behavior."

He shook his head. "No. It's not that. My mother has progressive views on legal marijuana."

"Then what is it? Are you embarrassed by me?"

He chuckled. "Definitely not embarrassed by you. I'm so proud of you, actually."

I let out a little snort.

"Here's why I've been hesitating. I was going to ask you to go up to Tampa for Noche Buena." Because his family was Cuban American, they had a big, traditional pig roast on Christmas Eve. Since I loved pork in all forms, I'd secretly longed to be invited and was disappointed when I hadn't been. "I wish we could've all gotten together then."

"If wishes were fishes, we could all have a fry," I said. Noah looked at me funny. "My mom used to say that."

The holidays had been the first inkling that something was amiss, since he'd gone up there and I'd stayed here. We had spent New Year's together, however.

He hauled in a breath, as if what he was about to say required extra oxygen. "Right before that, Mom called to tell me about a job opening. The chief job in Tampa."

Chapter Nineteen

M y breath caught in my throat. Noah had worked at the Tampa Police Department for years, prior to becoming chief in Devil's Beach. His father and grandfather had worked there too.

"Oh," I croaked. "I guess it would make sense for you to apply, since you were a big shot there previously, and you know so many people—"

"Lana."

He was leaving me. That's why things had been so strained for the past month. Somehow, in a matter of days, everything and everyone I cared about had seemed to crumble before my very eyes. It made me feel a little dizzy, and I gripped the edge of the sofa cushion.

"You were born and raised in Tampa. You love it there—you always talk about it. Plus your whole family's there, your mom and sister and nieces and nephews—"

"Lana."

"You have no roots here in Devil's Beach, and maybe you feel like an outsider here, even though everyone loves you. But that's okay, I know what it's like to go home, and it makes total sense. Plus it's small here and can't compete with a big city." I was on the verge of tears now, fighting them mightily but about to cry anyway. The stress of the poisoning at Perkatory, Erica's revelation about Joey, Gus's murder—and now this?

Noah hung his head, shaking it from side to side. I swallowed a lump of phlegmy tears in my throat. "I get it," I whispered. He'd been weird this past month because he didn't know how to break it off with me. My heart felt like it was splitting in two.

He lifted his gaze and stroked my hair. "You don't get it, not at all."

I sniffled miserably in response, and a fat tear rolled down my cheek. He brushed it away with his thumb.

"I'm not going anywhere, cupcake. The reason why I didn't invite you to Tampa for Noche Buena was because my mom was pressuring me to apply. I needed to gently tell her that I wouldn't apply, that I was happy on Devil's Beach and that I'd met someone here."

He reached for a napkin on the coffee table and handed it to me. I honked into it. "You told your mom about me?"

"I did. She wants to meet you. I needed a little time to get her used to the fact that I'm staying here. I think she's lonely since Dad died. Of course, she thinks I should apply for the chief job, marry you, move to Tampa, and give her grandbabies. She really, really wants grandbabies."

I gaped at him, a mix of terror, hope, and confusion. Our relationship seemed much more serious all of a sudden. This conversation was going far better than I'd anticipated. *Go me.*

Noah chuckled softly and kissed my forehead. "I told her that one, maybe two of those things are very possibly in the future."

"Moving to Tampa?"

"You're so funny."

I snuggled into his warm body, and he wrapped his strong arms around me. He kissed the side of my head. This is what I loved about him—he didn't hold back his affection.

"As soon as things calm down, we'll plan a trip up there, okay? We'll take Stanley with us, maybe go out on the boat with my brother-in-law. Mom will probably want to have lunch with you alone, so she can make sure you're serious about me."

"Sounds perfect," I said. "And I'm extremely serious about you. I hope you know that."

He hummed an affirmation into my hair. "So what did you have to tell me? Is there something else?"

I mashed my face into his chest, inadvertently wiping my nose on his shirt. "Um, well." My voice was muffled by his muscles. "Yeah, I wanted to share a few things."

"About?"

I unstuck my body from his and reached for my hot toddy, hoping the alcohol would fortify me. The spicy, aromatic liquid was the perfect temperature now, and I took a glug. "It's about Gus. I've discovered some things."

His expression remained neutral, which I took to be a good sign. "Go on."

For the next ten minutes, I told him everything. Probably it sounded like word salad or, worse, the conspiratorial rantings of a half-cocked amateur sleuth. The look on his face was still impassive and unchanged.

Then I showed him the texts between Gus and Yates.

"Bridget never told me all this," he murmured. "Nor did she inform me about Gus's distrust of law enforcement or that she had knowledge of his brother's situation. We did know about his brother in prison, though."

"Not really a surprise, I guess. What do you think of it all?" I twisted my fingers together nervously, hoping I was doing the right thing by telling Noah everything I'd discovered.

Noah set my phone down on the table. "I think you've done a helluva job."

"Really?" I beamed.

"Really. I'm impressed."

"How much of it is new info to you?"

"Definitely the texts. Oh, and the Joey link?"

"Yeah?"

"It's not Erica's Joey. It's his uncle. He's named after the guy. The uncle is Joey V. Apparently Erica's boyfriend is Joey Junior."

I let out a soft gasp. "Oh, thank goodness. Erica's going to be so relieved. *I'm* so relieved. I guess I knew he had an uncle, but I didn't know his name."

"Lives on the mainland, owns a bingo hall. Kind of a sketchy past. But has a rock-solid alibi for Sunday because he was helping out at his church."

"Did you know Joey's dad was a big mafioso in New York? He got out of the life and opened the Square Grouper."

"I'd heard something about that. Joey's clean, though, by all accounts. Well, Joey Junior, is. The jury's still out on Joey V."

"Ah. And Erica? Do you still suspect her?"

Noah scratched his head. "How do I put this?"

"Tell me. Please."

"Fine. Since you're not doing an article and since I know you're relentless. She's not my top suspect. But she is still a suspect. And we're still investigating the Julian situation—don't forget that."

A twinge of relief washed over me. This wasn't an exoneration, but it wasn't an indictment either. "Who is the main suspect in Gus's death?"

"I can't say, Lana." He pulled me toward him, and I grinned into his arm, contemplating whether I should barge into Erica's room to tell her the good news. "Will you stop investigating now?" he asked.

"What if I say no?"

He didn't answer for a couple of minutes while he stroked my arm.

"Noah?" I prodded. "What if I don't stop looking into this?"

His hand worked its way into my hair, and he sighed. "I have to admit that you often come up with good details."

"Mm-hmm." I tried to keep a triumphant tone out of my hum.

"I don't know if that's because you stumble on them or what."

"I'd like to think it's my superior sleuthing skills."

"No comment. But if you're going to keep poking around, I have a couple of requests. Don't put yourself in danger, okay? I'd rather you not interview people unless you're doing an article. Which you're not." He paused. "Are you?"

"Not at the moment. I don't know about the future, though." Part of me wondered if Jeri and Perry would want me as a special correspondent or guest on their podcast. I was itching to take a run at Mickey Dotson, considering all I'd learned. Which is why I didn't want to make promises to Noah that I couldn't keep.

"Let's make a pact. If you find out something significant—say, online, in public records—feel free to tell me, okay? I can't believe I'm saying this, but I'd rather us work together than have you out there as a lone wolf."

Lone wolf. I liked the sound of that. I sat up, the corners of my mouth tugging upward. "I'm glad you're acknowledging my worth."

"I've always acknowledged your worth. I don't want you to jeopardize your safety or your life. I'm serious, Lana. We've had too many close calls in the past."

I held up my right hand. "Promise."

He gently clasped my wrist and pulled me close. "Seal the deal with a kiss?"

I nodded, and pressed my mouth to his. Then pulled back. "Oh. One more question. Can I open Perkatory tomorrow morning?"

"Well . . ." He pondered for a few seconds. "Can you stay closed at least until noon? I should have the results from the toxicology tests of all the ingredients by then."

Not optimal, but better than staying closed for an entire day. "Sure. That works."

He brushed the backs of his fingers down my cheek, leaving pleasurable tingles in their wake. "Cupcake, it's been quite a haul today. What do you say we move into the bedroom and watch a movie on your TV in there. In the dark. In bed."

Of course, I was unable to resist that particular idea.

*   *   *

At six the next morning, I was wide awake. That figured—since I had half a day off, and I could've easily slept in. Noah had left an hour earlier, and I'd stayed under the warm covers and fallen back into a light sleep. His news that Erica wasn't the main suspect had left me rejuvenated and ready to tackle every possible obstacle.

First I made a double espresso, then knocked on Erica's door. "Room service," I trilled.

223

Stanley barked once, and the door swung open. The dog bounded out to greet me, and I held out the cup and saucer to Erica, who was squinting like a pirate with one eye closed. Her short, black hair was mussed, and she was wearing a long-sleeved, plaid flannel nightgown, like a grandma would wear in the dead of winter. In Vermont. I grinned.

"Hey," she growled, taking the coffee. "Thanks."

I followed her inside. "I have good news. We can't open the café until noon, on Noah's orders."

"That's good news?"

"Yes. Because I have more good news."

She slurped her coffee. "Oh yeah?"

I told her what Noah had said the previous night, about how she wasn't his top suspect and that the Joey in question was actually her boyfriend's uncle.

"Whoa. I met that guy once. Do we think *he's* a suspect?"

I lifted a shoulder. "Could be. We need to look into him online."

Her eyes opened all the way. "Alright, alright, alright. Now we're getting somewhere."

"We need to focus on a few people now. Anyone connected to that boat business, especially. One: Mickey Dotson."

She nodded, and I continued.

"We need to find out who this Yates character is. I have a lesson with Honey at five, so I'll try to pump her for more information."

"Yes. She might be the key to some important details. What did Gus do before he came to Devil's Beach? Did he own businesses? Did he make enemies?"

"Those are solid questions. But it seems like whoever killed him knew about his leaf-blowing habits, which apparently only began when he moved to the island. I think that rules out a lot of people from his past."

"Makes sense, I guess," Erica said.

"And about the other case. I think you should try to remember who was at the café yesterday while Julian was there, maybe go through credit card receipts. Did anyone leave their business card in the raffle fishbowl?" We kept a fishbowl near the counter where people could drop their business cards. Once a week, we selected one to receive a free coffee.

"I think someone did. I'll look this morning and see if it jogs my memory."

"But your main task today is to talk with Joey. Find out more about his uncle, and see if he had an alibi for Sunday. Joey adores you. He'll tell you anything."

"If he doesn't, I'll wear him down."

Stanley pranced around my feet, which was my cue to take him outside for his morning constitutional. I told Erica I'd meet her at the café at noon, and braced myself for a day of fact-finding.

Chapter Twenty

The rest of the day was mercifully smooth—I did paperwork in the morning, then opened the café at noon, after Noah gave the all-clear. We were soon brisk with customers. Something about the sunny, mild afternoon brought everyone in, seeking caffeine. Most of the tourists wanted to grab an iced brew or the Orange Blossom Special, and head to the beach, where they could sip and stare at the waves.

Obviously, the Lion's Roar wasn't on the menu. Neither Erica or I mentioned the drink to each other, much less to anyone else.

It didn't seem as though word of Julian's poisoning had gotten around. Yet. The *Devil's Beach Beacon* didn't have an article, and I wasn't about to tell Mike the news.

A couple of regulars heard a man had collapsed, but most assumed it was someone from out of town who'd had a heart attack. When anyone asked, I murmured, "Medical privacy," and "The gentleman will be okay," and "Thank you for your concern."

That seemed to quell any further inquiry, but I knew from experience that at any second, the island could explode with gossip, and business would be reduced to a trickle.

Erica came up with a list of five people who had been in the café yesterday morning when Julian collapsed. In a show of good faith, I texted the information to Noah, who returned my text with a thank-you and a heart emoji.

When two o'clock rolled around and Dad and Barbara arrived for their shift, Erica and I huddled in the back room to go over the plan.

"Joey flew in this morning and is at his restaurant, preparing for the evening shift. I'm going over to say hello, and I'll grill him about his uncle then," she said.

"Are you going to tell him you're a suspect? He's been away for this whole saga." Although I'd gone to high school with Joey—we'd both been band geeks—I had no idea how he'd respond to Erica's questions.

She waved her hand. "He's apologized about fifty times for the charcuterie argument. He says he bought me a gift in Vegas and can't wait to see me. Plus, get this: I remember him talking about an uncle, and he's not on good terms with him. I hope it's the same uncle who co-owns the boat."

"Cool, cool, cool. I'm going to stop by the post office and send some bills, and then I'm meeting Honey for a skating session."

Erica smirked playfully. "I think you're going to buy a pair of skates before the month's out."

"No," I scoffed.

"I'm in the presence of a budding Instagram star."

I rolled my eyes and pushed the back door open. "See you back at home. Oh. I'm also planning to stop by the hospital to see Julian after my lesson. Visiting hours are from six to eight. I'm hoping he's up for talking and that he remembers more now."

She winced. "Tell him best wishes from the woman who served him the delicious mushroom coffee."

"You sure you don't want to come with me to see him?"

She wrinkled her nose. "Considering I'm a suspect, probably a bad idea."

"Good point. Later."

Once outside, I was assaulted with bright sunshine and a brilliant blue sky, making me wish I'd brought sunglasses. Oh, well. It felt good to be outdoors, and I was secretly excited about zipping around the sidewalk by the beach on skates. I'd even worn a pair of stretchy jeans and a Perkatory hoodie today, hoping to look casually cute.

Because I had an hour before my appointment with Honey, I could take my time walking through town. Today I didn't have to try to avoid people, and I popped into several stores to say hi to folks. Part of the reason I loved living here was the connection with the locals. Some were people I'd known since childhood, while others were newcomers. Most everyone liked to chitchat, and the longer I was back, the more I realized I enjoyed a bit of gossip myself.

Was I turning into Dad? This was exactly what he used to do when I was a kid—wander downtown during his breaks from his real estate office and chew the fat.

I figured this was also a way to find out what people were talking about, whether it was Gus or Julian.

No one seemed to know about the latter. Only one person—a clerk in a card shop—mentioned that she'd seen an ambulance. I gave her the stock answer about a medical emergency, and she seemed to accept it.

Gus was another matter altogether. Everyone had heard about his grisly, unusual death, and seemingly everyone but Erica and me were longtime fans of Jeri and Perry's true crime podcast. Three people asked me about Erica: the florist; a clerk in a bookstore; and a friend of Dad's, who was sitting on a barstool at the local watering hole downstairs from the *Devil's Beach Beacon* offices.

"Do you think Erica did it?" the gossipy florist asked.

"If she did, I think she'd have been arrested by now," I said confidently.

"Is Erica okay?" the bookstore owner asked. "She comes in here all the time for her science fiction fix. I haven't seen her in a week. I'm worried about her."

I reassured him that she was fine.

Next I encountered Dad's buddy, Rusty. He was a retiree who carved pelicans out of sandstone. He was also a serious day drinker. Today he lurched down the street and minced no words when he asked about Gus's murder. "Anyone who leaf blows daily deserved to die. Heck, I've wanted to strangle my own neighbor who uses the power washer too much. Tell Erica I'll buy her a beer anytime."

Whoa. Until now, I'd had no idea that people felt so strongly on the topic. I smiled weakly and moved along, crossing the street to the post office. I could barely fit inside, it was so packed.

I checked my watch. I only had fifteen minutes to get to the splash pad, which was a couple blocks away. By the looks of things in here, it could take a half hour. Everyone, it seemed, was in a chatty mood, wanting to talk about the mild weather, the winter tourist rush, and Gus. The postal clerk, a person I didn't recognize, leaned in to a customer I pegged as a tourist because of the Hawaiian shirt and cargo pants.

"You should check out that true crime podcast. There's going to be a part two about the leaf-blower murder."

I sighed and turned to walk out. This was getting out of hand. I'd have to return tomorrow or try to remember to hand the bills to the mail lady when she made her rounds in the morning. The bills could wait one more day.

I strolled on the beach side of the street, reveling in the cool, salt air. Seagull cries and soft waves hit my ears. At the splash pad, which was closed for weekly maintenance, no one was around. I parked myself on a bench and checked my emails, social media, and texts. One was from Noah.

Hey, cupcake. Hope you're having a good day. I stopped by and your dad said you were already gone. Miss you.

"Aww," I said aloud, grinning like a fool. That's what Noah did, caused me to talk to myself in public. For a second, I tilted my head back and soaked in the sun, feeling loved and complete.

Miss you too. I sent that text, then tapped out another. *Hey, any word about Julian and how he's doing?*

"That's the smile of a woman in love."

I looked up, and there was Honey, gently gliding to a stop in front of me. She was wearing a neon-pink sweatshirt and bell-bottom jeans. A large tie-dye pack was strapped to her back, and she wore round, rose-colored sunglasses, the type John Lennon would wear if he were an Instagram roller-skating influencer.

"Hey there," I beamed.

"How's it going, Laura?"

"Uh, Lana. My name's Lana."

"Lana! Yes. Gosh, I'm so sorry. You know how I am about names."

"Don't apologize. I've been called much worse." I laughed.

She did a little spin and then sat next to me, pointing to my phone. I was amazed at her agility while wearing a backpack. "So, who's the guy? Or girl?"

"My boyfriend." I debating telling her more, but perhaps letting on that I was dating the police chief wasn't the best idea at this juncture, in case she was actually Gus's killer.

"Is it serious?" Her big blue eyes and chummy tone made it feel like we were fast friends—despite the fact that she couldn't get my name right.

I shrugged. "Possibly. We're talking about taking it to the next level."

"Be careful. Men are difficult. You don't want to get in a situation like I did. Divorce sucks."

"Don't I know it. I'm actually divorced."

We exchanged mournful, what-can-you-do looks. "So, how are you doing with the Gus situation? It must be difficult, going through a divorce and then him dying."

I didn't add that there were a few days during my own divorce that I would have cheered if I'd gotten the news that my ex had died. Fortunately, those days had passed, and I no longer harbored any anger or sadness when it came to my ex.

She took a breath, sighed it out, and slipped her rose-tinted sunglasses off her face. I got the distinct impression that she leaned toward the dramatic. "I'm okay, I guess. His mom's flying in for the funeral. She always hated me, so I'm not looking forward to that. And Bridget's making things hella difficult. She's such a mean person."

The thrill of gossip surged through me. "How so?"

"She wants to be part of the planning of his memorial. His mom wants us both there."

Yikes. That sounded like an unpleasant scene. My face crinkled into a grimace. "If you don't want to be there, why go?"

She bobbed her shoulders. "I'm contesting his will, that's why. He tried to change it to leave everything to Bridget. Or she coerced him into changing it, and then killed him."

"I see." I didn't, but thought it best not to challenge her. "Do you really think she killed him?"

She looked toward the beach. "Actually, no, I don't. She loved Gus. A lot. Probably more than I ever did. But still. I was his wife and gave up so much when I left Fort Lauderdale to move here with him. I deserve something from his will. I spent three years with him, and I'm not getting those years back."

"Of course you deserve something, but I'm sure you have many more wonderful years ahead," I said chummily. "Hey, I was thinking about something yesterday. You said Gus sold the pirate cruise ship to a group of men. Does the name Joey Rizzo ring a bell?"

Her eyes squinted to slits. "Maybe? It sounds familiar. Does he live here on Devil's Beach?"

"No, on the mainland. Probably in his forties or fifties. He might have something to do with boats."

I could see the wheels turning inside her head. "I think so. Smokes cigars. Looks like he's right out of central casting of a mafia movie. Yes, Joey Rizzo. Why do you ask?"

"There's been a lot of talk at my café recently about Gus and the men who bought his pirate cruise business." This wasn't entirely a lie, but all the talk came from Erica, Dad, or me. "Some folks were trying to figure out who bought it, and Joey's name came up, along with Mickey's and, uh, another guy's."

I paused for dramatic effect, then snapped my fingers. "A guy with the last name Yates, I believe."

"Oh yeah. Doug Yates. Real nice guy. Well, nice to me. He was quite mad at Gus after the sale. Don't know why. That's what Gus told me once, anyway. Yates thought Gus stiffed him in the business deal. Knowing Gus, he probably did."

"What do you mean?" I played dumb.

"Gus told me he gave the buyers some falsified profit statements. So they bought the pirate cruise for more than it was worth. Also, the ship needed repairs, and Gus only made some cosmetic changes. I'm sure the new owners had a rude awakening once they found out what was really going on."

"He cooked the books?"

"Is that what you call it? I guess. Doug Yates was upset when he found out, but Gus insisted he'd done nothing wrong. At least he insisted that to his lawyer and in court. He told me otherwise. That's one of the reasons I left him. He had no integrity. He tried to scam everyone. I shoulda known when we had our first dinner together. He ate all but one bite of his meal, then claimed there was a hair in it and argued with the manager, to get the dish for free."

A real catch, that Gus. "Oh my."

Their divorce was now understandable. We were definitely getting somewhere with the info, which made my mood soar. I tapped my finger on my chin. "Doug Yates. Yes, that sounds familiar." Another small fib.

"Yeah, apparently he invests in a lot of businesses, does some day trading. He's kind of a digital nomad. I think he's pretty wealthy." She shrugged and reached for her enormous backpack. "Anyway, I have your skates in here. Size seven, right? Funny how I remember that, but not your name. I swear, I remember the strangest details. Hey, are you wearing socks?"

As she spoke, a lightning bolt of recognition zapped my brain. Doug. *Digital nomad.* Could it be *our* Doug, the customer who worked almost every day from Perkatory? He called himself a digital nomad. But his last name was Rogers, not Yates.

A squirmy feeling invaded my stomach, and I had the urge to text Erica. She'd found Yates's name online, as part of the corporation paperwork. "Great, thanks. Socks? Yes. I am wearing them. Listen, I want to send a message to a coworker before we start, okay? We've had a heck of a week."

"No problem. Here are the skates. I'll be over there warming up while you lace up." With a sunny smile, she set the skates on the ground and stood up, gliding away as she slipped the backpack on again.

My hands shook as I navigated to my messages app, bringing up Erica's name. Our last message had been from before Gus was killed. It was about whether she should buy Stanley a new pack of mini tennis balls and whether they should have a squeaker or not. Simpler times, when we were both sweet summer children.

Hey, I typed. *Do you remember Yates's initials on that state paperwork?*

She answered almost immediately. Yeah. *D.R.*

Doug Rogers Yates. The saliva in my mouth evaporated. This had to be significant. He'd threatened Gus. He was also Perkatory's best customer. What was going on? I needed to talk to Erica now and figure out whether Doug had been involved in Gus's murder, or if I was jumping to conclusions.

Okay, thanks. I'll be home soon.

I slipped my phone back into my bag and searched around for Honey. She was doing a one-legged glide around the fallow sprinklers of the splash pad. With the backdrop of the beach, she looked like an impossibly cool advertisement for jeans.

I waved and called her name.

She rolled over. "What's up? Why haven't you put on your skates? Don't they fit?"

"No, they're probably fine. I'm really sorry, but something big has come up at, uh, work. I need to go, unfortunately. We had a medical incident at our café, and, uh, I need to fill out some OSHA paperwork."

"A slip and fall? Oh no." Her face fell, and I didn't correct her assumption. "I was looking forward to our lesson."

"Me too." It was true. I'd so much rather be skating than sleuthing. Well, maybe not—if that current of adrenaline running through my body was any indication.

I pulled out a wad of cash and she shook her head. I stood up and thrust the money toward her. "No, really. I'm sorry to waste your time, and I feel terrible that you cleared your calendar for me. I have a lot going on and can't ignore this situation that's unfolding. Let's plan on next week, okay?"

She looked forlorn as I started to power-walk away.

"Okay, but we'll have to schedule around Gus's funeral and the wake," she shouted.

Chapter
Twenty-One

I jogged back to my house, taking back streets to ensure I
wouldn't run into anyone I knew. At home, Erica and Stanley
were playing fetch in the backyard, and she looked up as I burst
out the back door.

"What's shakin', bacon?" she asked.

As she flung the ball, I breathlessly told her about Doug Rogers
Yates. I plopped onto a lounger and stretched out, wrapping my
chunky sweater around my body.

She sank onto the steps leading to the deck. "No way. Doug?
Nice Doug? The one who buses the tables for inconsiderate people
who get up and leave cups and glasses behind? The one who leaves
us the best tips? Oh, man, it better not be Doug."

"Remember how he helped you sweep up that sugar spill a few
months ago? The two of you laughed so hard."

She let out a long, wounded sigh. We sat in silence as Stanley
tottered up to us with the ball in his mouth. He sat in between us
but didn't release the puppy-sized ball from the grip of his tiny jaws.

"Doug's there every day," Erica said. "Where was he that
Sunday?"

"Barbara and Heidi were working that afternoon. Let me ask them." I pulled out my phone and tapped out a text to the group message I maintained with the staff.

"Was Doug at the café on Sunday?" I read aloud.

A message, from Barbara, came almost immediately: *He came in for his usual iced coffee but didn't stay. I remember because Bernadette, the police dispatcher, was also there. With her parrot. The parrot swore at Doug, and we all laughed.*

I relayed the message to Erica and she groaned. *About what time did all that happen?* I typed.

Noonish, I think, she replied.

"That fits the time line. He could've gotten his coffee and then slipped into Gus's garage and tampered with the leaf blower," I said.

"Right when I was working only a few feet away in our garage. That's bold."

"And scary."

The idea of Doug prowling around while Erica was reupholstering her boat cushions shook loose something in my memory, and I sat up, fear shivering through me.

"Holy Pup-Peroni. Erica," I gasped.

"What now?"

"Doug. He was at Perkatory when Julian was poisoned."

Her eyes bulged. "So? What are you trying to say? Why would he poison a total stranger? Are you saying he did it?"

My heart sped up. "This is totally conjecture, and completely insane. But hear me out. What if he was trying to frame you?"

"Why would he do that?" Her brows drew together. "He likes me."

I snorted. "Why does any criminal do anything? It doesn't need to make sense. This is Florida. Does anything make sense ever?"

"Right. So he picked me out of thin air." She shook her head.

"Maybe not. Maybe you were the most convenient scapegoat. People who want to deflect attention from themselves are liable to do anything."

She chewed on her bottom lip. "Wait, what about the Mickey Dotson theory? He seems pretty likely, too, given his experience with actual landscaping tools. Doug once told me that he isn't handy, and he can't do a do-it-yourself project to save his life. He said he ruined the drywall in his place when he was hanging a photo."

"You're right. Mickey is still a possibility. I wouldn't put anything past him. He's such a snake. Do you think they worked together to kill Gus?"

"I guess it's possible. I don't know anymore. This is all too wild, even for my imagination."

"What did Joey say? Did you see him this afternoon?"

"Yeah. He hasn't talked with that uncle in two years. They got into a fight over some business stuff. Apparently his uncle felt like he had some claim on the restaurant, and Joey didn't want him involved. Joey wouldn't put it past his uncle to whack someone. That's how he put it. Whack."

"Whoa. Interesting. So maybe Mickey, Doug, *and* Joey killed Gus."

"Let's call him Uncle Joey to distinguish him from my Joey, okay?"

"Agreed. Uncle Joey it is."

"What are we going to do next?" she asked, leaning over to pick a leaf off Stanley's head.

I fiddled with my phone, checking the time. It was almost five, and the late-day winter sun cast long shadows. It was going to be a gorgeous sunset.

"Let's bring the puppy inside and grab our jackets." I stood up.
"Why?"

Erica and Stanley followed me to the back door of the house. A plan formed in my mind, one that involved drinking and pirates. Fortunately, Erica and I both had tomorrow off.

"Because we're going on a sunset booze cruise."

* * *

"Ahoy mateys, welcome aboard the *Royal Conquest*. I'll be yer captain today."

Erica and I guffawed as we boarded the ship along with a couple dozen tourists, many of them seemingly already drunk.

"Hey! You two wenches!" the captain roared. Erica and I looked around, panicked.

"You talking to us?" Erica asked, pointing at her chest.

"You forgot yer drinks," the captain said, pointing at a woman in a short skirt and puffy-sleeved top that seemed to cover more of her arms than her midriff.

"Can't have that." Erica lunged for the cocktails, which were in white plastic cups emblazoned on the front with a pirate holding a knife in his teeth. She handed one to me and lowered her voice. "Especially since we spent fifty bucks each on this cruise."

"Isn't that the Tampa Bay Buccaneers' old logo?" I pointed at the mug.

"Who are the Buccaneers?" Erica asked, slurping her first sip. She didn't follow sports, even on a casual level.

"We got them in bulk at a closeout sale," the waitress said. "So maybe they are."

I took a sip. The purple concoction had no discernable flavor other than sugary sweet alcohol. I tapped on the plastic cup with my fingernails. "I'll give these to Noah. He'll love them. He's a huge Bucs fan, being from Tampa and all."

Erica and I drifted over to the side of the ship that faced the marina. The rest of the crowd was on the other side, staring at the sunset over the water.

"Did you tell Noah we're here?"

I shook my head. "I'm planning on explaining everything after our voyage. It's not like it's that long—it's only a couple of hours."

My words were drowned out by the captain, on a megaphone, telling us what to do if the ship encountered rough seas or capsized.

"We're toast if this thing goes down," Erica muttered, taking another big gulp. "God, this is disgusting. They didn't skimp on the alcohol, though."

I surveyed the scene. Back at home, it had seemed like a grand idea to come aboard the *Royal Conquest* to fact-find. Now that we were aboard, it felt like a tacky tourist trap filled with drunks. I'd counted five ship employees, who were all dressed in various pirate outfits.

They were our latest, and possibly only, hope for gleaning information about Doug, Mickey, and Uncle Joey.

"There are life jackets underneath the rows of seats over here," the captain said, pointing toward the front of the ship, where there were four rows of white benches. "Also on the ship's stern, which is in the back. But nothing's gonna happen on this voyage, unless you count drinking your booty off!"

The crowd, which seemed to be comprised of drunk college-age tourists and even drunker baby boomers, whooped and hollered. Erica and I stared at each other.

"Maybe this wasn't the best idea," I said, eyeing one of the faux pirate staff members hauling up the gangway.

Erica hunched her shoulders. "The cocktail's not so bad after the first few sips."

A molar-shaking explosion startled me, and when everyone around us laughed and hooted more, I realized that it was the fake cannon on the ship. Apparently this signaled that the voyage was underway.

I shouldn't have been so shocked by the noise; I'd heard it almost every day since I'd moved back to Devil's Beach several months ago. But the sound was muffled on shore, whereas here on the ship, it sounded like a real cannon.

Erica swirled the ice in her drink and peered into the glass. "Let's go explore the ship while everyone else is up here oohing and aahing over the sunset."

I nodded, glancing toward the tourists, who were all snapping selfies against the setting sun. It really was a gorgeous sunset tonight, a clear, orange-sherbet sky.

We wandered toward the stern, where a group of people all in the same red sweatshirts were doing shots. "This is the Smith family reunion," one guy hollered at us. "Do you ladies want to join us and be honorary cousins? We've got tequila!"

"Not right now, but maybe later, thanks," Erica said with a friendly wave. "We're trying to find the bathrooms."

"They're down below, through that door. Past the gift shop," the guy yelled. Why he was so loud, I wasn't sure, since we were only two feet away.

I gave him a thumbs-up, and we walked to the only door. The handle turned easily, but it wouldn't budge.

"Let me try," Erica said.

In a second, she tugged it open. "How'd you do that?," I asked. "Impressive."

"Doors on boats are often sealed tight. You have to know how to pull."

We slammed the door shut behind us and crept down a short hall. I poked my head into the first open doorway and was greeted by rows of T-shirts, postcards, and assorted pirate-themed knickknacks.

A young woman behind the counter looked up from her phone. "Welcome to Pirate's Cove, the most swashbuckling store in the Gulf of Mexico." Her voice sounded even more bored than she looked.

Erica gave me a little shove into the store. I almost lost my balance and dropped my drink from the swaying motion of the ship. Fortunately, I was able to right myself by clutching a rack of T-shirts emblazoned with the ship's likeness.

"These are cute," I said, trying to make small talk.

"Two for one, today only." The woman went back to her phone. "Oh, and we've got a special on this saltwater taffy."

She gestured to a basket near the counter, without looking up from her cell. The taffy was from Darla's shop. Well, at least someone on the island had made a positive connection with Doug, Mickey, and this tacky pirate ship.

While we perused the gift store, I gathered a couple of questions in my mind. Then I glanced to Erica and gestured with my eyes toward the woman at the counter. Erica nodded once.

I plucked from a rack a book called *From Havana to Tampa: Pirates of the Gulf Coast* and brought it to the glass counter, setting it down.

"This looks really good," I chirped. "I think I'll get this for my boyfriend. He loves history, especially being Cuban American and all."

The woman blinked. "Cash or credit?"

"Credit." Setting my glass down on the counter, I reached for my wallet and took another stab at small talk. "You know, I've lived on Devil's Beach for a long time, and I've never been on this cruise. It's really cool. Isn't it cool, Erica?"

"It's fab," she replied, coming to join me at the counter.

"Who all owns this, anyway?" I asked the clerk.

"Three guys. Locals. Well, two are local to Devil's Beach. One's on the mainland."

"Really? Maybe we know them?" I looked to Erica, and she nodded as if this were the most scintillating conversation in the world.

The woman sighed. "Some guy who owns that coffee shop downtown. Not the good one, Perkatory, but the other one— Mickey; he owns a place called Island Brewnette." She leaned in. "The coffee's not great at his place."

I swelled with internal pride and nodded. It was confirmation— no, *validation*—of Perkatory's superiority. We had the best coffee shop on Devil's Beach. Even random strangers agreed. Heh.

"Yes, Mickey. I think I know him."

"There's some other guy named Joey—I never see him. I often see Mickey and the other guy."

"What's his name?" Erica fiddled with a keychain featuring a parrot.

"Doug Yates."

"That sounds familiar," I said, squinting at Erica, who nodded. "I think he's a pretty wealthy businessman. Am I thinking of the same guy?"

The clerk perked up. "He invests in a lot of different companies. The month he bought our ship, he also made a million day-trading on the stock market. I didn't believe him, but then he gave us all a bonus, so that was cool."

"Must be nice having a great boss like that," Erica said.

"Oh, that didn't last long. This is my final week here because I can't take it. Doug turned out to be not such a great boss, after that bonus."

"What's the problem? I was thinking about applying here since it seems fun." I slurped my drink, my eyes wide with rapt attention. Some of the slushy concoction hit my nose, and I wiped it away without a trace of embarrassment. This clerk had seen much worse, I was certain.

"Doug and Mickey, they're way too intense. They micromanage everything. Plus I hate Florida. I feel like I have no friends, and I miss my family up north in Missouri. It's difficult getting to know people here." She looked at us suspiciously.

"Hmm, that's too bad," Erica said in a noncommittal tone.

"You know, I believe I've seen Doug and Mickey around town." I was babbling now. "Maybe last Sunday? At Island Brewnette?"

The woman slipped the book into a bag. "Mickey was definitely here on Sunday. He showed up all greasy."

Erica inspected a talking statue of a pirate and pressed a button on the side. It let out a loud "Argh!," and she fumbled, almost dropping it. I ignored her. "Greasy?"

"Yeah, like he'd been working on an engine or something. It was weird. I asked him if he'd been changing oil, and he grunted at me. Told me to mind my own business. That's when I decided to quit and go back up north."

"How about Doug? You see him around?" Erica asked.

The woman waved her hand in the air, in the direction of the door. "Oh, I saw him when I boarded today. I think he's here somewhere. Maybe in the office? Sometimes he likes to hang out up on deck with the tourists, and drink."

Eep. We hadn't anticipated this.

"Oh, good to know," I said. Stuffing the book into my backpack, I edged away from the counter. "Well, good luck with your move back up north."

"Where's the little girls' room, anyway?" Erica asked. For some reason, she always adopted a thick southern accent after one drink.

The clerk pointed. "Out the door, to the left, third door on the left. Past the office."

Erica and I quickly walked out and then took a left, just as a few loud women walked into the gift shop.

We huddled outside the doorway. "What if we run into Doug?" I hissed.

"Don't sweat it. We'll make small talk."

"Okay, let's get back upstairs."

"No, I really have to use the bathroom."

"Oh. Okay." We wandered down the hall, and at one open door, we spotted a messy office. There was no one inside. A few paces away, a sign over a door said "Wenches."

"I'll be right back," Erica said. "You go into the office and snoop around."

I pointed to my chest. "Me?"

"Yeah." Erica stared at me like it was the most natural thing in the world to ask someone to poke around in a random office. "I have to relieve myself."

"Fine. Be quick."

She went into the bathroom, and I tiptoed back down the hall, to the office. As a reporter, I'd never done anything like this, preferring to rely on ethical, legal methods of getting information.

But I was no longer a journalist, and if anyone interrupted me, I'd claim I'd gotten lost on my way to the restroom.

My sneakers made no noise as I crossed the doorway into the office and gently shut the door. Goodness. Where to begin? It looked worse than my own office, with clear plastic bags of colorful beads, a stack of kid-sized pirate hats, and bricks of printed brochures.

I moved toward the desk, going behind it so I could keep an eye on the door. At first I didn't touch anything, only scanned the papers on the desk. I spotted a planner book that was open to the current month, and there were only a few items on various days, things like *Order rum* and *Pay quarterly taxes.*

When my gaze landed on a stack of letters, I couldn't resist rifling through. Those were uninteresting, envelopes stamped with businesses' return addresses.

I kept looking, going through what appeared to be a stack of liquor invoices. Man, the company really went through a lot of booze. It was probably why the ticket prices were so high. I kept rifling through the papers, becoming more disgusted with myself by the moment.

This was a huge risk, being in here, and for what? Looking through some bills—

Wait. What was this?

The words *Circuit Court* snagged my attention.

I used my speed reading ability to glean the important details, and nearly gasped. It was a protective injunction. Gus had sought a judge's order to keep both Mickey and Doug away from him.

"Would you look who it is!"

A familiar male voice boomed through the door. I froze with the paper in my hand, unable to breathe.

"Doug! My word! What are you doing here?"

Holy guacamole. My jaw hung open.

"Erica, you vixen, you! What are *you* doing here?" Doug's voice sounded warm and friendly, almost to a creepy degree. Or maybe it felt that way now that I suspected him of murder.

"I told Lana that I'd never been on a tourist cruise, and she insisted we come. We also have tomorrow off, so we can tie a few on, if you know what I mean. Walk the plank and all."

The two laughed like old chums. My eyes grew wider.

"Where is Lana anyway? In the bathroom?"

I looked around, wondering if there was any escape route. There was only a porthole, which revealed the indigo sky of twilight.

"No, Lana's upstairs waiting for me. Come on, have a drink with us."

"I'd love to. First I need to grab something in here."

The doorknob rattled and I felt my bowels loosening. *Noooo.*

"Wait—we need to rescue her *now*. I only left because I had to pee, but some really drunk guys were harassing her. Please?"

"Oh wow, we can't have that. Not with the girlfriend of the island's police chief. Don't want her to tell him we've got something nefarious going on here."

He and Erica dissolved into laughter.

"I guess I can come back down to my office anytime," he said.

"You work here?"

"I help out a bit with some bookkeeping. No big deal. I use this as an office sometimes."

Why was he lying? He co-owned this ship. Things were getting curiouser and curiouser.

"Pfft. Office, schmoffice. Doug, it's time to have a drink with your favorite baristas."

"Do you two do rum shots?"

"Do we ever!" Erica boomed. "We are rum shot experts."

"Good, because we have this one called the Florida Man. Hope you're not planning on driving tonight. Ooh, Erica, what's this? Your arm in mine?"

"I'm already a little unsteady on my feet and thought you could help me up those stairs, sailor." Her laugh was lusty and throaty.

Erica was doing her best impression of Stella from *Streetcar Named Desire*, while I was in here scared witless. Great.

Their footsteps faded down the hall, and I let out the breath I was holding. *Crud, that was close.* I gulped in a few mouthfuls of oxygen and quickly used my cell to snap a photo of the restraining order. Then I cracked the door open a couple of inches.

When I was sure no one was right outside the office, I thundered down the hall, past the gift shop and up the stairs, wondering how we would toss back shots with Doug for the rest of the cruise without blowing our cover.

Chapter Twenty-Two

The party was in full swing when I arrived upstairs. Nineties rap played in the background, people were dancing badly, and everyone seemed to be wearing eye patches. Needless to say, more than a few people lost their balance and ended up rolling around on the wooden deck.

Erica and Doug were at a high-top table at the stern of the ship, three shot glasses filled with electric-blue liquid in front of them. Erica wore a black pirate hat, and she tipped it at me when I approached.

"There's our little wench." Erica slid a shot toward me. "That's a Florida Man shot."

"Hey, Doug. Wow!" I pasted on a giant smile. It was crucial that I act surprised to see him. "Fancy meeting you here. Erica, I never would've imagined that Doug would be here."

"Doug keeps an office on the boat," Erica said.

"Oh, cool." I looked to him and pretended to be impressed. I was about to ask the obvious question—why would he keep an office on a tourist pirate ship?—but decided to shut up and roll with it.

"So what's in these?" I picked up the shot glass and held it in a toast to my drinking companions.

"Coconut rum, pineapple juice, blue curacao, and a splash of vanilla vodka," Doug said.

Sounded like a recipe for a raging hangover. "Yum," I replied.

"Batten down the hatches, friends," Erica cried, pounding her shot. Doug and I followed.

I was instantly hit by two things: nausea caused by potent liquor hitting my empty stomach, and a panic attack.

If Doug had truly poisoned Julian, what would stop him from spiking our drinks here? My heart raced. Really, I should've thought about this before I tossed back the shot. I was such a dummy.

The only thing I could do now was let someone know where we were, and tell them to come look for us if we didn't get off this boat and return home.

"Ooh, I think my man is texting me," I said, feeling an anxious need to get in touch with Noah. "Excuse me."

Erica snickered.

"Are you single?" Doug leaned toward her.

I swear, it seemed like he was interested in her. So why would he try to pin a poisoning on her? Nothing made sense. I turned away, frantically swiping my thumbs over the keyboard. I looked up when a server came over and plopped three more electric-blue shots in plastic glasses on the table. The tops were sealed with little tinfoil caps, like the juice drinks in little bottles from my childhood.

"Interesting," I murmured.

"They come premade," Doug tapped the top of one bottle with his finger. "Cheaper that way."

That's when I saw three foil tops crumpled on Erica's side of the table. Hopefully, she'd peeled off the tops, and I didn't have to worry about being poisoned by Doug with some random, deadly mushroom powder.

Still, I felt the need to alert Noah to where I was.

Erica and I are on a tourist booze cruise, and we are drinking heavily. If I don't call you in an hour, please come looking for us.

His response came immediately. *What? Are you okay?*

We're fine. Doing shots.

You'd better not be driving.

No, we're walking from the marina to my house. I'm worried.

About what, Lana? Now I'm worried too.

I paused, wondering if I should tell him about my spiked drink fear. Probably not the best idea.

There are a lot of drunk, forward men on this ship. That's all, I texted back.

Call me immediately if things get out of hand.

I will. The cruise isn't long, and we'll be headed back to the marina in a while.

If I don't hear from you by 20:15 I'm coming to look for you. Aww, cute: Noah used military time.

I smiled at my phone, feeling a little sense of relief. *Thanks. I owe you one.*

The only thing you owe me is to stay safe and to not stick your nose where it doesn't belong. He included a wink emoji.

Too late for that nose-sticking business. "Heh," I mumbled aloud, suddenly a bit tipsy from the drink and the swaying of the boat.

"Everything okay?" Erica lined up the shots in front of us.

"Peachy." I looked to Doug and laughed. "So what brings you here? Oh, right. You have an office here. That's interesting."

He chuckled. "Perkatory will always be my main office, though. Time for another shot!"

"Amen to that," Erica said.

We all slammed the blue liquid, and I shuddered. "That really packs a punch."

Erica, who seemed stone-cold sober, tapped the table with her index finger. "You know, Doug, you never told us why you chose Perkatory as your preferred coffee shop. Let's do some market research. Why us, and not, say, Island Brewnette?"

Oh my. Was she being a bit too bold? I clammed up and steadied myself for his answer. It was an excellent question, though. If he was in business with Mickey Dotson, why didn't he hang at Mickey's café? Another thought popped into my head: Doug didn't know that *we* knew he co-owned this ship with Mickey.

This was going to be a task keeping everything straight while half drunk. Probably it was for the best if I shut up.

"That's a simple answer. I like the coffee and the music better at Perkatory." He hoisted a shoulder. "Although, Lana, I have to admit, I'm not digging the music your father's been playing lately."

"You and me both. Dad's gone rogue with the tunes."

We talked amiably about Dad for a while, with Doug recounting the time Dad did an impromptu Reiki healing at Perkatory on Doug's left calf, which he'd apparently injured while running.

"He's quite the healer, Peter Lewis," Doug said, signaling the server, then calling out, "Another round of shots."

"Yeah, he was really upset about what happened to Julian," Erica blurted.

Eep. Okay, well, if she was going there, so was I. "Dad's an empath. He feels things deeply. So when Julian was poisoned, he was devastated."

"Julian?" Doug asked, his features tight with confusion. "Poisoned?"

"Yes, the man who passed out at Perkatory yesterday and was taken out on a stretcher by the EMTs," I said.

Doug shook his head. "I don't remember that. I think I was at lunch, at a business meeting."

My eyes doubled in size. Was he gaslighting me? Did he not remember? What the heck? "No, you were there. I walked in, and we talked as the paramedics were working on Julian while he was on the floor."

"No, you must have mistaken me for someone else in all the confusion. It wasn't me." Doug smiled tightly. "Yesterday I was at a lunch with my business partner."

I opened and closed my mouth several times, shocked that Doug would deny this detail. Did he really think he could make me question my memory? A frisson of anger bubbled in my chest. I didn't dare look at Erica because I'd be unable to shoot her a knowing, pointed look.

Now was not the time to confront Doug, but his response was confirmation that we were dealing with someone incredibly sketchy. And given how Mickey Dotson was also a questionable character, I was almost certain they'd teamed up to kill Gus.

I couldn't wait to tell Noah my theory.

"Yeah, probably I was mistaken—sorry," I said casually. "Now, where are those Florida Man shots?"

*   *   *

We spent the next forty-five minutes talking about superficial things like local pirate lore, pounding another round of shots, then pouring water down our throats in hopes of staving off an epic hangover. I didn't bring up Julian or Gus or the fact that Doug co-owned this ship—and he didn't raise the issue either.

"I want to officially thank the universe that we have tomorrow off," I muttered as the boat approached the dock. A rager of a hangover loomed, and my stomach wasn't feeling all that hot either.

"Well, Erica, Lana, I guess that means I won't be seeing you tomorrow at Perkatory," Doug said. "Or maybe I'll take tomorrow off too."

"You work so hard. You need time off," Erica purred. "You've actually seemed stressed lately, dude."

"You don't even know the half of it," he responded, sliding off his stool.

"Oh, we might." Had I said that aloud? He looked deep into my eyes, and I smiled from instinct. Inside, I felt a chill flow down my spine. "We're all so busy these days, I guess."

With a flourish, he whipped off his pirate hat. "It was a pleasure, ladies."

"See you around!" Erica cried. "We're going to get mushroom pizza. Want to come?"

I gasped a little. Was she out of her mind, bringing up mushrooms like that?

"No, I've got some things to do." Doug stared at her, then shifted his gaze to me. There was no warmth in his eyes. "I mean, I have to get home. It's late."

"Us too," I said. "Egad, the idea of pizza was making me a little queasy. Erica, we'll make some cinnamon toast at home."

With a half smile and a weak wave, Doug disappeared into the crowd, which was making its way to the gangplank off the ship and down to the marina.

"Ready, dudette?" Erica asked.

"I can't believe you said that about the mushroom pizza. Let's scram." I nearly fell while climbing off my stool, and as we moved down the gangway to the dock, Erica and I held onto each other for support. Neither of us seemed particularly steady on our feet.

"Crud. I forgot the buccaneer cup for Noah," I mumbled.

We lurched down the dock, toward the beachfront sidewalk. Erica still wore her pirate hat, and I had an eye patch on an elastic string around my neck, like a particularly funky pendant.

"That was so weird," she cried. "I haven't had a night like that since you and I went to the Dirty Dolphin with Stanley that one time."

"Shh. Don't yell." For some reason, she and Dad were similar in that they needed to tell the whole world what they were thinking, at high volume. My breath seeped out of me in one long, frustrated sigh.

"Doug is a liar," she hissed.

"Shh. I know. He was there at the café when Julian was poisoned. I know he was. I saw him."

I pulled Erica away from the departing passengers. Who knew if Doug was lurking? I didn't see him anywhere, but my powers of observation were clearly impaired, and it was dark. "He's a total gaslighter. I had an entire conversation with him when I walked into Perkatory yesterday."

"He straight up lied. Like a rug," Erica chortled.

"Doug is so creepy. Why didn't I notice that before, when he was in the café?"

"He didn't seem all that different to me." Erica shrugged. "But I'm definitely willing to entertain him as a possibility in Gus's death."

"Well, you should because I have more to tell you," I whispered.

"Um, let's see. You're hungry? Want to stop by Joey's restaurant? He can make some cheese fries for us. I could go for some grease to cut through all that sugar in my stomach."

I pantomimed a gag at the thought of eating gooey dairy over fried potatoes after those shots. "No. Not hungry at all, but I could use some water. Listen, I found a clue in the office." The last word came out as *offitthhhh* because the liquor was really catching up to me.

Erica tugged me under a palm tree, and I nearly stumbled while stepping down from the walkway and onto the sand.

"What did you find?"

I pressed my back against the trunk of the tree. "Gus got a restraining order against Doug and Mickey. I got a photo of the document."

"No way. What did it say?"

I fumbled for my phone, dropping it in the sand. My back ached as I bent to retrieve it, then wiped the cell on my jeans. "Crap. It'll be easier to show you on my computer at home."

"'Kay. Let's go."

We stumbled toward the street. It was only a few blocks home but seemed like the length of a marathon. I pondered whether to call an Uber and wrapped my cardigan around me tighter. Temperatures seemed near freezing.

As we were about to cross Main Street, a police car pulled up, flashing its red and blue lights. Erica shielded her eyes. "What the heck? Are we under arrest for walking while intoxicated?"

The passenger window of the cop car went down, and Erica and I peered in.

"Evening, ladies." It was Noah.

"Oh, hey." I waved, trying to act sober.

Erica snorted with laughter. "Do you always have to check up on her?"

I swatted her arm. "Shush."

"I do when she texts that she's worried about her safety. Get in. I'll take you home."

"I'm not getting in the back of a cruiser." Erica folded her arms.

"I'll get in the back. Come on. I don't feel like walking," I pleaded with her.

She climbed into the passenger seat, and I collapsed into the back. It was my experience that being in the back of a police car was a rather grimy experience—I'd ridden along with more than a few cops during my time as a reporter in Miami—but Noah's car was squeaky clean.

"This back seat doesn't get a lot of action, does it?" I asked. Noah's eyes met mine in the rearview mirror.

"I don't arrest many people and transport them, if that's what you're asking," he said.

"Not even slightly tipsy girlfriends?" I teased.

"You're the first."

Erica sighed and slumped against the window. "Those shots were hella gross. I'm glad we didn't get the cheese fries after all." She let out a soft burp.

"Please don't throw up," Noah said.

She snorted in response.

We rode the rest of the short ride in silence. When Noah pulled into the driveway of my house, Erica turned and flashed a genuine smile at him.

"Thanks, dude. You know, I've been meaning to ask you. Do you have a cop nickname? I heard cops give each other nicknames."

Where did Erica get this stuff? I groaned while Noah turned in his seat to tilt his head. "Actually, I did, back in Tampa."

Interesting. I leaned forward. "Tell us."

He sighed dramatically. "I can't believe I'm telling you two this."

"Spill it," Erica cried.

"The Dragon."

"What? Why?" I asked.

"I started on the night shift in Tampa. The guys in my precinct thought I looked like a nerd who played Dungeons and Dragons. So an older sergeant gave me the nickname and it stuck."

"That's actually pretty cool," Erica said, opening the door. "I think I like you more now. Thanks."

"Welcome," he said as she lurched out of the car and shuffled up the walkway to the front door.

He turned around to look at me. "C'mon, let's go inside and you can tell me all about your night and what you found."

"Okay, but I'm going to make myself some cinnamon toast." Probably I should've been embarrassed for being so tipsy around him, but I was past the point of caring.

I tried to open the car door, but it seemed to be stuck. I tapped on the window and saw Noah peering at me from the outside. He waved playfully.

"Hey, let me out!"

He easily opened the door, and I tried to exit the cruiser with as much dignity as possible on rubbery legs. "Why did you trap me back here?"

A guffaw escaped his mouth. "It's locked because it's a police car. Most of the people in the back of the cruiser are the ones we don't want escaping."

"Oh. Good point." I held onto his arm as we made our way up to the door. Then I stopped on the bottom porch step and squinted, one eye closed.

"Wait—did you play Dungeons and Dragons?"

He smoothed the hair back from my face. "I did, actually. Is that too geeky of a detail for you?"

I kissed his cheek. A warm fuzzy feeling settled in my stomach, although that might have been from all the shots. "No. It's perfect. And it's a badass nickname."

Chapter Twenty-Three

"No, please don't give us a pep talk while we're hungover." I pressed my forehead into the cool wood of the kitchen table while Erica groaned.

"Now that you're both somewhat sober—"

Raising my head, I interrupted Noah, who was looking maddeningly chipper for this ungodly early hour. He was munching on an English muffin topped with peanut butter. "Who says we're sober?"

Erica made another unintelligible noise, seemingly incapable of forming words or sentences. Noah had roused me out of bed at seven, then made me wake Erica up so he could "have a serious talk" with the two of us.

He'd skipped his usual morning beach run, which was an indication that he wasn't messing around.

His head volleyed to me, to Erica, then back to me. "The two of you are banned from sleuthing, investigating, or researching."

"What about interviewing? Studying? Examining?" I asked.

"Probing?" Erica croaked.

His glare silenced us. "No fooling around. No more. This isn't your place. You're not detectives. I saw the whiteboard, in the garage, with the list of suspects."

The ding of the toaster punctuated his last statement. Because he burned so many calories during his days, he ate not one, but two English muffins. I shuffled over to the toaster to take the toasted bread out of the slots and plopped them on his plate.

"Why are you snooping around my garage?" I asked in a cross voice.

"Because I always put the recycling out for you early Thursday morning when I stay over, and the bin is in the garage."

"Well." This was all true, and terribly endearing on his part. I made a humph sound, attempting to sound indignant, but it came out phlegmy, like I was clearing my throat.

"Lana? Erica? Did you get that? No more investigating. I'm serious. I'm trying to conduct a homicide investigation here, and the two of you are running around the island trying to collect clues."

"We wouldn't investigate if Erica wasn't a suspect. And we believe that Doug and probably Mickey are key to both Gus's murder *and* Julian's poisoning. Doug lied to us last night. He said he wasn't at Perkatory when Julian was poisoned, but he was. I remember him. I talked to him. He's heckin' sketchy."

Erica grunted a third time while I scooped peanut butter out of the jar and globbed it onto the bread. The smell made me queasy, and my stomach felt so unpleasant that I didn't even want coffee. That's how I knew I was severely hungover, and I vowed never to drink again.

"Don't you think I know that, Lana?"

I set the plate with the English muffin in front of Noah. He murmured a thanks.

"So does that mean Erica's off the hook?" I tried to fix a stern gaze on Noah, but one of my eyes watered uncontrollably. Lovely.

Noah angled his body against the counter and sighed. "Officially, no. Unofficially, yes. At least for the Gus investigation." He ate one half of the muffin in two bites.

Erica's nostrils twitched. I could tell she was refraining from defending herself, or maybe she was also so hungover that she was unable to utter one of her trademark snappy comebacks.

"Okay, well, that's definitely something." I cast a wan smile in her direction. "I promise we won't get into trouble and that we'll stop all sleuthing activities. There. Are you happy?"

I followed up with a weak squeeze of his bicep, which was formidable under his long-sleeved, button-down white shirt. On most days he didn't wear a police uniform, opting instead for a professional look with a shirt and tie. I adored his fashion choices.

He turned to kiss my forehead. "Reasonably happy. I'll text you later. Gotta run, cupcake. Erica, have a good one."

Erica gave a weak wave from where she was slumped at the table. We watched as Noah strode out and Stanley tottered in.

"God, I love when he looks like that."

Erica rolled her eyes. "Too sweet. Too early. Please stop objectifying your hot boyfriend."

"I was talking about Stanley," I protested. "I love when he looks all sleepy like that."

Stanley yawned and did a downward dog yoga pose, stretching his paws in front of him and hiking his back half into the air.

"Oh yeah, you're right. He's the cutest." Erica giggled, a throaty, raspy noise that devolved into a coughing fit. "Anyway, are we really going to listen to Noah and stop sleuthing? What are you doing today?"

"I plan on taking a couple of aspirin and returning to bed. But first"—I reached for my phone—"I'm going to call Mike to see if he's heard anything and to tell him what we found out. I might not be able to sleuth or write a news story, but I can be a tipster."

The call rang and rang. *Come on, Mike.* Finally, it went to voicemail.

"Hey, it's Lana. I've got a lot to tell you about Gus's death. So many tips—too many to list here on voicemail. Call me back ASAP, okay? Okay. Later, gator."

I tapped the phone's screen to end the call. It occurred to me that since leaving journalism, I was on the verge of becoming one of those ex-reporters who was hounding the local paper with information. As someone who used to break important stories, that didn't sit well with me.

For the first time in months, I felt like a loser. I'd given up on journalism. Or it had given up on me.

Perhaps this was my hangover talking. I yawned. "I'm headed back to bed."

"Me too," Erica mumbled.

I scooped up Stanley and slogged my way back to the bedroom.

*   *   *

I woke hours later, at one in the afternoon. Miraculously, my hangover was gone, and I felt excellent. Sitting up, I stretched and scratched Stanley on the head. He was still in bed, chewing on his favorite de-stuffed bunny.

"Maybe we can salvage this day, little dude. How about we go to the park?"

He cocked his golden head and stared, rapt, with his button-like, espresso-colored eyes. He wasn't familiar with many words, but he knew that one; the island's dog park was one of his favorite places.

I quickly showered, donned my cutest Florida winter outfit—jeans, chunky oatmeal-colored sweater, fake Ugg boots—and went into the kitchen to make a quick espresso.

A horrible realization washed over me: I had no coffee.

"Crap. I'll have to go to Perkatory for a cup," I muttered to myself. In the meantime, I drank a glass of water, telling myself I needed both more self-care and hydration.

The house was oddly quiet, and I wondered if Erica was still out cold. I rapped softly on her bedroom door, figuring she'd want to come to Perkatory with me. No answer.

A quick check of my phone revealed no message from her. Noah hadn't messaged either. Dad had, though.

I know it's your day off. Why don't you meet me at two for the monkey protest? We're starting at City Hall and heading through Main Street to the cop shop.

I bunched my lips into a pucker at the thought and texted him back: *We'll see. I just woke up, headed to Perkatory now. I also promised Stanley a visit to the dog park.*

Okay, munchkin. You can bring Stanley to the protest, and we can get some shots for his Instagram channel. Dad included a monkey emoji, which was impressive since he'd only recently grasped the basics of texting. I let out a sigh because I'd forgotten all about Stanley's Insta channel.

I'll think about it. Love you.

PTTP, he responded.

I stared at his text for several long seconds, trying to decipher the acronym. Primates That Teach Peace? Professional Theatrical Thundering Protesters? Plodding Toward The Primates?

I give up, I texted. *What's that mean?*

Power to the Primates! He included a sloth emoji, which further confused me.

"Okay, whatever, Dad," I muttered, glancing over at Stanley, who was standing by the door, wagging his tail. "Buddy, I'm going to grab a coffee first. You know I shouldn't bring you to the café. The town's cracking down on animals in stores. I'll be back in a flash."

He whimpered, and I knelt to kiss him. "Be back soon, okay?"

For a change of pace, I stuck my earbuds in so I could listen to music on the short walk. Noah had made me a playlist of Cuban salsa, but despite its happy, infectious rhythm combined with the crisp winter air, my mind drifted to darker things.

Namely, Gus and Julian. Something didn't sit right with me about either case, and I was still convinced that Mickey and Doug had something to do with both. I had to put my faith in Noah that he was going to arrest someone soon.

As I walked, I tapped out a text to Erica. *Hey, I'm headed to Perkatory. Want to meet me there for coffee?*

She hadn't answered by the time I arrived at the café, and I immediately forgot about her because one of my baristas—Barbara, the local artist who was about Dad's age—greeted me with a hug.

"Why so cheerful?" I said with a grin, taking out my earbuds.

"No reason. I'm always happier in cooler weather."

"I hear you on that." I explained that I'd come in because I was out of coffee.

"The horror. Let me make you something. In the mood for hot or cold?"

I felt particularly cozy in my sweater, and my cheeks felt an unusual sting from the cool breeze. "Definitely hot."

Barbara knew my flavor preferences, and a few minutes later she handed me a perfect flat white with a pretty leaf design in the foam atop the drink.

"Stunning. I'm going to sit by the window and check my emails. Anything going on today?" As I made my way to the seat, I scanned the room for Doug but didn't see him. A twinge of awareness went through me. Had he been arrested?

Barbara followed me, her long silver-blonde ponytail swaying from side to side. "It's been smooth as butter today. Joey called, looking for Erica. He thought she was working today. He sounded weird."

"Weird how? Joey always sounds weird."

"Like frenzied. I don't know." She shrugged. "Let me get back to the counter. I don't want Heidi to handle all those customers."

A line had formed at the counter, and I noted that it was almost the entire staff of the nearby insurance office. They must be having some sort of meeting.

I turned back to my coffee, wondering about Joey. And Erica. Where was she, if not with him? I sipped my creamy, full-bodied espresso for a while, staring out the window at the busy downtown of Devil's Beach.

My gaze snagged on a familiar-looking, tall guy with a shock of salt-and-pepper hair. He was crossing the street, coming from the beach, but not using the sidewalk.

It was Mickey Dotson.

I licked my lips. He was only about thirty feet from where I sat. This was too good a chance to pass up.

Yes, I'd told Noah I wouldn't investigate. But running into a fellow citizen and having a friendly chat on a Main Street sidewalk didn't count as "investigating," did it?

I snatched my coffee and slid off the stool, rushing over to Barbara. "This is delicious, but can you hold it for a second? I have to go chat with someone outside."

She accepted the cup with a puzzled look and a nod, and I tore out of Perkatory and headed across Main Street at full speed.

Mickey was passing by the bookstore now, swaggering in his cowboy boots like he was headed for a shootout at the O.K. Corral. I called his name, breathless.

He turned with an expectant look that crumpled into a frown when he saw it was me.

"Wait! I need to talk to you." I huffed to a stop.

"If it's about sponsoring this year's barista competition, I can't tell you yet. I know you're on the welcoming committee." He went to turn as if he was about to walk away, and I reached for his arm.

"No, this has nothing to do with that."

He glared at my hand on his arm, and I yanked it away.

"Sorry." I paused to inhale. "This is about Gus. He's my neighbor, a fact you probably know. *Was* my neighbor."

His mouth worked into a bitter pout. "Can't talk out here. Come with me."

He whirled and stalked down the street so fast that I had to scurry to keep up. Why didn't he want to discuss this in public? What did he have to hide? And where was he taking me?

It didn't take long to find the answer. We reached his coffee shop, Island Brewnette, in three blocks. He pulled open the glass door.

"After you."

Entering was like crossing into enemy territory. The entire place was done up in minimalist black and white, and a loud electronic beat wafted through the air. It was the kind of music Dad liked.

Still, I noted that there weren't as many customers here now as there had been in Perkatory. That left me with no small amount of satisfaction, and I smiled, tight-lipped, at Mickey.

"Would you like a cup?" he asked.

"Sure, I'll try an espresso." Since he wasn't being nasty, I figured it was my cue to be gracious as well. Mickey and I—and Mickey's daughter and I—had a long history of ill will. Starting with his daughter's bullying me back in high school.

Mickey approached one of his baristas and asked for two espressos, then returned to me and gestured to a secluded table in the back corner.

I sat, and Mickey returned to the counter, hovering over his barista while he made coffee. He obviously made the barista nervous with the way he licked his lips repeatedly, like Stanley did when faced with a bigger dog in the park.

Jeez, was I like that with my staff? I needed to check my manners with them.

A minute later, Mickey returned with the two espressos. He set one down in front of me, planted the second on his side, then extracted a cell phone from his back pocket and added that to the table.

"Did you want sugar?" He asked this in a flat, bored tone that indicated he'd prefer to be anywhere but here with me.

I shook my head.

He plunked across from me and stirred his espresso with a small spoon. I did the same, noting that the crema on this espresso looked thin and weak. Score another point for Perkatory.

"Why do you want to talk about Gus? Are you doing an article?"

I couldn't read his tone, mostly because I expected him to be nasty. But he wasn't.

"No. I'm curious for my own reasons."

"Because he was your next-door neighbor or because Erica's a suspect?"

"How did you know that?"

He lifted a shoulder. "Rumor around town."

I calmly sipped from the cup, wondering if he'd helped spread that rumor. "She didn't do it."

"I know. That's what I told Noah."

I almost choked on my coffee. "You? Defended one of my baristas? I would've thought you'd have made something up to implicate her further."

Mickey shifted uncomfortably in the hard, black plastic chairs. "Is it that difficult to believe, Lana? It's not like someone asked me who serves the best coffee on Devil's Beach. If I'd been under oath for that, I couldn't tell a lie. As you can taste."

He gestured toward my cup, which made me snort. "Come on. The crema is watery. And let's get it all out on the table. You've always disliked my family; your daughter has always disliked me; and Erica and I beat the two of you in the barista championship last year. We'll do it again this year too. And to be honest, I wouldn't put it past you to pin a murder and an attempted murder on Erica. You're that kinda guy."

His already long face dropped. "Real talk here. You actually think I killed Mickey?"

I rubbed my lips together, thinking of his experience as a landscaper. Suddenly the evidence against him seemed thin, although his lawsuit against Gus, and Gus's restraining order, sure seemed to point in his direction.

"Where were you the day he died?" I tried, and probably failed, to keep the accusatory tone out of my voice.

Chapter Twenty-Four

With a smirk, Mickey plucked his phone off the table and began to scroll. After a second, he flashed the phone at eye level so I could see the screen.

I leaned forward and squinted. The picture was of a woman and a baby in what was obviously a hospital. I almost visibly winced but caught myself. There, on the screen, was my nemesis. "Paige? She had her baby?"

"That's where I was the weekend Gus was murdered. Up in Tampa, celebrating the birth of my first grandchild." His eyes softened.

He swiped left to another photo of the newborn in his daughter's arms, then to a picture of him beaming and holding the baby. My heart fractured because I knew the father of the child—it was my murdered barista, Fab. That poor child. Poor Paige.

"What an adorable little baby," I cooed, then sat back. "Congratulations on becoming a grandpa. How's Paige?"

"Doing quite well. She and the baby were out within two days. They're settling in at Paige's mother's house in Tampa." He set the phone down. "So that's my alibi."

Although I'd already finished my espresso, I pretended to take one final sip because I wasn't sure what to say. Mickey's revelation had left me stumped—being in a hospital while his daughter gave birth, and having photos of that event, sure was an excellent and solid alibi.

"I'm sorry. I'd heard you owned a landscaping business, and because Gus died from an exploding leaf blower, I thought I'd put two and two together. My apologies. I guess it's time I stop thinking the worst of you."

He pondered my words for a few seconds and nodded. "Same goes for me. I have a rough exterior, but really I'm not a son of a gun."

I still wasn't so sure of that, but considering all he'd been through recently with Paige, her pregnancy, and the death of the father of her child, I smiled sympathetically. "Who do you think killed Gus?"

He nodded grimly. "The police thought I did at first. But I owned that landscaping business twenty-five years ago, and we didn't even have leaf blowers back then. I wouldn't know how to tamper with one if I tried. But honestly, Gus was a piece of work—a horrible person—and I wish I'd never bought that tourist ship from him. Wish I'd run the other way."

"Can you tell me more about what happened with him? I'm incredibly curious."

He stared at me warily. "You sure you're not writing an article?"

"I wish I were, but no. Mike Heller at the *Beacon* thinks I'm too close to the case and Noah—well, he's not in favor of me poking around on this one."

"Can't say I blame him. Gus was involved in some wild stuff."

"Really? What do you know?" In the span of a few minutes,

I no longer disliked Mickey and wanted to pump him for all the information I could. My mind briefly drifted to Noah. Did this count as sleuthing?

Mickey opened his mouth, and I forgot all about Noah. "Gus purchased that business about five years ago, when he lived over in Fort Lauderdale. He'd come over every few months to check on things, had a great manager who lived here on the island—I knew the manager from the local Chamber of Commerce. I got to know Gus when he and his wife came into the shop. When he moved here and said he was interested in selling the ship, I gathered a couple of guys to pool our money for an investment. I figured that it would be easy profit. Who doesn't like pirate tourist cruises?"

A memory of those Florida Man shots I'd done on the boat last night came to mind. My stomach sure didn't like them. But I didn't say that aloud, only nodded. "It does seem to be a popular tourist attraction. I went last night and it was packed."

His eyes glittered. "That's why I wanted to buy it. And that's what Gus's financials showed when we were pulling together our business plan and getting the bank loan. Everything went through, and we took possession of the ship, and that's when we found out that Gus had cooked the books. He vastly understated how much he spent on alcohol—and on other expenses. We were underwater from our first sailing, so to speak. We're in the red and not sure if we can get out. The three of us stand to lose a considerable amount of money, several hundred thousand dollars." Mickey sighed miserably.

"Oh, dear. So that's why you sued him."

He nodded. "And you know what that jackwagon did? He got a restraining order against us."

"Us? Meaning, you and . . .?" I tried to play dumb.

"Me and my partner, Doug Yates."

"I heard you had a third co-owner. Joey Rizzo."

"How do you know that?"

"Erica's dating his nephew. Who's also named Joey."

Mickey nodded. "Joey's a silent partner. A financial investor. It's mostly Doug and me running the show."

"So why did Gus say you and Doug were stalking him?"

"Exactly what your boyfriend asked me. Maybe you should be a cop, you know?"

Or a journalist. I shot him a little smile.

"I haven't seen Gus since he signed the paperwork. He stopped coming in here the minute he sold the business. Even his wife stopped coming in, but I figured that was because she was distancing herself from anyone acquainted with him. Can't blame her for that. But Doug . . ." He sighed and shook his head. "He was the one who triggered that restraining order."

"How? What did Doug do?"

"He took the whole situation much harder than I did. I've owned businesses before and have bought some real clunkers. Sometimes you gotta press through, spend the money, and try to make it work. Sometimes you take the loss. Doug doesn't see it that way, and he became obsessed with Gus. He took it real personal."

Oh, now this was getting interesting. I scooted my chair closer to the table, so the edge was pressing into my midsection. "Whoa. Really?"

"At first it was some strongly worded emails, which I approved of. Then he started calling Gus a lot. Several times a day. Texting. That's when Gus began ignoring him, and Doug and I retained a lawyer. I thought that would be the end of it, but Doug continued trying to engage with Gus, tried to get a rise out of him. When he found out that Gus and his wife had split, he took one of Honey's roller-skating classes and asked her out on a date. Creepy stuff like that."

I grimaced. "Is that when Gus got the restraining order?"

He shook his head. "Doug mailed him some inappropriate things. Like a voodoo doll. Stupid, childish stuff. Gus loved his lawn—you know that—and in the middle of the night, Doug went and dug up a patch of it, to annoy Gus."

"When was that?" And where had I been when all this clandestine lawn activity was going down?

Mickey scratched his chin. "Two months ago? I think it was right around the time that Doug ran into Gus at the post office, and they nearly had a fist fight. The restraining order came right after that. I thought it was a bit unfair to include me."

"Why did it include you? Judges are usually pretty strict about those."

"Well, I might have helped Doug with the lawn prank. But that was the only thing, I swear. And only because I thought it was hilarious." He held up his right hand.

"But as you point out, those were juvenile pranks. How does that translate into Doug tampering with a leaf blower to kill Gus?"

"I don't think Doug intended to kill him. I think it was likely another prank, but this one went wrong. Doug talked to me about how he'd like to hurt Gus, how he'd like to give him a permanent reminder of what he did to us."

It still seemed tenuous, but plausible, I supposed. Certainly I'd heard of weirder motivations for crime in Florida. "When was the last time you talked to Doug? Where was he the day Gus died?"

Mickey shifted his head back and forth. "I talked with him the Thursday before Gus was killed. Doug was ranting and raving about how Gus took his new girlfriend, the librarian, out to an expensive dinner. I told him I didn't care, and he hung up on me. Then I left for Tampa on that Friday and didn't return until yesterday. I only heard about Gus's death from reading the paper and talking to my manager here." He gestured to a lanky barista guy wiping down the counter.

"You told all this to Noah?"

"I hesitated because I didn't want to accuse my business partner of a crime. But I couldn't overlook his behavior. Otherwise, I'd be complacent. Or worse."

"A coconspirator."

He nodded grimly, and I stared into my cup while letting all this information sink in. All signs were pointing to Doug, and I hoped an arrest was imminent.

"It's so weird . . . Doug is one of my best customers," I said softly. "Hey. That reminds me. Why does Doug come to my shop instead of yours? He's your business partner."

Mickey rolled his eyes. "That used to annoy the crap out of me."

"Did you ever ask him?"

"Doug said you had better coffee." His face hardened into a grimace.

Do not smirk triumphantly. Do not smirk. Do not . . .

"Well, everyone has their preferences."

"I guess so," he grumbled. "So did that answer your question? I didn't kill Gus."

"It did. Thank you for being so forthcoming. And congratulations on your grandbaby. Please tell Paige I said hello and congrats." I thought about asking when she'd be back on Devil's Beach, but figured that might be a sensitive topic, considering she had a somewhat rocky relationship with her father, according to what I'd heard around town.

I rose, and so did Mickey. "I'll see you around. Oh, I wanted to ask about something else, something I heard about Perkatory," he said.

"What's that?" I moved around the table, and Mickey and I began to walk toward the door together. A chill went through me. Had he heard about Julian's poisoning?

"Did your barista, Erica, really turn Doug down? He asked her on a date."

I stopped in the middle of the café. *"What?"*

"Yeah, he's been enamored with her for months now. That's the other reason he goes to your shop every day. He's in love with her."

"He is?" I gaped at Mickey, who nodded.

"A couple of weeks ago he got up the courage to ask her out. But then she said no."

Holy Pup-Peroni. Could this be the reason he'd tried to pin Julian's poisoning on her? I needed to talk to her about this right away. "She has a boyfriend. Joey. So I'm sure she politely told Doug no."

"Doug doesn't like that word," Mickey said. "I'd tell Erica to watch out. Or hope that Doug's arrested for Julian's death."

I swallowed hard and thanked him again as I power-walked out of the café. Once outside, I took a few steps down Main Street, then stopped to dig out my phone.

I need to talk to you now, I texted Erica. *Where are you? I got some really interesting information about Doug.*

As I stared at my phone, waiting for a response, I heard someone call my name. It sounded like it was filtered through a bullhorn.

I looked around. There, in the middle of the street, was a crowd of people, many of whom were wearing monkey costumes. A lot of them carried signs such as "Save the Primates," "Relocate Tourists, Not Wild Animals," and—my personal favorite—"Stay Out of Our Monkey Business."

People on the beach side of Main Street and on the business side stopped to stare at the procession, which was blocking traffic.

Horns honked angrily. A few people appeared to be taking photos and video with their phones. Several people laughed and pointed, and one man near me said, "Stupid animal rights activists. Who cares about wild monkeys anyway?"

I was going to chide him, but the screech of bullhorn feedback bounced off the brick walls of the buildings on Main Street.

"Is this thing on? Lana Lewis, come join us to help the primates. The primates need you, Lana! Walk with our rally to the police station to tell officials to keep our monkeys on Devil's Beach. I see you, munchkin."

I gaped in disbelief and deep embarrassment.

There, at the front of the procession was my father. He was dressed in a black-furred gorilla costume, with only his face showing, and pointing a bullhorn in my direction.

Chapter
Twenty-Five

Throughout the course of my life, my father had done many things to embarrass me. Like showing up to a parent–teacher conference in grade school, looking like an extra in Miami Vice (those were the days of pastel suits, woven huaraches, and no socks). Like chaperoning homecoming and disco dancing with the soccer team coach while the entire high school looked on and laughed.

More recently, he'd smudged Perkatory last month with sage, practically smoking out the customers drinking lattes while he waved the herb stick in the corners of the café, claiming that the ritual had to be done on the afternoon of the winter solstice.

I'd rolled with all of the above with laughter and only a hint of embarrassment. Usually I could deal with Dad's wackiness. But today—with the bullhorn and furry suit on Main Street—was a whole other level of mortifying.

For a few seconds, I tried to pretend that I hadn't heard him, and stuck my face in my phone. But Dad was relentless and called my name twice more.

A woman standing nearby sidled up to me and elbowed my arm. "I think that crazy guy in the ape suit is talking to you. He's pointing right at you."

With a heavy sigh, I marched up to him. By now the protest was blocking an intersection, much to the ire of a few motorists. Horns blared angrily, but the protesters either ignored the drivers or waved signs.

"Hi, munchkin," Dad said through the bullhorn as I approached.

I pointed in his direction. "Put down the megaphone, please."

Fortunately, he did, and I fell into step with the marchers, shooting a frosty glance at a nearby protester wearing what looked like a lemur suit, so he would step aside and allow me to walk next to Dad.

His gorilla costume smelled vaguely like mothballs and marijuana, and I wrinkled my nose as I glanced at the outfit. It looked a little threadbare and worn, especially under the arms.

"What?" Dad asked.

"You smell funky. Or maybe it's the fur on that costume. It also looks a little matted."

"I got this from a buddy of mine, who used to protest anti-union corporations. This gorilla suit's gotten a lot of use over the years. You know Stew?"

We shuffled along, heading down the street toward Noah's workplace. Dad clicked on the megaphone and shouted something about saving the primates.

I groaned in frustration. "No. I don't know Stew. I don't have time for this now."

"Are you going to march with us the three blocks to the cop shop?"

I imagined Noah's expression, peeking out the police station window and seeing me leading three dozen people in primate outfits toward his office. "No, definitely not. I'm trying to find Erica. I found out some important and possibly crucial information about Gus and Doug Rogers Yates. Or whatever his name is—I'm not even certain right now. Have you heard from her?"

He shook his head, which made the fur on his suit shimmy. "Maybe she's at the marina. She talked about checking on her sailboat repairs this week."

I snapped my fingers. "Ooh, good idea. I'm going to head over there now. Uh, I'd kiss you goodbye, but not in that suit, okay? It's a little smelly."

"No worries, Lana. Love you." He raised the megaphone. "I say monkeys, you say matter! Monkeys!"

"Matter," yelled the crowd.

I took this as my cue to sprint out of the crowd and down the street, deciding to power-walk back home to grab my car and check to see if Erica was home. Perhaps her phone wasn't working.

The house was empty save for Stanley, so I let him out to do his business in the backyard while I texted Erica again. Why wasn't she responding to me?

Are you okay? Where are you?

While Stanley zoomed around the backyard, I made an espresso and ate two Oreos. I stuffed a third into my mouth and dialed Perkatory. Barbara answered.

"Hey, have you seen or heard from Erica yet?" I plucked a fourth cookie out of the sleeve.

"No, but Lana, did you hear the news about your dad?"

Oh goodness, the entire island knew about his protest. "Yeah, I saw him about a half hour ago at the primate protest."

"Well, apparently he's at the police station and is doing a sit-in, and he might get arrested."

I lost my grip on the cookie, and it fell to the counter and cracked in two. "What?"

"Yeah, someone came in and let us know. You might want to go down there, seeing as you're a calming influence for both your dad and Noah."

I gulped in a steadying breath. "Dad's been at tons of protests, and he knows how to handle himself. I have to find Erica. If you see her, let her know I urgently need to talk with her, okay?"

"Sure thing, Lana."

I thanked her and hung up. Dad didn't need me running interference with Noah. If he was actually arrested—which I doubted Noah would do—he'd call me, I'd post bail, and then collect him from jail. We'd set these ground rules years ago, when he attended protests in Miami about climate change.

From the back door, I called Stanley inside while shaking a bag of doggie beef sticks. While I was offering him one, my phone dinged.

I lunged for the cell. It was Erica.

H

That's all the text said. *H.* I scowled at the screen, stumped. Was that a typo? A cryptic message? Fat thumbs?

Is this some new code I'm supposed to decipher? I texted back. *Or was that a butt text?*

I couldn't tear my eyes from the phone as I waited for a response. Five minutes passed, and I paced the living room. Still no text.

Call me ASAP, I messaged to Erica, then patted Stanley on the head and flew out the door.

* * *

My first stop was the Devil's Beach Marina, where Erica lived on her sailboat.

It was also the location where her boat was in dry dock, undergoing repairs to the fiberglass hull. I figured that perhaps the work was finished and the boat was back in its slip, and she was polishing the teak deck—something she did when she felt stressed or anxious.

The marina was different from the one closer to downtown, where the *Royal Conquest* was berthed and where all of the water-based tourist attractions were. While that marina was something out of a picture postcard, this was more hardscrabble, home to a few dozen live-aboard sailors. Some, like Erica, were young people looking for a cheaper place to live. Others were sketchier, crusty individuals who had sailed the Florida Straits during legal and not-so-legal voyages.

This wasn't the kind of place to ask a lot of questions, but I didn't care.

I parked and walked over to where her boat normally was docked. It was empty. Then I made my way to the boat repair berth and asked the guy behind the counter if Erica's boat was finished, or if he'd seen her.

It wasn't, and he hadn't. The guy shook his head but didn't offer more information, no matter how much I pressed him. With a sigh, I left the boat repair business.

I checked my phone five more times while walking back to my car. There was only one explanation for Erica's absence, and it came in the form of a redheaded, black-rimmed-glasses-wearing, hipster restaurant owner named Joey Rizzo.

Joey's house was on the other side of the island, near the bridge to the mainland. While Devil's Beach wasn't that big, I figured I'd stop somewhere closer first. Joey owned the Square Grouper, a popular restaurant that had been started years ago by his mobster father.

I knew that sometimes Erica went there to have a drink and hang out with Joey, who often tended bar, like his father had when he started the restaurant.

Rumor had it that his dad had used the money he'd made in the mafia up in New York to open the eatery, but since it was Devil's Beach, Florida, no one asked many questions, mostly because since the moment the doors had opened, the restaurant had served the best grouper sandwich on the Gulf Coast.

The Square Grouper was near downtown, and I pulled into the parking lot. Since it was three PM, there were only a few cars there in the lull between lunch and dinner. I barged into the restaurant, slightly breathless.

Since there was no one at the hostess station, I went to the bar. Joey was there, chatting with two customers drinking beer.

"Lana, hey!" He came around the bar and we hugged. "We were just talking about your dad. Heard he has a sit-in happening at the police station. Has he been arrested yet?"

I pressed the heels of my hands to my forehead. "Not sure. I have more important matters to deal with. Listen, have you heard from Erica today?"

He shook his head. "She told me she was going to drop by today, but I haven't seen her. She texted me a few hours ago and said she had something important to take care of first. I was kinda disappointed, since I've only seen her once since I got back from Vegas."

"Did she say what was so important?"

"Lemme see . . ." he reached into his back pocket and took out his phone, and then burst into laughter. "Ah, here we go. She said she was going to talk with an unsalted walnut. Isn't that hilarious? She's so brilliant with her descriptions, and that's why I'm wild about her. An unsalted walnut. What is that even?"

Unsalted walnut was one of Erica's unique phrases. She used it to describe people who were dry and humorless, and occasionally to refer to people who were sour and nasty.

Joey was still chuckling when he looked up from his cell, but I wasn't.

"Oh no," I whispered. Had she gone to talk with Doug by herself?

"What? What's wrong?"

"Erica. I think she's going to confront someone that she shouldn't."

As I was about to show him the cryptic text I'd received from her, my phone rang. I pulled it out of my bag, hopeful that it was her. Instead, it was a number I didn't recognize.

I answered on the second ring.

"Lana?" the male voice said.

"That's me?"

"Hey, its Shawn. Your Jet Ski friend!"

My shoulders sagged, and I couldn't hide the disappointment in my tone. "Oh, hey."

He didn't seem to notice, because his voice had an out-of-breath quality. "I felt like I had to call you because something really weird happened. I was at my kiosk, selling paddleboard tours, and I saw your friend Erica near the pirate ship. You know, the one we were talking about the other day, the *Royal Conquest?*"

I inhaled and held my breath. "Oh? When?"

"Around a half hour ago. I tried calling Perkatory to tell you, but you weren't there, and I finally convinced them to give me your cell. And here's the strange part. This guy kind of pulled her down the dock, toward the boat. Like forcefully almost? I don't know. It felt odd, you know? But not enough to call the cops. The two of them went onto the ship. I'm not sure if I'm using my intuition here, but I always go with my gut and share out of a spirit of honesty . . ." I stopped listening because Shawn was talking about being his authentic self and because my heart was pounding against my ribcage.

"Shawn, I'll be right there, okay?" I hung up and looked at Joey, who was blinking in confusion. "We need to go rescue Erica. Now."

Chapter
Twenty-Six

I t took us all of ten minutes to get to the island's other marina, which was close to downtown and Perkatory. We drove in Joey's car, so I could try to reach Noah.

He wasn't answering. A strangled groan slipped out of my mouth. "He's probably arresting my father."

Of all the times to have a raucous monkey protest!

Trying not to panic, I texted Noah instead, telling him that Erica had likely sought out Doug, for reasons I couldn't fathom, and that she wasn't answering calls or messages. I also included the details about the cryptic text and, most importantly, the scene Shawn had recounted, about Doug possibly pulling Erica onto the boat. When I read over my message before sending, I erased the word *possibly* and sighed.

"What?" Joey asked while trying, and failing, to stay at the speed limit as he drove toward downtown.

"What if we're overreacting? What if it wasn't Erica Doug was pulling into the boat? What if Shawn was mistaken?"

"Erica's pretty well known around town. And she kind of stands out."

"True, true," I muttered. Erica, in her tropical goth clothing of black shorts, black T-shirt, and black boots (sometimes black flip-flops) was unique on Devil's Beach, where people tended to wear bright colors and casual—even wrinkled—clothing.

"If something's happened to her, I swear to God . . ." Joey slammed his hand on the steering wheel. "We had a fight before I went to Vegas, and I keep kicking myself for being such a jerk. I really care about Erica. I've never felt this way about anyone."

His voice cracked, and so did my heart. I'd gone to high school with Joey, and we'd both been band geeks, which meant we'd had a casual friendship for decades. His concern for Erica was palpable, and it mirrored my own.

"I'm sure she's okay. Erica's tough. She can handle herself." Part of me said those words to soothe not only Joey but myself. I was trying to tamp down my free-floating anxiety, which had spiked my heartbeat and caused my feet to sweat uncomfortably in my furry boots.

Soon we were downtown, and I directed Joey to Perkatory so we could park in my spot in the alley behind the café. The spaces near the downtown marina were usually full, and I figured we could sprint the block and a half. Which we did. On our way, we heard sirens and saw two cop cars rip past us, going in the direction of the police station.

I sent a silent prayer to the universe. *Please don't let those sirens be for Dad. Please don't let Dad make too much trouble at his protest.*

I simply couldn't handle bailing Dad out of jail and extricating Erica from . . . whatever it is she'd gotten herself into.

Shawn was in his thatched-roof, tiki hut–like kiosk, where he rented canoes, kayaks, paddleboards, and Jet Skis.

"Where did you last see Erica?" I said, without even a hello.

"Over there, near the walkway to the pirate ship." Shawn gestured to my right, to the dock where Erica and I had been aboard the pirate ship and then disembarked the other night.

Except today the dock was empty, and the ship wasn't in its slip at the end of the dock.

"Where is she?" Joey cried with more than a hint of panic in his voice.

"Who's this dude?" Shawn asked me.

"Erica's boyfriend." I made a quick introduction, as I scanned the blue water beyond the marina. "Holy crap. Is that the pirate ship?"

I pointed in the distance at the black-hulled, three-masted ship. We all squinted, shielding our eyes from the bright sun in the azure sky.

"Where's he taking her?" Joey yelled, his hands pulling at his spiky red hair.

"I've gotta try Noah again." I dialed his number, but the call immediately went to voicemail. I left a rambling, disjointed message, telling him where I was and that I'd wait for him at the dock.

"Oh—and we weren't sleuthing. Well, I wasn't. I don't know what Erica was doing," I added to Noah's voicemail, then hung up. For good measure, I also dialed 911 and got Bernadette.

"You think your friend's been kidnapped?" she asked skeptically. "Noah's in a meeting in the back."

"Please go into the meeting and tell Noah to contact me ASAP. Or send someone down to the marina. Thanks, Bern."

"I'll see what I can do," she grumbled before I hung up. That didn't leave me with a promising, hopeful feeling.

"So what are we going to do? Wait for the cops?" Shawn asked.

"Call the Coast Guard? The Fish and Wildlife officials? Don't they have a boat?" I racked my reporter's brain, thinking of the authorities who had jurisdiction in the Gulf of Mexico.

Joey stood with his hands on his hips. "We can't stand around and wait."

I threw my hands in the air. Shawn stepped toward us. "I've got a Jet Ski."

"Yes!" Joey clapped Shawn on the shoulder, and Shawn beamed with pride, as if he'd offered the wisest idea since the invention of the cappuccino.

"That one over there, the black one, can take two passengers."

Joey clapped his hands. "Let's do it. Can it take three?"

I was about to interrupt with a few obvious questions regarding safety but Shawn broke in with a question for Joey. "Do you know how to drive one, bro?"

"Sure do. I had one but sold it for a new PlayStation last year."

"Cool, cool. C'mon." Shawn gestured for us to follow him down a dock, where a sleek-looking personal watercraft was tied up.

Joey toe-heeled his shoes off and pointed at my furry boots. "I'd take those off if I were you."

"Lemme go grab some life jackets." Shawn ran up the dock toward the kiosk.

"You sure you know what you're doing?" I eyed Joey as he rolled up the pantlegs of his black jeans. His pale, freckled feet and legs almost glowed in the bright sun.

"Sure do. You know, you can stay here and wait for Noah. I can go alone. I'll try to keep my cell dry and send you my location when I get the ship in sight. I promise I won't do anything stupid."

A thousand questions ran through my mind. Would Joey on a Jet Ski be able to catch up with the ship? Would the ship accelerate and leave Joey in its wake? What if those cannons on the ship were real?

And, most importantly, what was Doug doing to Erica?

A sick, helpless feeling settled in my stomach like a lump of undissolved sugar. I thought of my high school friend Gisela, and how I hadn't been able to do anything to save her from an unknown fate—and how that powerless feeling had left me with guilt for years.

"No, I'll go with you," I said quickly, pulling off one furry boot, then the other.

"Can you swim?" There was a hint of doubt in Joey's tone.

"Of course." I wasn't a bad swimmer, but I did prefer a pool. And those swim-up pool bars. I enjoyed those a lot. "I came in third in my age group in a swim meet on North Beach once."

Joey scrunched up his face, as if he were trying to recall that event. "When was that?"

"Seventh grade."

By now, Shawn was back with the red life jackets, and I slipped it on over my bulky sweater. I handed him my purse and phone, wondering if I looked like a tomato with arms. Joey looked far sleeker, like he was wearing a hipster vest.

"If Erica or Noah calls, pick up. Also monitor the texts."

Shawn nodded, then gave Joey a few quick instructions on how to operate the machine. From the lightly confused look on Joey's face, I doubted whether he had the Jet Ski experience that he claimed he did, but whatever.

With the cool air tickling my ankles, I padded down the dock in my bare feet after Joey and Shawn. With the grace of a Cirque du Soleil performer, Joey slid his slim frame onto the watercraft, which was tied up to the dock. Still, it bobbled softly in the water.

"Okay, now you, Lana." Shawn pointed at the black seat behind Joey. The entire contraption looked futuristic, angular and downright dangerous. A little like a floating motorcycle.

I hesitated, long enough for Joey to ask, "Have you ever been on one of these?"

"Absolutely, several times." It was the truth. I'd been on a few in high school and once in the Bahamas when my ex-husband and I were on our honeymoon. My ex had thought it would be fun to rent one and pretend we were extras in *Baywatch*. After zipping through the water, he'd taken a hard left, and I'd ended up in the warm, electric-blue water.

Probably I should've taken that as an omen for our marriage.

"I love Jet Skis." I tried to sound enthusiastic, but I was lying like Stanley after a rotisserie chicken binge.

"Well, climb aboard," Shawn said heartily, holding onto the handlebar of the vessel to steady it.

Gingerly, I held onto Joey's shoulder while straddling the watercraft. Somehow I made it aboard without falling into the water, and I wrapped my arms around Joey's thin frame.

Shawn explained how to turn on the Jet Ski. "And this is an emergency engine cutoff on a lanyard. Put this around your wrist."

He handed Joey an orange wristband, which attached to the engine switch via a fob. "So if I fall off, this will cut the engine?"

Shawn nodded, and pointed out that there were whistles and tiny beacons attached to our life jackets. He opened a plastic case on a lanyard and asked for Joey's phone, then slid it into the case and the lanyard over Joey's head.

"That's your dry container. Only take it out if you really need to call for help."

"Gotcha. I think we're ready." Joey nestled the fob attached to his wrist into the starter, and the watercraft rumbled to life.

"Shouldn't we wear helmets?" I yelled.

"No time," Shawn yelled back. "Good luck!"

Shawn loosened the rope that tethered the Jet Ski to the dock.

"Er, Lana?' Joey turned his head.

"Yeah?" I was wrapped tightly around him, like a barnacle.

"You don't need to strangle me. We haven't even moved yet. Ease up, at least until we get out of the wake zone."

I let up on my grip and Joey twisted the right handlebar, propelling us forward.

"Oh my goodness," I yelped.

For a couple of minutes, we moved slowly through the water. It would have been a pleasant ride if it wasn't for the cool air and my tight jeans that were getting wet at the ankles.

Oh, and the fact that we were trying to locate my best friend, who had apparently been kidnapped aboard a fake pirate ship.

"Hang on," Joey yelled once we were a couple hundred feet from the dock. "I'm going to put the pedal to the metal."

I gripped his waist tightly from behind as he twisted the throttle, sending us across the water at seemingly top speed. My hair flew back, the skin on my cheeks rippled, and I let out a yell.

"It's okay—we're cool!" Joey screamed.

I was not cool. Truthfully, I was terrified. My teeth clacked together from a combination of the sharp wind and fear, and now my legs were soaked. That didn't feel so terrible, mostly because the water in the Gulf was warmer than the air.

Still, I briefly pondered the possibility of hypothermia as we hurtled across the light blue water. The pirate ship loomed in the distance. It didn't seem to be moving that fast, or possibly at all. But maybe that was my warped perception, considering that I had one eye closed, and the other was blurry from the saltwater spraying all around us.

As we got closer to the ship, logic suddenly struck. What were we going to do once we reached the ship? Overtake it like pirates? Scale up the hull and have a fistfight with Doug? Implore Erica to jump into the water, where we'd scoop her up and whisk her away?

"What are we doing?" I hollered to Joey. The wind whipped my hair everywhere, but I was too afraid to let go of Joey and push it back.

"I don't know," he yelled back over the roar of the engine.

Great.

After about ten minutes, we came about two football fields away from the ship, and Joey slowed the Jet Ski to a crawl. The tourist boat seemed a lot larger out here in the open water—especially compared to our tiny Jet Ski—and my tight chest labored to take in air.

"Okay, I've got a plan," Joey said. "I'm going to zip by the boat like we're tourists, then I'll pass it and we'll turn around for another look. Hopefully no one aboard will notice. Try not to stare too much. Once we get a decent look, we'll call Noah and Shawn with the coordinates and then follow the ship as long as we can, until authorities get here."

I was impressed with his line of thinking and gave him a squeeze around the midsection, which elicited an *oof.* "Excellent idea, dude!"

He revved the engine, but not as fast as before. We reached the ship and skimmed past. Oddly, it wasn't moving at all, as if it were anchored. Perhaps it was.

We didn't see anyone on deck, which made me wonder where Erica was. Also, who was piloting a ship that large? Was Doug an experienced captain? Or was someone else helping him?

The icy grasp of fear clutched at me, and I shivered. Poor Erica. We needed to put an end to this, now.

Joey zipped past the ship and continued a couple hundred yards beyond, then slowed. I winced as he made a wide turn, hoping I wouldn't topple into the water. Somehow we stayed afloat, though, and he maintained a slow speed as we headed closer to the ship.

It didn't seem safe to be this close to the ship; we were perhaps only five or six feet away. Joey slowed the Jet Ski so the engine sounded like a low purr.

"We're too close," I muttered.

"What?" he yelled.

We moved along the ship, past the fake skull and bones painted in white on the black hull. On one side there was a row of portholes. Perhaps one was the one I'd seen when I was in the office the other night.

As we approached one porthole window, I saw a flash of motion. "Wait, slow down." I patted Joey's chest to get his attention.

He did. We bobbed in the water, and I pointed up at the porthole.

"Erica!" I cried.

Her face, streaked with tears and mascara, was pressed into the round glass. She banged with her hand on the window, and Joey yelled her name.

"Shh," I said.

We floated for a moment next to the porthole as we all stared at each other. Without thinking, I stood up, my feet supported by the Jet Ski running board.

"Are you okay?" I mouthed, pointing at her and then at my other hand, making the okay gesture.

She shook her head.

"Hey, you," came a male voice. "Get away from my ship. Wait. Lana?"

We looked up toward the deck, almost directly above us. It was Doug. His hair was messy, and even from this angle, I could tell there was a large, angry scrape down his cheek.

"Let her go, Doug. Please! Let's talk over coffee." I figured I'd try to plead with him first.

He hollered something unintelligible and said Erica's name. That's when we saw the glint of a machete blade in his hand and I gasped, a jolt of pure terror washing through me.

"Nooo," I yelled.

"That's it. I'm getting on that ship to get Erica. I'll kill that guy!" Joey screamed, and gunned the Jet Ski. This sent me flying into the air, arms and legs splayed.

The last thing I saw before I fell backward into the water was the sight of another boat in the distance, one with flashing red and blue lights on its bow.

* * *

"Here. Drink this. It'll warm you up."

Noah thrust a Styrofoam cup into Erica's hand, then one in mine. An oversize orange thermos sat on a table, and an officer poured liquid into a cup for himself but didn't acknowledge us, even though Erica and I were sitting on a bench nearby.

Noah turned his back to us, barking into his cell phone.

"I've got four officers on a boat headed in with the suspect now. We're also getting a warrant to search his house, and the Fish and Wildlife agents are securing the ship for processing," he said in a stern tone.

Erica and I were in the back of the massive police boat, huddled together under a silver blanket that looked like a giant piece of tinfoil. Joey had been taken away in another police boat, and we hoped he wouldn't be arrested for interfering with an investigation. Heck, I was hoping the same thing for me.

I rested my head on Erica's shoulder, much warmer now that I'd ducked below deck to strip off my sopping wet sweater and donned Noah's police bomber jacket. The boat also had a stack of clean men's sweatshirts, sweatpants, and socks. While they didn't fit, they were dry and soft against my chilly skin.

The sun was setting and the air was crisper than when I'd left home. It left a brilliant red-orange sky in its wake. It was the kind of evening on a boat that tourists paid good money for, and here I was, snuggling with my best friend while swaddled in a crinkly thermal blanket, trying to avoid my boyfriend's stink-eye.

"I really like this blanket. I feel like a sweet potato in the oven," Erica remarked, wrapping the mylar blanket around us tighter. "Mmm. Sweet potato."

"I'll get you a blanket like this for your birthday."

She laughed and sipped from her cup. "Warm lemon water. How very on brand for Chief Noah Garcia."

I giggled until I started coughing, thinking of how he ordered this concoction every day at Perkatory. Noah whirled and scowled in my direction, still talking on the phone.

"We're in deep doo-doo," I muttered to Erica. "Why the heck did you have to go and sleuth?"

"I couldn't help myself. I had to confront Doug. And get this: he told me everything. He used Darla too."

"What? Who?"

"Our regular at the café, the taffy woman. Turns out she's an expert gardener, and he asked her for help with a leaf blower. Once she showed him the inner workings, he tweaked it so it would explode. He claims he didn't mean to kill Gus, only scare him, hurt him a little."

"Whoa. That's quite a plan. But it explains why Doug and Darla seemed to get so close for a while." I pondered this for a moment. Now I was even more thankful that we'd gotten Erica out of Doug's clutches—and that he hadn't done anything to harm me or Joey. "That doesn't explain Julian, though."

"I was going to try to get that out of him. But he locked me in the office before I could ask."

"My brave friend." I exhaled a long sigh. "Wait, what about your text today? The one that just had the letter H? Were you trying to call for help?"

Erica hummed. "Yeah, actually I was. But Doug grabbed my cell and tossed it in the water at the marina."

Like her phone, I'd also had an inelegant fall into the Gulf of Mexico. When Joey realized that he was missing a passenger, he'd turned the Jet Ski around to scoop me up, but that turned into a bit of a farce. When he extended a hand to me so I could climb on the Jet Ski, I ended up accidentally pulling him into the water.

By the time Noah arrived in the first of a dozen police boats, Joey was gasping, draped over the watercraft seat, stomach down. I was clinging to his leg while bobbing in the water. Fortunately, we were immediately able to show Noah and his officers where Erica was being held hostage.

We were hauled aboard Noah's boat, and from there, things moved quickly, if not uncomfortably.

Officers from four jurisdictions surrounded the ship and told Doug to surrender. For a moment, I feared he might try to fight or hurt Erica, but in the end, he gave up. I watched, rapt, as a stream of cops boarded the boat and handcuffed Doug—then cheered when they brought Erica out and helped her down a ladder to the police boat.

Noah ended his call. "You two okay? We're going to head back now."

"I'm good," Erica said.

"All fine on my end," I added.

He stared at us for a beat and shook his head.

"Sorry, Noah," Erica piped up. "Lana wasn't investigating. I was. Don't hold this against her."

He sighed and ran a hand through his dark hair. "I'm glad you're both okay. Good grief. This day has felt like an entire year."

His phone rang again, and he answered it with a clipped, "Garcia."

I turned to Erica. "You sure you're okay? Doug didn't hurt you? When I saw him, he had a machete in hand."

She shook her head. "Maybe an arm bruise when he pulled me onto the ship and stuffed me in the office. I got in a solid punch and a scratch. And a kick to the shin."

"I saw his cheek. Nice going." I lowered my voice. "I actually did do some investigating today. Talked to Mickey, and he revealed a lot of details. Did you know Doug was in love with you?"

"He was? Huh. He asked me out, but I didn't take it seriously. I also didn't think he'd kill someone and then try to pin attempted murder on me, so what do I know?"

"Do you think that's what he was doing? Trying to frame you for Julian's poisoning because you wouldn't go on a date with him?"

"I guess we'll soon find out, right? It seems like the evidence in both cases points to Doug. Hey, Noah, c'mere." She motioned with her head for him to join us.

Noah was off the phone and standing several feet away, staring in the direction of the pirate ship while massaging his temple with one thumb. I could feel the exasperation coming off him in waves. Honestly, his annoyance with Erica and me was justified, and I couldn't wait to be alone with him so I could apologize profusely.

He turned in our direction as an officer started up the boat motor from the stern. We pulled away from the pirate ship with a throaty acceleration of the motor.

Noah sank in the seat next to me and squeezed my damp leg. "What's up?"

Erica leaned over me, which made the blanket crinkle like tinfoil. "How did the Devil's Beach Police afford this huge fishing boat? This is hella pricey."

"Drug seizure. Traffickers used this boat to transport hash," he said.

We both nodded, impressed. "Learn something new every day," I remarked, hoping to diffuse the tension in the air.

"Listen, Lana, when we get to the marina, I'm going to take you home to change, and then we're headed to the mainland."

"Why?" I tilted my head to avoid the salt spray coming from the water. "Are we going to dinner?" My stomach ached with hunger.

"Nope. No dinner for a while. You need to bail your father out of jail."

"Oh dear," I muttered, scooting away from him a few inches.

The boat skimmed across the water toward the sun setting in the west. Erica and I were silent while Noah took out his phone and focused on the screen.

She jabbed me on the thigh under the silver blanket.

"Ow. What was that for?"

While fighting to free herself from the crackling blanket, Erica leaned into me and whispered. "I'm gonna leave you alone with Noah."

"Wait—"

By the time I could say anything, she rose and walked over to the officer who was behind the wheel, steering the boat. "How many horses on this engine?" she said.

"Two engines, fifteen hundred hp each."

Erica looked genuinely impressed.

I scooted closer to Noah and held out a corner of the silver foil wrap. "Want some blanket?"

He shook his head, and my stomach sank. How angry was he?

"Were you the one who arrested Dad?" I asked.

Slipping his phone into his pants pocket, he focused his gaze on me. "I was. Didn't want to, and I asked him to leave. He refused and started hooting like a monkey. I'm sorry, Lana."

I cringed, filled with secondhand embarrassment. "It's okay. I understand. It's not the first time Dad's been arrested for protesting." I paused for a second. Dad had gambled and lost.

"I doubt if the prosecutor will press charges." Noah yawned and stretched his arms above his head, then lowered his right arm around my shoulders.

"Was Dad angry at you?"

"No, he told me that I should pursue a different line of work. That being a fishing guide was a better fit for my aura."

"Yeah, he mentioned that to me as well."

Noah rubbed my upper arm. "It's not a bad idea, actually. I'd probably have way more fun. Except I wouldn't be able to rescue you when you get into scrapes while playing detective."

I snuggled into his side, thankful that Noah wasn't too upset with me. "I'm sorry about that. I probably shouldn't have chased after Erica on the back of a Jet Ski. It wasn't my best moment."

"Oh, Lana. I don't know what to say. No. You shouldn't have been on the water. You could've gotten hurt or worse. But you did do a good job with all the details of this case. Somehow you always seem to find the important information. Maybe I should hire you as a consultant on the next homicide here on Devil's Beach."

Now that was an exciting prospect. For a millisecond, I imagined Noah and I investigating side by side, combing through case files and interviewing witnesses. I was about to reply with an excited *are you serious*, but refrained. He was staring at me with that handsome grin of his, obviously joking.

"Let's hope there won't be another murder for a long, long time."

He kissed my temple. "Let's hope not, cupcake."

Epilogue

From the bench closest to the rink at the Hot Wheels Skate Shack, I laced up my brand new roller skates as joy spread throughout my body. Tonight was my first-ever public group disco skate, and Honey had invited me to join her skate crew.

She'd even hired a professional video crew to capture the evening, and while I was a little skeptical of being on Instagram or YouTube, I accepted her invite because I'd been bitten hard by the roller disco bug.

Recently, Noah had surprised me with a new pair of skates—they were straight out of the 1970s, with a bubblegum-pink glitter boot and fat black-and-pink wheels. They molded perfectly to my feet and left no nasty blisters.

The skates also looked perfect with my leggings, which were black and adorned with dayglow planets. A black, fitted tank top completed the outfit, and earlier, Erica had worked for an hour and a half with my hair, curling it into a perfect Farrah Fawcett flip. I topped it all off with glittery blue eyeshadow, clear lip gloss, and a rainbow terry-cloth sweatband.

Probably the entire outfit was a bit ridiculous, but I didn't care. I was having the time of my life, and I hadn't even skated a lap yet.

Dad, who was sitting in the bleacher behind me, poked his head over my shoulder. An invisible cloud of weed odor followed. "You know who you look like, munchkin?"

I twisted in my seat, expecting him to say something wacky, like a Muppet, or some obscure 1970s actress. "Who?"

"Your mom. She had hair like that when I met her. It was all loose and feathery like yours is now."

At one time, this mention of Mom would have made both of us weep. Tonight, we both smiled while good memories washed over us. She definitely would've loved all of this, with the disco ball sending shards of light everywhere, the Kool and the Gang tunes, the smell of popcorn. I spotted Perry and Jeri a few rows away, waved and blew a kiss, before turning back to my father.

"Thanks, Dad."

He squeezed my shoulder. "I can't wait to see you skate again. I haven't seen you do this since you were a little girl. I'm glad this is your new hobby. You needed something other than Perkatory. Life's too short to spend on work, even if you love your job."

"I'm coming to realize that." I'd spent all of my twenties in Miami, obsessed with being a journalist. Then, when I'd been laid off, I was unmoored, adrift. When I took over Perkatory, I'd thrown myself into the job with a fervor, never once stopping to think that I should perhaps take time for balance and joy.

Since Doug's arrest a month ago, I'd sought more joy. Maybe it was Gus's death, or the fact that life can change in the blink of an eye, but I'd decided to schedule fun into my days.

I'd been coming to the rink almost every day. Roller skating had become my therapy. Whizzing around the rink or zipping along the sidewalk near the beach allowed me to live in the moment. When I donned my skates, I forgot about my mounting responsibilities at Perkatory and also stopped thinking about the what-ifs of my dead journalism career.

It had been a long time since I'd done something purely for the pleasure, and at first, skating had felt incredibly decadent—selfish, even. But Noah, Erica, and Dad had encouraged me, especially since in the immediate aftermath of Doug's arrest, I'd yearned to write an article. But couldn't.

Within days of his arrest, Doug had confessed not only to Gus's murder but to Julian's attempted murder. As it turned out, Doug hadn't intended on pinning anything on Erica; he'd killed Gus out of sheer rage because he'd lost so much money in the pirate ship deal. When Doug had tinkered with Gus's leaf blower, he wasn't aware that I lived next door or that Erica was staying with me.

As far as Julian, that was a rage-based crime as well. When Doug had watched Erica chat with Julian, only a couple of weeks after she'd turned him down for a date, Doug became blinded by jealousy.

What we didn't know about Doug was that he was also fascinated with growing mushrooms, and an expert in identifying poisonous fungi. He'd used his mushroom expertise to befriend Darla from the saltwater taffy shop. She loved plants and showed him the inner workings of the leaf blower that would kill Gus.

While talking to the detectives, Doug revealed what he'd told Erica while holding her captive: that he'd tried to poison Julian.

He'd sprinkled a little powdered *Amanita verosa*—one of the world's most dangerous mushrooms, which grew right here in Florida—into Julian's coffee while Julian was in the restroom.

It was a miracle that Julian hadn't died, and toxicology confirmed Doug's confession. Fortunately, Julian had gotten world-class treatment in Miami and made a full recovery. He and his family also weren't holding the incident against me and were keeping Perkatory as a client. Noah and I had plans to visit Julian for dinner during a coffee convention coming up in a few months at South Beach.

Since Doug's case had occupied Noah and the Devil's Beach Police for weeks, Noah and I had to cancel our Valentine's Day plans for a mini vacation in the Bahamas. Instead, we enjoyed a double date with Erica and Joey at a fondue restaurant on the mainland.

Noah and I did make plans for the spring: to take a trip to Tampa so I could meet his family. We were even thinking about bringing Dad along, but were treading lightly on that front ever since Dad had been arrested during the monkey protest.

Dad hadn't held it against Noah, because Dad had a forgive-and-forget attitude. Noah had also taken it in stride, and I was relieved when the state attorney declined to press charges. Still, I wasn't sure if his mother was ready to meet my hippie, pot-smoking, monkey-advocating father. I preferred to face Noah's mom alone before unleashing Dad's eccentricity on them.

Noah, being the amazingly kind boyfriend that he was, had left the decision up to me.

The Kool and the Gang song ended. Before another one started, I heard a wolf whistle.

I whirled in the direction of the sound. It was Erica and Joey, coming toward Dad and me.

"Doesn't she look hot?" Erica said, pulling Joey toward my bench. "I did her hair and makeup. I think she looks like a Lisa Frank illustration come to life."

Joey tilted his red head. "Or maybe a Care Bear."

I chortled. "Uh, thanks, dude. I guess that's a compliment."

Erica swatted his arm. "So how does this work tonight, anyway? Do you get a trophy if you win?"

"I'm part of Honey's roller disco crew. We all skate and dance together. That's it. It's very low stakes. There are other roller disco groups, but no—no trophy. No award. Just people skating. I think some will be synchronized, but Honey said we don't need to be."

Honey and I had become friends over the past month, mostly since I'd been taking twice-weekly skating lessons. She was an unusual person, and I wondered if she was bottling up her grief about Gus or if she truly didn't have a sad bone in her body. Fortunately, she and Gus's lover Bridget had come to a truce. They'd each gotten lawyers and had agreed to split the proceeds from the sale of his house.

Which meant I was getting a new neighbor. Several people had come to look at the place, and Jeri, Perry, and I paid close attention to every new potential resident. Since Doug's death, I'd become tight with them and even sat in on one of their podcasts, an episode updating listeners about Gus's homicide.

Erica and Joey took seats next to Dad, and the three of them began chatting about the monkeys.

"Did you hear what the judge said?" Dad said, the excitement obvious in his tone.

"Yes, I read about it in the *Beacon*," Erica said. That might have been my biggest triumph of all in recent weeks: Erica had started reading the newspaper.

"No, what? Are the monkeys in court?" Joey asked. He was probably the only person who wasn't up to speed on the intricacies of the monkey case, and I knew Dad couldn't wait to share every detail.

"A coalition of animal rights groups brought a suit against the city and the state, arguing that this is the monkeys' habitat. The judge issued an injunction against Devil's Beach and the state of Florida. They can't relocate the monkeys until the case is over."

Right then, I spotted Noah coming through the crowd. We locked eyes, and as if on cue, Barry White's "You're the First, the Last, My Everything" blared over the sound system.

I giggled aloud, and he laughed as he slid onto the bench next to me.

He kissed my cheek and whispered in my ear. "You look so gorgeous."

A zing of desire shot through me. Goodness, I adored this man. I was about to smooch him when he pointed to the rink. "I think someone's looking for you."

I glanced up, and there was Honey in pink hot pants and a cropped top with a rainbow on the front. She flipped her long blonde hair and smiled. "You ready, Lana?"

"Sure am." I stood up and waved at Dad, Erica, and Joey, who all hooted and cheered.

I did a little pirouette and stopped in front of Noah, bending over to rest my hands on his knees so our faces were close.

"Knock 'em dead, cupcake," he murmured.

There was only one way I could stop grinning. I pressed my lips to his for a long, lingering kiss.

But we couldn't kiss all night. That would come later. I turned to skate onto the rink, the shimmering light of the disco ball filling the room—and my heart—with little sparkles of joy.

Acknowledgments

Thank you to my agent, Jill Marsal, for her help on this book. My gratitude also goes to Lyn, Saundra, Margaret, and Heather, for their eternal friendship. And to my husband, Marco: I love you.